Hyde & Seek

BAEN BOOKS
by SIMON R. GREEN

ISHMAEL JONES MYSTERIES
The Dark Side of the Road
Dead Man Walking
Very Important Corpses
Haunted by the Past

JEKYLL & HYDE INC.
Jekyll & Hyde Inc.
Hyde & Seek

For Love of Magic

Hyde & Seek

Simon R. Green

HYDE & SEEK

This is a work of fiction. All the characters and events portrayed in this book are fictional, and any resemblance to real people or incidents is purely coincidental.

A Baen Books Original

Baen Publishing Enterprises
P.O. Box 1403
Riverdale, NY 10471
www.baen.com

ISBN: 978-1-9821-9338-6

Cover art by Todd Lockwood

First printing, May 2024

Distributed by Simon & Schuster
1230 Avenue of the Americas
New York, NY 10020

Library of Congress Cataloging-in-Publication Data

Names: Green, Simon R., 1955– author.
Title: Hyde & seek / Simon R. Green.
Other titles: Hyde and seek
Identifiers: LCCN 2023054039 (print) | LCCN 2023054040 (ebook) | ISBN 9781982193386 (hardcover) | ISBN 9781625799623 (ebook)
Subjects: LCGFT: Paranormal fiction. | Novels.
Classification: LCC PR6107.R44 H93 2024 (print) | LCC PR6107.R44 (ebook)
| DDC 823/.92—dc23/eng/20231127
LC record available at https://lccn.loc.gov/2023054039
LC ebook record available at https://lccn.loc.gov/2023054040

Printed in the United States of America

10 9 8 7 6 5 4 3 2 1

Hyde & Seek

✣ ✣ ✣

Whatever happened to all the old monsters? There was a time when everyone believed in vampires and werewolves, and all the other creatures that lurked in the darkest parts of the night to prey on Humanity. But suddenly they were only legends, familiar stories that no one believed in anymore. Which made life so much easier; for the monsters.

Daniel Carter started out as a cop. It was all he ever wanted, all he ever believed in. To be the knight in shining armor who protected people from the bad guys. But his career didn't turn out the way he expected, and he ended up sitting behind a desk pushing bits of paper around.

So when he got a chance to do some off-the-record undercover work, by shutting down a particularly nasty group specializing in illegal transplants, he jumped at the opportunity to do something real, something that mattered. He should have known better. In a blood-soaked cellar, surrounded by the gutted bodies of abducted homeless people, Daniel came face-to-face with the Frankenstein Clan and the things they had made; and found that monsters were still very real.

Disgraced, broken, and crippled, he was thrown out of the police force; not least because no one believed him about the monsters. And then he met the head of Jekyll & Hyde Inc., who told Daniel the truth about vampires and werewolves and all the other monster Clans. How they chose to disappear into the underworld of crime, moving out of history and into legend so they could continue to prey on people undetected. Only one refused, because he wouldn't lower himself to be just a criminal. Who insisted on being a plain-dealing monster. So the only one left to fight the monster Clans was . . . Edward Hyde. He offered Daniel a place in Jekyll & Hyde Inc. All he had to do was take Dr. Jekyll's Elixir, and he would become strong enough to fight the monsters who'd destroyed his life. And that was how Daniel Carter became Daniel Hyde.

Teamed up with the glamorous, outrageous, and very deadly Valentina Hyde (always Tina, never Val), Daniel went to work with a vengeance. Together they destroyed the Frankenstein Clan, the Vampire Clan, the Clan of Mummies, and the Werewolf Clan. And finally they killed the greatest monster of them all, Edward Hyde—because he had lied to them about what they were fighting for.

When the war is over, what do you do? If you're a Hyde, you go looking for a new war. With all the Clans gone, who will move in to take their place? What could be more of a threat to Humanity than monsters?

Aliens.

Whatever happened to all the old aliens—the Martians, the Bug-Eyed Monsters, the Reptiloids, and the Greys? Daniel and Tina Hyde are about to find out there are worse things than monsters.

✣ ✣ ✣

Chapter One
THEY DON'T ALWAYS WAIT FOR YOU TO START A WAR

✣ ✣ ✣

AFTER KILLING EDWARD HYDE, for many good reasons, Daniel and Tina went out on the town and partied till they dropped. Rampaging through London's clubland, they made the scene at all the best establishments and the very lowest of dives, drinking, dancing, and starting fights just for the hell of it, before finally lurching home in the early hours to break any number of beds with their passion.

They visited underground fight clubs and took on all comers, barged into celebrated restaurants and ate their way through entire menus, and even broke into a bank vault just so they could throw the money around and have sex on top of it. After a while London tried to hide when it saw them coming, or claim it was out, but Daniel and Tina were just celebrating being alive—and being Hydes.

Eventually they calmed down a little, and decided to take some time apart. So they could work out what they wanted to do with their lives, now the war with the monsters was over.

Daniel went to the Purgatory Club—so called because it was considered to be halfway between Heaven and Hell. One of those very private establishments you can only find if you know where to look, down the kind of back streets that might not have names but certainly have reputations. The Purgatory—where everybody knows what you are. A home away from home, for those who couldn't pass for normal on the best day they ever had.

The air in the club was thick with smoke and all the scents of temptation, and full of the kind of people who had good reason to believe they'd seen everything; but they all turned to look when Daniel Hyde walked in. He nodded politely to the scowling old vulture who ran the Purgatory, and had done since time immemoral. Old Man Trouble was a withered old stick, wearing nothing but a collection of black leather bondage straps, possibly to hold himself together. Time had scoured all the character out of his face, leaving nothing but hollows and shadows, and eyes sunk so deep they barely caught the light. But when Trouble smiled at Daniel and showed his teeth, it quickly became clear he could still be dangerous at need.

He extended a dried-up hand, so Daniel could kiss his ring. Daniel jerked the ring right off the finger and examined it, in case it might be worth something. The Gehenna Girls hissed angrily at him. The identical twin Goths were Trouble's bodyguards, famine thin but burning with fierce energy. Their faces were so white Daniel thought at first it must be makeup, but it was just them. Long dark hair, black lipstick, and so much mascara they looked like pandas on the pull, the Gehenna Girls wore night-dark catsuits and their fingers ended in implanted steel blades. They started to rise from their seats, but quickly fell back again when Trouble looked at them.

"Not just yet, my little gore crows," he said smoothly. "He is a Hyde, and must have his little ways."

He caressed both Gehenna Girls impartially as he spoke, but they didn't even glance at him. They kept their gaze fixed on Daniel, just in case Trouble decided to let them off the leash, and they could test the Hyde's reputation for themselves. It was rumored they ate their kills.

Daniel tossed the ring back to Trouble, who caught it deftly and slipped it back onto his desiccated finger. One of the Gehenna Girls took the opportunity to slash the back of Daniel's hand with her razor-sharp nails, and blood rose up in thin crimson lines. Daniel kept his eyes fixed on Trouble.

"I'm just visiting."

"I didn't ask," said Trouble. "You want a drink, it's on the house. Anything or anyone else, you pay standard rates."

"I won't be here long," said Daniel.

Trouble showed his teeth in something that didn't even try to be a smile.

"That's what they all say."

Daniel looked around the low-ceilinged room, his eyes easily piercing the smoky atmosphere, and made his way through the packed tables to a booth at the back, where someone was waiting for him. Scarlett had been on the game for most of her life, and it showed. She had to be in her late forties by now, with a handsome face and long red hair, and a certain shop-soiled glamor. She dressed in bright primary colors, and despite her easy smile she had the eyes of a predator.

"Thanks for coming," she said, and put a hand on his thigh. He looked down, and she took it away.

"You were my best confidential informant, back when I was starting out," said Daniel. "You knew everything, and everyone."

"And you were wise enough to know you didn't know anything," said Scarlett.

"We had each other's back," said Daniel.

"Among other things," said Scarlett.

"So," said Daniel. "Why reach out to me? It's not like you to need someone else's help."

She looked him over for a moment, as though considering making an offer.

"You look good. Being a Hyde suits you."

And then she took in the scratches on the back of his hand, raised it to her mouth, and lapped at the scratches, her tongue rasping pleasantly against his skin. Because she knew what chemicals the Gehenna Girls used to smear their blades. They would have killed anyone who wasn't a Hyde, and of course Scarlett wasn't bothered because she'd used much worse in her time. Daniel let her finish, and then took his hand back.

"Why am I here?" he said.

"Because something bad is coming," said Scarlett.

"Worse than a Hyde?"

"Maybe."

Daniel smiled. "I never could resist a challenge."

"I know," said Scarlett.

They sat together, almost like old friends, as they waited for the Bad Thing to show up.

Daniel watched interestedly as Purgatory's featured singer took the stage. She grabbed hold of the microphone stand as though she needed it to hold her up. The Nightingale was a terrible broken figure, her face a mess of scars. There were those who said she did it to herself because she wanted the outside to match the inside. She had gone all the way into the dark, and found hope waiting for her. Now she sang at the Purgatory, with a voice like a fallen angel, to tell everyone that if she could survive the darkness, so could they.

Daniel studied the club's patrons, sitting quietly at their tables. The flotsam and jetsam of civilization's underside—the sirens and the nephilim, the throwbacks and the mutants, the weird and the wonderful. The Purgatory was one of the few places where a Hyde could just sit quietly and be accepted, because everyone there had seen worse. Normal people were never admitted, no matter how extreme their fashions or fetishes. The Purgatory didn't cater for tourists. It was just a watering hole for those who needed to get away from the everyday world, and its disapproving eyes.

Daniel gave Scarlett an impatient look, and she nodded slowly.

"The Purgatory is under threat, from something that wants to make the club its own personal feeding ground. The last of the great monsters: the Ghoul. Not the lesser creatures, used by the other monster clubs to clean up the messes they made; I know you already dealt with those. This is something that has learned to feed on the suffering of others. And the pain of the Purgatory's patrons offers an endless feast."

Daniel looked at her thoughtfully. "And you're afraid of it?"

"We all are," said Scarlett.

She broke off, as the club suddenly went quiet. Something was walking unhurriedly through the smoky air, drifting through the murk like a shark entering the shallows. Daniel sat up straight, and Scarlett's hand clamped down hard on his arm, warning him to keep still and not draw attention to himself.

"I'm not worried," said Daniel. "I'm a Hyde."

"But that," said Scarlett, "is the Grinning Ghoul."

As the creature emerged from the curling smoke, Daniel could see how it got its name. The Ghoul's mouth was stretched in an unrelenting smile so wide it would have been painful on a normal face. The head was hairless, the face pale as death, and it had no eyes—only empty sockets. But it could see. It still wore the suit it had been buried in, spotted with grave-mold and rotting away in places.

The Grinning Ghoul glided smoothly through the smoke as

though moved by willpower rather than muscle. The patrons it passed flinched back, and turned their heads away. The Ghoul headed straight for Old Man Trouble, and the Gehenna Girls braced themselves, though they must have known there was nothing they could do. Trouble stabbed a finger at Daniel, and the Ghoul turned its empty gaze on him.

Daniel stood up. Scarlett edged away from him, and Daniel didn't blame her. No one in Purgatory could face the Grinning Ghoul—because they all had too much pain to offer it. Daniel nodded easily to the Ghoul as it closed in on him, and stared right into its empty eye sockets.

"What manner of thing are you?" said the Ghoul, in a voice like dead leaves rustling in the gutter.

"I'm a Hyde," said Daniel. "And there's nothing in me for you to feed on, because I left all my pain behind me, in my old life."

"Then what are you doing in a place like this, with things like these?" said the Ghoul.

"Looking out for an old friend," said Daniel. "Because somebody has to."

He hit the Grinning Ghoul so hard in the face the blow ripped the creature's head right off its shoulders. The body just stood there, until Daniel put a hand on its chest and pushed it over backward. Daniel looked down at the head, which was still trying to say something. He stamped on it again and again, until the skull collapsed in on itself, and then he nodded easily to Old Man Trouble.

"Burn the head and the body separately, and then scatter the ashes in running water. That should take care of the problem."

"What do I owe you?" said Trouble.

Daniel smiled. "On the house."

He turned to leave, and Scarlett rose quickly to her feet.

"Looking for some company?"

Daniel stopped her with a glance. "Thank you. But I'm spoken for."

He walked out of Purgatory and didn't look back once. Because he knew he didn't belong there.

Daniel's old flat was a dingy second-floor walk-up in a permanently unfashionable part of town. He'd lost his key long ago, but he just gave the door a friendly shove and the lock exploded. He walked into a room full of shadows and looked around, taking his time. He'd been gone so long he barely recognised the place; or remembered the man who used to live there. Just another plainclothes policeman whose career hadn't worked out the way he thought it should. Who'd gone head-to-head with the world for the best of reasons—and found out just how dirty the world could fight.

He drifted unhurriedly through the empty rooms, picking up things that used to mean something to him, and putting them down again because they didn't anymore. He remembered the broken, crippled man who should have died after everything the Frankenstein Clan did to him, dragging himself painfully from room to room. Another person, in another life, left behind when Dr. Jekyll's Elixir made him something better.

The flat felt cold and abandoned, like something he'd outgrown. The dusty gray chrysalis that produced a monstrous butterfly. He stopped before the mirror on the wall, half expecting to see his old Daniel Carter face looking back at him, only to find he was having trouble remembering what that man looked like. Daniel Hyde stared back out of the mirror: big and brutal, dark-haired and dark-eyed, handsome as the devil, larger than life and proud of it. His Savile Row suit emphasized the powerful form within, and his slow smile was a dark and dangerous thing. And then his reflection winked roguishly back at him.

"Feeling nostalgic, are we?" it said nastily. *"For a life you hated, and a career that wasn't worthy of you? Come on—you couldn't wait to throw them away."*

"He was a man who believed in all the right things," Daniel said steadily. "I'm still him; there's just more of me now."

"You're a Hyde," said his reflection. *"A self-made monster who doesn't have to care about the rules any more, because Hydes can do whatever they want and get away with it. What are you doing here, Daniel?"*

"Reminding myself of my roots. Of all the things that made me who I am."

"The Elixir made you what you are. Everything else was just the warm-up act. So: now you've killed all the monsters, and the big bad daddy figure... what are you going to do next?"

Daniel shrugged. "Damned if I know. Something worth doing."

"Something good?" his reflection said archly. *"I think we've moved on from that, haven't we?"*

It laughed at Daniel, loud and mocking, until he smashed the mirror with one blow from his fist. But there was no breaking of glass, no fragments falling to the floor, just a wall with a big crack in the plaster. Because there had never been a mirror on the wall.

Daniel turned away, and did his best to call up all his old dreams and ambitions: of becoming a policeman so he could protect people from the villains who preyed on them. To bring hope to all the dark places of the world. He still wanted to take down the bad guys, but in a more hands-on kind of way. He needed to feel their bones break and shatter in his hands, and smile as he watched the light go out in their eyes. He no longer had any faith in the law, not after the way it abandoned him. And yet . . . if he could do anything he wanted, and never have to worry about the consequences, what was there to keep him from becoming just like the monsters he'd fought so hard to destroy? His conscience, in a mirror that wasn't really there? Daniel smiled briefly. He knew what Tina would say.

Hydes don't do consciences.

He remembered her sumptuous apartment, in a much more upmarket area of London. Where every comfort and luxury came as standard, and the bills never came due. He'd spent a lot of time there with Tina, in and out of bed, but it had never once occurred to him to invite her back to his place. Not just because it would have made him feel very much the poor relation, but because it would have felt like a step backward.

To a life he'd walked out on, without thinking twice about it.

He left the flat, not bothering to close the door behind him because he had no intention of ever going back. The flat was his past, and he had to look to the future. He made his way across London, hardly seeing any of it, intent on his own thoughts. Until finally he found himself standing before the front entrance of the Jekyll & Hyde Inc. building. A pleasantly old-fashioned edifice with a businesslike façade, and the lower windows heavily tinted so no one could see in. He paused for a long moment, wondering why he'd come back. He finally decided it was because he missed the only person he could still talk to, who could understand what it meant to be a Hyde. He had no doubt Tina would be here, for the same reason as him. Because she didn't have anywhere else to go.

Daniel kicked the door open and strode into the lobby. A great open space, with streams of light shining in through the higher windows, it was all very empty and very quiet. Daniel supposed he shouldn't be too surprised. It wasn't like Jekyll & Hyde Inc. was still a going concern, after everything he'd done to it. The lobby felt haunted—by the memory of the way things used to be.

He moved over to stand before the ornate wooden scroll on the wall, bearing a long list of company names. Jekyll & Hyde Inc. was right at the top, set proudly forth in dignified gold leaf. None of the other names were real, just covers for the various departments that served the bigger cause—everything from an extensive armory to tailors who could clothe an oversized Hyde body and still make it look stylish. But these days the departments were as empty as the lobby, their servants scattered to the four winds. Daniel smiled, as he remembered how he and Tina had beaten the hell out of them, after Edward pressed guns into their hands and drove them into the lobby, in one last desperate attempt to protect himself. Now the building was abandoned; for all practical purposes Daniel and Tina were Jekyll & Hyde Inc. If only they could decide what to do with it.

Daniel took the elevator up to the top floor, and made his way to Edward Hyde's office. The reception area was all thick carpeting, bland art prints on the walls, and an oversized desk with no one left to sit behind it—because at the end Edward had killed and eaten his receptionist. Daniel breezed into the inner office and there was Tina, tearing the drawers out of the main desk, and searching quickly through their contents. She nodded briefly to him, before turning the drawers upside down to make sure there was nothing attached to the undersides.

"Why?" said Daniel.

"Because that's where I would have hidden something," she said.

"What are you looking for?"

"I'll know it when I find it."

Daniel nodded, and took his time looking around what had been a comfortably old-fashioned office . . . before he and Tina trashed it in their efforts to bring down Edward Hyde. Most of the furniture was still in pieces, and there were great scars in the walls. Daniel picked up an overturned chair, set it on its feet, and sat down. He remembered sitting on it when Edward offered him Dr. Jekyll's Elixir, and changed his life forever. It didn't seem that long ago.

Daniel crossed his legs, and fixed Tina with a speculative eye. "Do you really think you're going to find something worth finding?"

"Don't you?" said Tina. She threw the last desk drawer at a wall, with such force the heavy wood shattered into splinters. "Edward always was a great one for secrets. As we found out to our cost."

"But why are you looking here," said Daniel, "when he had a whole building to choose from?"

Tina planted her fists on her hips and glared around the office. "I had to start somewhere. What brings you back to the scene of so many crimes?"

"Probably the same reason as you. Two lost lambs, finding their way home."

"This was never home," said Tina. "Just somewhere we worked."

"But our work is done," said Daniel. "It died with the last of the monster Clans. So what do we do now? Hydes aren't meant for retirement, and the easy life. We need a new challenge. Something we can sink our teeth into, deep enough to draw blood."

"We could rebuild Jekyll & Hyde Inc. in our image," said Tina.

"And do what with it?" said Daniel.

"There must be something else out there worth fighting!"

"But what's left that's worthy of a Hyde?" said Daniel.

Tina folded her arms under her magnificent bosom, and glowered at him sullenly. At six and a half feet tall, she was a few inches taller than Daniel, with a physique like a bodybuilder and the sleek grace of a predatory animal. She had gone back to her favorite business suit, complete with black string tie and a silver clasp in the shape of a skull. Just standing there, Tina looked seductive and glamorous and deadly as all hell. Every inch a Hyde, and loving it. Her great mane of crimson hair cascaded down around her shoulders, and her green eyes were unremittingly fierce. Her full mouth widened suddenly into a mocking grin.

"I suppose you've got something appallingly moral in mind."

"We could rebuild this organization into a force for good," said Daniel.

"Boring!" Tina said loudly. "You always were a Boy Scout at heart."

"You say that like it's a bad thing."

"We're Hydes!" said Tina. "We're not meant to be the good guys! We were made to hit people and break things!"

"All right," said Daniel. "What do you think we should do?"

"Make a whole lot of money, while having as much fun as possible," Tina said immediately. "We could rule this town, and have everyone bow down to us."

"And end up a monster like Edward?" Daniel said carefully.

Tina's smile disappeared. "We were always monsters. We were just better at it than the creatures we fought."

Daniel rose to his feet, so he could glare into her face. "I did not fight my way through armies of Frankensteins, vampires, mummies, and werewolves just to become the enemy! We have to be better than that, or everything we've done has been for nothing!"

"Don't you raise your voice to me!"

"What else can I do when you won't listen!"

It didn't matter which of them threw the first punch. They were Hydes, and all their arguments ended in a fight, or bed, or both. They hurled themselves at each other, and raged back and forth across the office, smashing through what was left of the furniture. They punched and kicked with vicious force, not bothering to dodge or defend themselves, because Hydes were built to take punishment. Finally, they slammed together like two runaway trains, and wrestled fiercely while sweat ran down their faces. They glared into each other's eyes, but they were both grinning broadly.

There was no telling how long the fight might have gone on. There was always a sexual element to their violence, a seductive dance in their conflict; but in the end Daniel threw a punch, Tina ducked at the last moment, and his fist shot past her head to open up a large crack in the wall behind her. Daniel immediately stopped fighting. Tina sniffed, and lowered her fists.

"Just when I was starting to enjoy myself..."

"You'll like this more," said Daniel. "I think I've found what you were searching for."

He gestured at the crack he'd made, and Tina grinned quickly as she took in the massive steel safe concealed inside the wall.

"I told you Edward was hiding something here..."

They tore the wall apart with their bare hands, until they'd opened up enough space to haul the safe out. It was heavy enough that when Daniel and Tina finally dropped it on the floor, the floorboards cracked. The safe was an old-fashioned affair, with thick steel walls and a blocky combination lock. Daniel looked at Tina.

"Did you see anything in the desk that might have been the combination?"

She shook her head quickly. "If I had, I'd have known to look for a safe, wouldn't I?"

"Don't get tetchy," said Daniel. "I see a simple solution to our problem."

He pulled back his fist and punched the combination lock so hard he separated the lock from the door and drove it back into the safe's interior. After that, it was easy enough for Daniel and Tina to wrench the door open and inspect the safe's contents. Which turned out to be one rather bulky file, and a laptop. Daniel and Tina checked hopefully for any valuables that might be lurking at the back, and then Tina sat down on the floor and flicked through the file, while Daniel opened the laptop and studied it dubiously.

"What could be so secret that Edward had to keep these things hidden inside a safe, inside a wall?"

"Information is always valuable," Tina said absently.

"Could there be more monsters that he never got around to telling us about?"

"Try the laptop," said Tina, not looking up.

"Probably password protected," Daniel said gloomily. "Unless he wanted us to find this, after he was gone."

Tina finally gave him her attention. "As in, last will and testament?"

"Or one last chance to manipulate us, like the vicious old puppet master he was."

Daniel hit the power button, and the laptop screen lit up to show Edward Hyde grinning out at the world. That familiar ugly face, with the low brow and prominent bone structure, and the unrelentingly evil eyes. The recording started automatically, and Daniel and Tina tensed as they listened to their master's voice.

"Hello, Daniel and Tina," Edward said cheerfully. "If you're seeing this, then I have failed to kill you and I am dead. However, while you may have won the battle, the war is far from over. Because as you probably already guessed, I didn't tell you everything. Jekyll & Hyde Inc. was never just about fighting monsters. There are more dangers, lurking in the wings.

"The file you are no doubt currently clutching in your greedy little hands has all the details. Basically, nature abhors a vacuum, and supernature even more so. With the monsters gone, something else will inevitably emerge to take their place. So, what could be worse than monsters? Aliens. Driven to hide in the cracks of the world, and wait for their chance. We're talking Martians, Bug-Eyed Monsters, Reptiloids, and Greys—the usual unusual suspects. And, of course, all the human crews that serve them.

"The only thing the monster Clans could agree on was to present a united front against the aliens, matching their every move with violence and sudden death, to make sure no alien force could ever invade our world. Because the monsters weren't about to share their prey with anyone else. But if you've done your job, all the monsters are gone... so there's no one left to bar the gates and barricade the doors.

"I found out about the aliens because each of them sent human emissaries to my office, to ask for Jekyll & Hyde Inc.'s help in their war against the monsters. You might wonder why any human would agree to serve creatures whose only purpose is to invade and destroy this world, but there's always someone ready to do anything, for money and the promise of power. A few did turn out to be True Believers, who worshipped their alien masters as supreme beings; they seemed more alien to me than the creatures they served. I would set this whole world on fire, rather than give up one inch of it to aliens. For all my sins, I have always been a very human monster."

He frowned for a moment, considering. "My only real regret is that none of the aliens ever turned up in person. I've fought everything else this world had to offer. And I always did wonder what alien flesh would taste like... Perhaps you'll get a chance to find out."

He grinned out of the screen, happy as some medieval gargoyle. "The human emissaries offered me money, weapons, power... but I already had all of those, and I always knew that even the highest kind of servant is still a servant. Once the human agents realized I was never going to agree, they turned to threats—against my organization, my people... even me personally. I just laughed in their faces. I'd spent more than a century plotting the destruction of the monster Clans, and savoring the thought of their deaths. I wasn't about to share that pleasure with anyone.

"The only thing that stopped me sending the agents' severed heads back to their masters as a warning... was that I had no idea where the aliens were. They weren't stupid enough to send me an agent who knew. Any of them would have given up their masters in a moment, after the things I did to them.

"So I sent my people out into London's underworld, to sniff out what traces there might be. They brought back whispers of very secret clubs where people went to fight aliens, or bargain for their technology, or have sex with them. People are strange. And bit by bit, rumor by rumor, I began to assemble a picture of the alien presence in London. Of who and what the aliens were, and how they might be stopped... and slowly and remorselessly I drew my plans against them. All the terrible things I would do... once I'd finished off the monster Clans.

"I always knew there was a chance I might not live to see that, but I have no doubt you will take up my war against the aliens. Because if you don't go after them, they will come for you, striking from the shadows and howling for your blood. Because they know you are all that's left, to stand between them and Humanity. So: kill them all, my children. Wade in their blood and glory in their destruction. Because that's what Hydes are for."

He laughed cheerfully, like the monster he was, and he was still laughing when Daniel slammed the lid down and shut him off. He looked at Tina.

"Martians? Really?"

"There's a whole chapter on them in this file," said Tina. "Apparently, what's left of the Martian civilization was driven underground long ago, and that's why none of our probes ever found them."

"I get that," said Daniel. "But... Martians? Really?"

"Isn't that what you used to say about vampires and werewolves?" said Tina. "Though to be fair, I always thought Bug-Eyed Monsters only existed in old-time movies."

Daniel frowned. "I have heard stories about Greys and Reptiloids, but I always thought that was just more conspiracy bullshit."

"If monsters can be real, why not aliens?" said Tina.

Daniel sighed wistfully. "If there had to be aliens, why couldn't they be happy little space friends, like ET?"

"I always thought he was seriously creepy," said Tina. "Like a scrotum with eyes. Look on the bright side: we have a new war! You did say we needed a new challenge."

"This isn't quite what I had in mind."

Daniel put the laptop down on the safe, and made a mental note to check through its files later, just in case Edward had a few other surprises tucked away. Daniel wasn't opposed to kicking the crap out of the alien menace, but he did wonder if fighting bad guys was all he and Tina had in common. What would happen to them, if they ran out of enemies? Would he have to create some new ones, just to hold them together? Daniel considered a life of never-ending wars, and smiled briefly. She was worth it.

He sat down on the floor beside Tina, and the two of them flipped swiftly through the file's pages. It seemed all the aliens had established secret bases on Earth, to prepare for their coming invasions. The only reason they never happened was because the aliens had been too busy fighting and sabotaging each other. Which was just as well, because the file seemed pretty certain all of Earth's armies put together didn't have the weapons or resources to stop them. Jekyll & Hyde Inc.'s various departments had argued that they should locate all the alien bases as a matter of urgency, and wipe out every alien they could find—to send a message that Earth was too dangerous to invade. But Edward just kept putting them off, so he could concentrate on his vendetta against the monster Clans.

Daniel sat back and shook his head slowly.

"When we destroyed Jekyll & Hyde Inc. as well as the Clans, we left Humanity defenseless against the aliens."

"Hydes don't do guilt," said Tina. "But we can do retaliation. Suddenly and violently and all over the place."

"Do we need to rebuild the organization, before we can take on the aliens?"

"I don't see why," said Tina. "We took down all the monster Clans on our own."

"With the assistance of the Hyde armory," said Daniel.

"We should take a look at what's in there," said Tina. "I'm betting we could lay our hands on all kinds of seriously unpleasant things. Especially now there's no armorer to slap our wrists and shout *Don't touch!* But first . . . I think we need to go up to the roof."

Daniel looked at her. "Why? So you can show me the kingdoms of the world, and say *All of this can be yours*?"

Tina grinned at him. "Something like that."

She broke open a concealed door at the back of the office, that opened onto a narrow stairway. Daniel followed her up the steps to a tall standing door that protruded from the roof like a turret; he couldn't help noticing that the door was extremely solid, with heavy bolts on the inside. Edward always did take his security seriously.

The roof itself was a great open expanse, flat and featureless, apart from a massive air-conditioning unit that glowered over the scene like some technological gargoyle. Steel spikes protruded from the sides, and it muttered menacingly to itself. Daniel gave the whole thing plenty of room, just on general principles.

More rooftops stretched away in all directions, but Jekyll & Hyde Inc.'s was taller by far, allowing an uninterrupted view on every side. Daniel was pretty sure that was no accident. The stars were out in the deep dark night, along with a cold and watchful half-moon. A chill wind was blowing, though neither Daniel nor Tina would lower themselves to shiver. Tina strode across the roof, and Daniel ambled along after her.

"You've been up here before, haven't you?"

"Edward liked to bring me up here," said Tina. "So he could show me London in all its ancient pomp and majesty—and then piss on it."

She didn't stop until she was standing right on the edge of the roof, with her toes protruding out over the long drop, and Daniel had no choice but to stand beside her. He wriggled his toes cautiously, maintaining his balance despite all the gusting wind could do to nudge him forward. He looked down, and the street seemed so far away it might have been another world.

Tina waved a casual hand at the cityscape of London. All the proud edifices and ancient monuments, skyscrapers and cathedrals, houses and offices, bars and clubs; and the endless maze of narrow streets connecting everything, that hadn't changed much in centuries.

"So many candles lit against the darkness," she said. "So many people going about their everyday lives, never knowing what lurks in the shadows. Just as well. If they knew all the things we'd saved them from they'd only get clingy."

"What are we doing up here?" said Daniel.

"Jekyll & Hyde Inc. became much more than it was ever meant to be," Tina said carefully. "Edward only ever thought of it as his own private army, but as it acquired more and more departments, its aims and abilities become more ambitious. It could have been a contender, leading the way in business and influence. And it still could. Why waste our time fighting aliens, when we could just as easily set them at each other's throats and let them do all the fighting, while we build something for ourselves? Look at that view, Daniel! All of it could be ours, to do with as we please."

"But how could we ever relax and enjoy ourselves, knowing aliens were planning to destroy it all?" said Daniel. "Besides . . . fighting the monsters was fun. Think of how much more fun we could have fighting aliens."

Tina laughed suddenly. "You always know the right thing to say, Daniel. What do you think we should do?"

"Find the alien bases," said Daniel. "And then stamp them flat, to send a message: Behave yourselves, or the nasty Hydes will come and get you."

"That does sound like a good time," said Tina. She looked out across the view and frowned slightly, as though she thought something might be staring back at her. "But eventually, we will run out of things to fight . . . and then, all of this could be ours. To play with till it breaks."

"You're still listening to Edward's ghost," said Daniel.

Tina frowned suddenly. "I can hear something . . ."

They both stepped back from the edge, and Daniel turned his head slowly back and forth.

"There's something out there," he said, "and it's heading our way. Helicopters—lots of them. But I'm not seeing any navigation lights. Why would a fleet of helicopters be flying undercover at this time of night?"

"I'm getting a seriously bad feeling about this," said Tina.

A dozen attack helicopters came sweeping in out of the night. Big black ships, bristling with weapons. Spotlights stabbed down, tracking back and forth across the roof until they found the two Hydes and pinned them in place, like insects mounted on a board. Daniel and Tina had to raise their arms to shield their eyes, while the downdraft from the pounding rotor blades sent them staggering back and forth. Until Daniel and Tina dug their heels in and refused to be moved. They dropped their arms and glared defiantly back into the spotlights; and the helicopters opened fire.

Heavy machine guns raked the rooftop, filling the night with the roar of massed gunfire. But Daniel and Tina were already gone, racing for cover behind the massive air-conditioning unit. Machine-gun fire followed them all the way, the heavy-jacketed bullets digging trenches in the rooftop before finally slamming into the unit. It shook and shuddered under the sustained fire, while Daniel and Tina crouched behind it. The helicopters spread out, sweeping around the roof so they could come at the Hydes from different directions. Heavy gunfire hammered into the air-conditioning unit, blowing it away piece by piece.

Daniel shook his head hard, half deafened by the ceaseless gunfire, and looked quickly around him. The standing door was within reach, but he could tell even his Hyde speed wouldn't get him there before the machine guns found him. He was equally sure that if he just stayed put, the guns would chew their way right through the air-conditioning unit, and sooner rather than later. So he grabbed one of the steel spikes protruding from the unit's side, hauled it out, stood up and threw it at the nearest helicopter.

The bulky javelin flashed through the air and slammed into the helicopter's rotors. There was a sudden explosion, a burst of fire and smoke, and one of the blades broke off and flew away, spinning end over end. The helicopter lurched to one side as the pilot struggled to compensate, and then it dropped out of the night and slammed into the roof. The nose dug in first, then the body tilted forward, and the remaining rotor blades tore themselves apart as they hammered against the roof. There was another explosion, and the whole craft went up in flames. Burning fuel splashed across the rooftop, and the sea of flames cast a flickering crimson glare to push back the spotlights.

Bullets came howling in from three different directions, and Daniel dropped out of sight again. Tina tore a spike out of the air-conditioning unit, popped her head above the unit, and threw the spike with all her strength. It smashed through the windscreen of an approaching helicopter and punched right through the pilot in his seat. The helicopter slewed sideways and slammed into a second craft, and both attack ships immediately went up in flames, before dropping to the roof like burning birds.

Tina crouched down beside Daniel and raised a hand to high-five him, but he was intent on another helicopter sweeping round in search of a better line of fire. He pointed urgently at the standing door, and Tina nodded quickly. They both ran for it, trusting to the chaos of the crashed gunships to buy them enough time to get there. But another helicopter rose up past the roof's edge, just beyond the standing door, and opened fire on the Hydes. Bullet after bullet slammed into Daniel and Tina, punching them this way and that and forcing them away from the door; but neither of them fell.

Blood and gore soaked the front of Daniel's clothes, and he howled with rage as the bullets kept coming. He turned to face the helicopter, lowered his head, and bulled his way forward despite all the guns could do to stop him, refusing to be slowed or turned aside. He cried out in pain despite himself as more and more bullets slammed into him, and his blood spurted thickly, but he made himself concentrate on the attack ship looming up before him. And when he was close enough he leapt into the air, and landed on the front of the helicopter.

He clung to the armored nose with both arms, and then hauled himself forward until he was kneeling right in front of the windscreen. He glared at the terrified pilot, and then grinned savagely at the horror in the man's eyes. He punched through the heavy windscreen, and thrust his arm in. He grabbed hold of the pilot, and safety straps tore like paper as Daniel hauled him out of his seat. The man cried out in shock and horror as Daniel dragged him through the shattered windscreen, snarled into his face, and then threw him away, laughing in sheer exhilaration as the pilot screamed all the way down the side of the building to the street below.

Daniel held on tight as the helicopter yawed back and forth, with no one at the controls. One of the attack ship's gunners howled like a terrorized animal as he tried to fight his way forward, to get to the controls. He aimed his pistol through what was left of the windscreen, but the helicopter dropped sharply and dove toward the roof. The gunman fell backward, firing into the ceiling, and Daniel jumped away from the helicopter as it augured in. He landed in a crouch, his leg muscles easily absorbing the impact, just as the helicopter smashed into the rooftop. A billowing fireball rose up, and spread out to engulf Daniel. He closed his eyes against the awful heat and walked steadily forward out of the flames, only opening them again when he felt the cold night air caress his face. And then he slapped out the flames on his charred suit, and looked around to see what Tina was getting up to.

Attack gunships swept back and forth across the roof like panicked birds, all sense of plan and purpose lost. Spotlights jabbed this way and that while the guns kept up their constant chatter, but the helicopters had to keep breaking away to avoid crashing into each other. One spotted Tina by the standing door, and she waved cheerfully, allowing the gunship to target her. Chattering ammunition dug a deep trench in the rooftop as the stream of bullets stitched a path to her. Tina ran straight into the gunfire, shrugging off repeated impacts and flurries of blood as she closed in on the helicopter. Its nose came up sharply as it fought to gain some height. Tina leapt into the air and grabbed an underside runner with one hand. She hung beneath the helicopter as it swayed this way and that, thrown off-balance by her added weight. A machine gunner leaned out the side door and aimed his gun at Tina, but she reached up, grabbed his arm, and pulled him out the door. She threw him at the rooftop with all her strength, and his scream broke off as he hit hard enough to break every bone in his body.

The helicopter bucked and swayed as the pilot tried to shake Tina off, but she just reached up with her free hand, grabbed the fuel lines running under the fuselage, and ripped them away. Fuel jetted out, steaming thickly on the cool night air. The helicopter's engines coughed and failed, and the attack ship dropped toward the roof. Tina waited till her feet made contact with the roof and then she braced herself, took a firm hold on the runner, and shook the helicopter the way a dog shakes a rat. The crew screamed horribly as they were slammed against the interior walls, and Tina laughed happily. One of the gunners leaned out the side door and emptied his machine pistol into Tina's chest at point-blank range. She held onto the steel runner, even though her whole body bucked and heaved as bullets tore into her. Blood spurted thickly, from too many wounds to count. Tina cried out despite herself, but wouldn't give up her hold. The gunner finally ran out of ammunition; and Tina was still there. She showed him a smile with blood on her teeth, raised her free hand, and punched him so hard in the face that his features exploded and her fist got stuck inside his head. When she jerked her hand free, the gunner's dead body came tumbling out the doorway after it. Tina took a firm hold on the steel runner and hammered the helicopter against the roof again and again until the fuselage collapsed in on itself.

Another helicopter came sweeping in, all guns blazing. Tina took cover behind the wreckage of the one she'd crippled, and then lifted the whole thing off the roof with one quick jerk. She threw it at the advancing gunship, grunting out loud with the effort. The two helicopters exploded in a single great fireball that lit up the night with hellfire. A rotor blade broke away from one craft, and came spinning end over end across the roof, heading for Tina like a giant buzzsaw. The blade dug deep furrows in the rooftop, but even that barely slowed it down. Tina stood her ground until the blade was almost upon her, and then stepped nimbly aside at the last moment; the blade shot past her and disappeared over the edge of the roof.

Tina put back her head and howled like a wolf. Daniel moved in beside her, and joined his voice with hers. The savage cry of Hydes at war. They moved to stand back-to-back in the middle of the roof, blood coursing thickly down from their many wounds to form a great pool at their feet. They glared defiantly at the remaining helicopters, and the gunships broke off their attack and shot up into the night sky, out of the Hydes' reach. They hovered over Daniel and Tina, their combined downdraft holding the Hydes where they were. And then all the helicopter doors slid open, ropes were thrown out, and a small army of mercenary soldiers came rappelling down.

Their uniforms had no identifying marks or insignia; nothing to give away who they were, or who they worked for. The soldiers opened fire the moment their boots hit the rooftop, and the sheer impact of so much firepower was enough to drive the Hydes backward. Bullets raked Daniel and Tina from head to foot, and blood fountained on the air.

Daniel urged Tina toward the standing door, and moved quickly after her, shielding her body with his own. Bullets hammered into his back again and again. He struggled on, light-headed from blood loss and pain, but damned if he'd let that stop him. He yelled to Tina to hurry, and she'd almost reached the door when it suddenly burst open, and more soldiers came storming out onto the roof. Tina shouted back to Daniel:

"Throw me!"

Daniel grabbed her by the hips, lifted her into the air, and threw her at the soldiers with all his strength. She slammed into them like a wrecking ball, sending broken bodies flying in all directions. Some of the guns kept firing, with dead fingers on the triggers, cutting down their own people.

Daniel was quickly in and among the few mercenaries still standing, striking them down with vicious force before they could aim their guns. Tina lurched back onto her feet, and she and Daniel plunged through the open doorway. The last of the massed gunfire punched hole after bloody hole in their backs, until Daniel could slam the door shut behind them and force home the heavy bolts, and then he and Tina collapsed at the top of the stairwell.

They sat slumped against the bullet-pocked walls, shaking and shuddering and breathing strenuously. Their ragged clothes were soaked in blood, running down to pool around them. Daniel had to grit his teeth to keep from groaning aloud. He hadn't hurt this badly since the Frankensteins did a job on him. The heavy door jumped and trembled in its frame as the mercenaries opened up on it with everything they had, but the door held. Daniel smiled tiredly. Edward Hyde had never been one to stint on materials, when it came to guarding his back.

Daniel was so exhausted he could barely keep his eyes open. His head fell forward and sweat dripped steadily from his face onto the floor, tinted with blood. He'd thought nothing could touch him now he was a Hyde, but a fleet of helicopter gunships and an army of heavily-armed mercenaries had proved him wrong. He raised a trembling hand to examine the aching wounds in his chest, and his fingers came away dripping with gore. But he was still alive, when anyone else would have been dead a hundred times over. Daniel frowned as he heard a quiet *tink-tink* sound; when he looked down he saw flattened bullets being forced out of his wounds, and falling onto the stairwell floor. Daniel laughed softly, and the pain surged up viciously, but for the first time he thought there was a real chance he might just walk away from this.

He forced himself up onto his feet, in a series of carefully considered stages, and once he was up Tina's pride wouldn't allow her to do any less. She had to press her weight against the wall to do it, leaving a bloody smear on the bullet-riddled plaster, but eventually the Hydes stood together, swaying slightly. Daniel looked down the stairs, and they seemed to stretch endlessly away before him. But he made himself clatter down the steps, and Tina went with him.

"Tell me we are not running away," she said hoarsely. Her face was deathly pale behind the bloody streaks, and she was hugging herself tightly, as though trying to hold herself together.

"Of course we're not running," said Daniel. "We're just advancing toward a better place to fight back from."

"I can live with that," said Tina.

They continued down the stairs, leaving a trail of crimson smears behind them, followed by a thunder of sustained gunfire as bit by bit the mercenary soldiers demolished the standing door.

Daniel and Tina lurched out of the stairwell and into Edward's office, and Daniel locked the door behind them. It actually felt heavier than the one on the roof, but even as Daniel slammed the bolts home, he could make out a great many footsteps descending the stairs. He grabbed hold of Edward's massive desk—and then swore viciously as he discovered he couldn't move the heavy weight on his own. He needed Tina's help to force it over to the door, and then wedge it into position. Daniel looked blearily around him, and then forced himself away from the desk and headed for the door. Tina moved in beside him, and they leaned heavily on each other as they staggered out of the office, through the reception area, and on into the corridor.

"Elevators?" said Tina.

"Better not," said Daniel. "The mercenaries might cut the cables. I'm not sure even we could survive a drop like that."

Tina managed a ghost of her old smile. "Might be fun to try, someday."

"Business before pleasure," said Daniel. "I need to survive, if I'm going to take my revenge on these bastards."

"And whatever bastards sent them," said Tina.

"Good point," said Daniel. "Listen! Do you hear that?"

"The soldiers are getting closer," said Tina.

"We have to keep moving," said Daniel.

"The stairs," said Tina. "If they can't see us, they might stop looking for us."

"Worth a try," said Daniel.

They made their way down to the next floor. Every time Daniel's foot crashed against a step, waves of pain juddered through him, but Tina wasn't making a sound so he couldn't. He paused at the door to the next level, and Tina stopped to listen with him, but it wasn't long before they heard heavy footsteps hammering down the stairs after them.

"Bastards," said Tina.

"Someone has put a lot of thought into this attack," said Daniel.

"When I find out who, they're going to wish they hadn't," said Tina. "Next floor?"

"Worth a try," said Daniel.

But by the time they reached the next door the mercenaries had already closed the gap.

"Oh come on!" said Tina. "Can't we get a break?"

"Determined little soldiers of fortune, aren't they?" said Daniel. He grinned suddenly. "Let's give them a run for their money, and see just how determined they are."

Tina grinned back at him as she got the idea. "There's a lot of stairs between us and the lobby, and I'm ready to bet the soldiers will be in much worse shape than us when they finally catch up."

The Hydes summoned up the last of their resources and raced down one set of stairs after another, faster than any human could have managed. Daniel still hurt like hell, but he was starting to feel like himself again. The pursuing footsteps fell farther and farther behind, and finally died away completely. Some of the more optimistic mercenaries leaned out over the handrails and sprayed bullets down the stairwell, but none of them came close to hitting their targets.

Daniel finally burst through the last door and into the lobby, with Tina right there at his side. And then they both stopped dead, as they discovered the lobby was packed full of mercenaries. For a moment both sides just stood and stared at each other—and then all the soldiers opened fire at once. The sheer impact of so many bullets threw Daniel off his feet and left him lying sprawled on his back. Tina crouched protectively over him, snarling defiantly as more bullets hammered into her. One soldier threw a grenade, and it landed right at Daniel's feet. Tina threw herself on top of it, just as the grenade exploded. Her Hyde body absorbed most of the blast, but it was still enough to toss her through the air and leave her lying dazed on the floor beside Daniel.

Fortunately, the explosion also filled the lobby with smoke, hiding Daniel and Tina from their enemies. They helped each other up, and then leaned heavily on each other for support as they glared around into the smoke. They were both soaked with fresh blood that was pattering heavily onto the parquet floor, but Daniel was sure he could feel his wounds healing, even if the pain was so bad he could barely breathe. He nodded brusquely to Tina.

"When I say run, we run right at the bastards. Get in among them before they can aim their guns, and then see how many of them we can take with us."

"Sounds like a plan to me, Sundance," said Tina. "How many are there, do you think?"

"Too many," said Daniel.

"No such thing," said Tina.

And that was when a trapdoor dropped open in the ceiling right over their heads, and a voice shouted down to them.

"Get your arses up here, before those soldiers make a meal of you!"

Daniel grabbed Tina and tossed her up and through the trapdoor, and she shot through without even touching the sides. Daniel jumped up after her, but only had enough strength left to grab the side of the opening with one hand. He snarled at his own weakness, forced himself up and through, and then closed the trapdoor and slammed the bolts home.

He lay on his back beside the trapdoor, breathing hoarsely. Tina sat slumped forward, her head hanging down. The trapdoor shook and shuddered as a great many bullets tore into it from below, but the door held off the attack with contemptuous ease. The massed gunfire died away, and Daniel slowly allowed himself to relax. In the sudden quiet, he could hear more *tink-tink* noises as his healing wounds forced more bullets out.

After a while, Daniel rose slowly and painfully to his feet, and reached out a hand to pull Tina up beside him. He looked around and realized they were inside the Hyde armory. A massive warehouse that took up most of the building's first floor, the great maze of open shelves and display cases were packed with all kinds of weird and wonderful weapons. Daniel smiled slowly.

"We should be able to find something here to ruin the mercenaries' day."

Tina spat out a mouthful of blood, and wiped the back of her hand across her mouth.

"Find me a gun," she said thickly. "I want a really big gun, with poisoned bullets."

"I'm not seeing anyone to ask," said Daniel.

"I heard a voice," said Tina. "Didn't you hear a voice?"

"I definitely heard someone," said Daniel. And then he gestured urgently at Tina. "Listen . . . They've stopped shooting."

"Why would they do that?" said Tina.

Daniel shrugged, and then stopped because it hurt too much.

"Maybe they ran out of bullets. They have been firing them off like there's no tomorrow."

"Wouldn't do them any good anyway," said Tina. "This armory was constructed to keep really dangerous stuff from getting out, so it should be strong enough to keep a few soldiers for hire from getting in."

"Emphasis on the word *should*," said Daniel. "I'm not feeling as optimistic as I used to be. I hate to admit it, but we got a little too cocky up on the roof. We could have died up there."

"Emphasis on the *could have*," said Tina.

And then the whole armory shook from end to end, in response to a series of explosions from outside. Daniel and Tina ended up lying facedown on the floor, as one tremendous blast after another shook the building. Daniel held Tina to him, his arms wrapped protectively around her, as the floor rose and fell and dangerous items were thrown off the shelves. The lights flickered, and some of them went out. Dust fell from the ceiling in a series of sudden rushes. Finally, the explosions came to an end, and the shelves stopped rocking.

Tina sat up, and threw off Daniel's arms. "I do not need protecting!"

"Next time, you can protect me," said Daniel.

Tina smiled briefly. "I'm not sure we could survive a next time."

They helped each other back onto their feet, and looked around them. Everything seemed very still.

"Is that it?" said Tina. "Is it over?"

"I hate to think there might be something else they could throw at us," said Daniel.

"It's so quiet . . . Do you think the soldiers have left?" said Tina. "I mean, you know I'm always up for a good fight, but those odds and that many weapons took a lot of the fun out of it."

Daniel hadn't realized how shaken Tina was, until he heard her admit to such a thought.

"How are you feeling?" he said.

"Fine," she said immediately. "It'll take more than a few explosions and a hailstorm of bullets to put me off my game. You?"

"I've got my second wind," said Daniel. "Let's go back down into the lobby, and see what's going on."

"Good idea," said Tina. "They might have left someone behind for me to hit."

Daniel pulled back the bolts on the trapdoor, hauled it open, and then stood quickly back out of range, just in case anything might come flying up. Daniel gave it a moment and then leaned cautiously forward to peer down through the opening. There was a lot of smoke drifting around, but no one reacted to his appearance. He dropped down through the gap, with Tina only a moment behind him. They glared quickly around them, braced for action, but the lobby was deserted.

The smoke started to clear, and Daniel growled loudly as he took in the sheer scale of the mercenaries' destruction. The walls were riddled with bullet holes, and the floor and ceiling were horribly scarred from shrapnel and blast damage. The wooden scroll of names had been mostly blown off the wall, so that only the top part remained; the gold-leaf lettering of Jekyll & Hyde Inc. was so scorched as to be almost unreadable. The interior doors had been blown off their hinges, and Daniel could hear fires burning deeper inside the building.

"I'm not seeing any bodies," Tina said quietly. "The soldiers took their dead with them when they left."

"Probably so they couldn't be identified," said Daniel.

"All this, and we don't even know who did it to us," said Tina.

"We'll find out," said Daniel.

He headed for the front door, hanging half out of its frame on shattered hinges, and Tina fell in beside him. They burst through the doorway, ready for anything . . . but the street was empty. Nothing moved in the dull amber streetlight. Broken glass crunched under Daniel's feet as he stepped slowly forward. All the lights in the surrounding buildings had been turned off, as though no one wanted to attract attention to themselves. Daniel frowned, as he realized the sound of crackling flames was actually louder outside the building. He turned around and must have made some kind of sound, because Tina immediately turned to look too.

The Jekyll & Hyde Inc. building was a wreck. Most of the windows had been shattered, and the entire frontage was cracked or bowed out. Fires blazed from windows up and down the length of the structure. The mercenaries had set explosives in just the right places. The rooftop was a mess, nothing but shattered concrete and protruding bent steel girders. Thick smoke billowed up into the night sky.

"Someone really doesn't like us," said Tina.

"This was a preemptive strike," Daniel said flatly, "by one of the alien groups. They must have decided we were bound to come after them now all the monsters are dead, and decided to get their retaliation in first."

"All our strength," said Tina, "and we still couldn't stop them."

"It's not enough to be strong anymore," said Daniel. "We have to be smart. Still, look on the bright side."

Tina tore her gaze away from the devastated building to stare at him.

"There's a bright side?"

"They couldn't kill us," said Daniel. "And they tried really hard."

"Trust me, I remember," said Tina. "I'm going to be digging bullets out of my arse for weeks."

Several ungallant comments passed through Daniel's mind, but he had enough sense not to say any of them.

"So," said Tina. "What are we going to do? What can we do, now the aliens have blown Jekyll & Hyde Inc. off the map?"

"All they destroyed was a building," said Daniel. "*We* are Jekyll & Hyde Inc., in every way that matters. And, we still have the armory."

Tina brightened. "A whole warehouse full of nasty weapons and horribly destructive dirty tricks. Just what we need to express our extreme displeasure to the aliens. Suddenly, I feel a whole lot better."

"Thought you might," said Daniel. He glanced up and down the conspicuously deserted street. "I think it's going to be a while before any of the authorities show up. No police, no fire engines, no ambulances . . . Because a full-on assault by a fleet of helicopter gunships, backed by mercenary soldiers, couldn't happen in the middle of London unless some very high-up people were warned and paid off in advance."

"At least that should give us some time, to search the armory for everything we're going to need to bring the hammer down on all the alien bases," said Tina. "No one does this to us and gets away with it."

"I still want to know who called out to us from inside the armory and saved our lives," said Daniel.

Tina frowned. "We're the only Hydes left; everyone else ran away."

"Apparently not everyone," said Daniel. He smiled briefly. "I suppose it could have been the ghost of Edward Hyde."

Tina shook her head firmly. "Hydes don't do ghosts."

Chapter Two
EDWARD HYDE'S LEGACY

✣ ✣ ✣

DANIEL TURNED AWAY FROM what was left of the Jekyll & Hyde Inc. building, because looking at it depressed him. He'd never cared much for the place, or the man who ran it, but the destruction of the building that had changed his life left a hole inside him he wasn't sure he would ever fill. A cold wind came blowing down the deserted street, surrounding him with the scents of fire and smoke and destruction, as though to remind him that the world doesn't care how bad you're feeling, you still have to get on with what needs doing. And then Daniel frowned and turned to Tina, as a thought occurred to him.

"Edward's file and laptop could still be up there, in his office," he said. "We're going to need that information, if we're to take on the aliens."

Tina glared at the top of the building. "Edward's office was right underneath the roof, and that's been blown to pieces. I doubt there's much left of Edward's inner sanctum."

"But we only skimmed the file," said Daniel. "There could be all kinds of useful information we never got to. Things we need to know."

"Are you seriously suggesting we tramp all the way back up those stairs?" said Tina. "You might feel up to that, but I sure as hell don't. I have used up my second and third wind, my inner resources have phoned in sick, and I would be hard-pressed to punch out a dormouse that wrinkled its nose at me funny. Who knew that having the shit shot out of you by soldiers with really big guns could put such a damper on your day?"

"I hurt too," said Daniel. "But I'm not giving up."

"Who said anything about giving up?" Tina kept her glare fixed on the wreckage where the roof had been, rather than look at him. "But even if we could haul our broken arses all the way up there without going into full meltdown, the odds are the mercs have already ransacked the office and walked off with the file and the laptop. If only to make sure we couldn't have them."

Daniel scowled as he considered the matter, though he was careful not to aim the scowl at Tina, who had a very short fuse when it came to feeling slighted.

"The file might be gone," he said carefully, "but the original information must still be out there, somewhere. So we'll just have to go and dig it up ourselves."

Tina managed a small sniff, because she didn't have the strength for anything more impressive.

"You can bet the aliens will have people waiting for us, so they can really ruin our day."

"Then we need to arm ourselves," Daniel said firmly. "Let's take a wander through the armory, and grab handfuls of nasty and destructive off the shelves."

"Because being a Hyde isn't enough anymore," said Tina.

Daniel didn't know what to say. He'd never heard Tina sound so beaten down before. In the end, she shook her head fiercely and straightened her back. It produced a series of low creaking sounds that made Daniel wince, but he thought Tina looked more like herself.

"We do need to check out the armory," she said, still not looking at him, "if only to find out who it was that called to us, and saved our backsides."

"I *would* like to know why," said Daniel. "I am not in a mood to trust anyone, just at the moment."

"Now you're thinking like a Hyde," said Tina. "Trust, but verify, and then kick the crap out of them."

When they went back into the lobby, it looked like someone had fought World War III there and not bothered to clean up afterward. A few traces of smoke were still drifting aimlessly on the air, not even trying to disguise the mass destruction and scattered rubble. But there was one change: someone had dropped a rope ladder through the trapdoor. It hung invitingly before them, looking strong and sturdy and not at all like a trap. Daniel and Tina walked slowly over to the ladder, and considered it thoughtfully.

"It would seem we're expected," said Daniel.

"'Welcome to my ambush,' said the spider to the fly," said Tina.

"I hate spiders," said Daniel. "Particularly those big long-leggity ones you find in the bottom of the bath. It's a good thing there weren't any giant-spider monster Clans, because I would have screamed like a little girl, bolted for the nearest horizon, and left you to deal with it."

Tina nodded understandingly. "I hate the way they dart out from under your furniture, and scurry across the carpet. They may serve a purpose in nature, but I am not having them in my home."

"Exactly," said Daniel. "If they come to where I live, they're asking for it."

They were just putting off going up the ladder, and they knew it.

"Whoever's up there is making this almost too easy," said Daniel.

"Right," said Tina. "They'll be offering us tea and cakes next."

"Actually, I wouldn't mind some tea and cakes," said Daniel.

"Never from a stranger," Tina said firmly.

"We need to get into the armory," said Daniel.

Tina looked at him. "Even though it's almost certainly a trap?"

Daniel smiled. "The best way to deal with a trap . . ."

"Is to walk right into it," said Tina. "Hyde 101. But that was before."

"I am feeling more and more in the mood to get back on the horse that threw us, and show it what spurs are for," said Daniel. "Come on, Tina: we took on a whole army, and a bucketload of bullets, and still walked away. That has to count for something."

"You would think so, wouldn't you?" said Tina.

"The horse is waiting, and starting to give you funny looks," said Daniel. "How strong are you feeling?"

Tina gave the rope ladder her best hard look. "Strong enough."

"Same here," said Daniel. "Let's do this."

Tina shouldered him out of the way so she could get to the ladder first, and he went up after her, trying not to feel seasick as Tina's weight sent the ladder plunging back and forth. She stopped halfway up, ostensibly to get her breath, but Daniel was having none of that. He rammed the top of his head against her bottom and gave it a good shove. Tina snarled something Daniel was pretty sure he was better off not hearing, and scrambled up the ladder. She hauled herself through the trapdoor, and Daniel made sure he was right behind her, not wanting to leave her on her own. Partly because it really might be a trap, but also because he didn't want her doing anything impulsive until they'd got a better feel for the lay of the land.

He found Tina holding herself in a defensive stance, her hands clenched into fists as she glared around in search of something worth hitting. The armory was still and quiet and apparently intact, preserved by its heavy walls and protections. At least half the lights were on, though there still seemed as much gloom as illumination. Daniel smiled briefly; the armory had always preferred to keep itself to itself, because people might not approve of what its contents got up to in the shadows. Daniel stood tall, and looked around him as though he meant to take the whole place by the scruff of the neck and shake it until someone fell out. He raised his voice.

"Hello! Is there anybody there?"

"And if not, why not?" said Tina.

Daniel looked round sharply, as he heard someone moving about. He strained his eyes against the gloom, but still couldn't make out anything. The sounds came again, but this time from a completely different part of the armory. Whoever it was, they were fast. Tina grabbed something large and blocky from a nearby shelf, and threw it in the direction of the noises. An item on a distant shelf toppled to the floor, but there was nothing to indicate she'd found her target.

"I'm not seeing anyone," Daniel said quietly.

"I'm not even sure what it was I heard," said Tina, "except that it moved like a greased weasel on amphetamines. Did it sound human to you?"

Daniel looked at her sharply. "You think something might have got in here?"

"More likely, something got out," said Tina. "Remember the rat?"

"How could I forget?"

Like all good scientists, Dr. Jekyll tested his Elixir on an animal before taking it himself. The result had been a rat the size of a Rottweiler, with teeth like knives and the disposition of Jack the

Ripper on a really bad day. Not surprisingly, Dr. Jekyll locked his lab rat inside a crate the size of a coffin, and left it there. A century later, Daniel and Tina stumbled across it in the armory while looking for something else, and accidentally let it out. The rat was still very much alive, and not in the best of moods. The three of them wrecked half the armory before Daniel and Tina were able to force the rat back inside its coffin and lock it up again. Because they weren't sure they could kill it. Now Daniel had to wonder if just possibly the explosions had been strong enough to shake the whole armory so badly that rat had broken loose again . . .

Footsteps moved quickly through the shadows, and Daniel felt a surge of relief as he realized they were definitely human.

"Someone is messing with us," he said quietly.

"You think?" said Tina. "Whoever that is, they're really quick on their feet."

"Maybe they're scared of us," said Daniel.

"That would make for a nice change," said Tina, just a bit wistfully. "Remember when people would actually fill their trousers, just because we were heading in their direction?"

"Ah, the good old days," said Daniel. "We need to get our mojo back."

"We need a lot of things," said Tina.

Daniel aimed his voice at the last place the noises had stopped.

"Who are you? Why can't we see you?"

"Because you're not looking in the right place," said a cold, measured voice.

From out of a deep dark shadow right next to Daniel stepped a very dark-skinned woman. Tall and lithe, with a cool, calculating expression, she had a gun in each hand aimed unwaveringly at Daniel and Tina. There was a time Daniel would have just slapped the guns out of her hands and crushed them into novelty paperweights; but his experiences with the mercenaries had taught him to be wary of unfamiliar guns. Especially now they were inside an armory that specialized in really unpleasant weapons. So he stood very still, with Tina seething quietly beside him, and watched for an opening.

Neither Hyde raised their hands, because they still had their pride.

Daniel left it to the mysterious intruder to make the next move, but let the look on his face make it clear that it had better be a good one. Daniel might not have been as strong or as fast as he was before a whole bunch of mercenaries shot the hell out of him, but he was pretty sure he could still jump out of the line of fire if the woman even looked like she was going to pull the trigger. Daniel gave her his best *make up your mind, we haven't got all night* look.

"Well?" he said. "Aren't you at least going to introduce yourself? Tina and I are being unusually patient, but given that we are Hydes there's no knowing how long that will last."

"What he said, only with several extra layers of menace," said Tina.

"You are not going to start anything, because those mercenaries really did a number on you," the woman said calmly. "It would appear there is a limit to how much punishment a Hyde can soak up, after all. I should take notes."

She put her guns away with a swift motion and Daniel relaxed, just a little. The woman looked them over carefully.

"Daniel and Tina Hyde: the final products of Dr. Jekyll's infamous Elixir. A tribute to bad living through chemistry. The Elixir brought out the beast in Edward, but on you it looks good. I've read his file, on how you took down the monster Clans. Ten out of ten for bravery and brute force, but minus several hundred for lack of subtlety. You were both obscenely lucky. Any number of things could have gone wrong with what I hesitate to describe as your plans; and tonight you found out what happens when you don't have a plan, you're improvising wildly, and your guardian angel has gone feral. In the past you could afford to coast on your reputation for being unstoppable, but I think we can safely assume that horse has bolted from the burning stable. Good Lord, look at the state of you."

Daniel looked down at himself. His suit was badly charred, and actually burned away in places. There were more bullet holes than he'd expected, along with a lot more bloodstains than he was comfortable seeing. He glanced at Tina, and if anything she looked even worse. Her smart business suit had been reduced to a thing of rags and tatters, held together by dried blood. The large areas of bare flesh on open display showed more bruises than skin. He caught Tina looking at him, and saw the same shock in her face that he was feeling. He tried for a smile.

"I look like I was used as a Guy on November Fifth, and you look like you've been fed feetfirst through a wood chipper."

Tina sniffed loudly. "But we are still here, while a lot of the mercenaries aren't."

"You're here because I intervened," said the woman. "If I hadn't, those soldiers would have scattered bits and pieces of you all over the lobby."

"Who are you?" said Daniel.

She took a step forward into the light, so the Hydes could get a better look. Almost as tall as Daniel, her skin was so black it had blue highlights. Her face had sharp-edged bones, her cold gaze was direct and challenging, and her mouth looked like it had never learned how to smile. She was wearing a black silk blouse over black slacks, with black leather gloves on her long slender hands. Her stance showed grace and strength, along with impressive levels of self-confidence—but not a touch of Hyde. It suddenly occurred to Daniel that she wasn't wearing any kind of holster, so he had to wonder where her guns had disappeared to when she put them away. It didn't seem like the right time to ask.

The woman nodded stiffly to Daniel and Tina, as though it was something she'd heard about but never actually done before.

"I am Patricia Mannering. I used to be the armorer here. I designed a lot of the weapons and devices currently lurking on these shelves. I left because Edward kept pressuring me to take the Hyde Elixir—to bind me more closely to his organization. I wasn't prepared to do that, because I didn't want to risk anything that might disturb the balance of my marvelous mind."

"A little old lady called Miss Montague was the armorer when I joined up," said Daniel.

"She trained me," said Patricia. She gestured brusquely at the stacks around her. "I'm here because you're going to need weapons to take on the aliens. And someone who can help you plan strategy. Because just being a Hyde won't be enough to get you through, this time."

"Why did you intervene to save us?" Tina said bluntly.

"Somebody had to," said Patricia.

Tina started to bristle, so Daniel quickly cut in before things could escalate.

"If you left the armory, what brought you back? And why tonight, of all nights?"

"What he said," said Tina. "Only even more suspiciously."

Patricia kept her gaze fixed on Daniel. Perhaps because she knew he was the one she needed to convince.

"I keep my ear to the ground. People still tell me things. I knew it was time to return when I heard Edward was dead."

"That was quick," said Tina.

"Good news travels fast," said Patricia. "And there was a whisper that something big and dramatic would be happening here tonight, so I let myself in through a back door only armorers know about."

She looked around, in a proprietary sort of way. As though she'd come home. Daniel thought her face showed an odd sort of nostalgia for a warehouse full of mayhem and mass destruction, but he had enough sense not to say anything. And then her gaze snapped back to him, so quickly he almost jumped.

"I believed in Jekyll & Hyde Inc.," said Patricia, "and all the things it could achieve, though I never had much time for the man in charge. Edward never got over being shunned by his fellow monsters. Did he tell you he refused to be a criminal? The truth is, he was never asked. None of the Clans wanted him. So he built this incredible organization, and then wasted it on a never-ending act of revenge.

"I stayed on because I thought I could change things for the better. That I could make the world a better place, with an army of Hydes to back me up. But Edward would only ever look back, never forward."

"You knew the other Hydes?" said Daniel. "I never got to meet any of them, only Tina."

"Because Edward killed them all," said Tina.

Patricia nodded slowly. "That happened after I left. I sometimes wonder if I'd stayed, whether I could have prevented that... but it was inevitable that the day would come when Edward could only see them as a threat." She paused for a moment, her eyes lost in yesterday, and then they snapped back to focus on Tina, who growled under her breath to show how not at all intimidated she was. For a moment Daniel thought Patricia might smile.

"So," said the armorer. "You are the last of Dr. Jekyll's children, and I am all that's left of the staff. Just what we need, to rebuild Jekyll & Hyde Inc. You'll go far, with me to guide you."

"Hold it right there," said Tina. "Who put you in charge?"

"You need me," said Patricia. "You make good agents, and better weapons, but you'll never get anywhere without someone to point you in the right direction."

"Hydes don't do authority figures," said Daniel.

"We trusted Edward," said Tina, "and that didn't work out too well for us."

Daniel looked at her. "I don't know that we ever actually trusted him. We just assumed that because he knew more than we did, he knew what he was doing."

"He betrayed us, by letting us think we were heroes," said Tina. She scowled at Patricia. "We won't be used again."

Patricia subtly shifted her line of attack. "I was careful to use the word *guide*, in my offer of assistance. I didn't come back to be your boss, just your armorer. I will provide you with the very best weapons, background support, and up-to-date intelligence to help you bring down the aliens."

"How much do you know about them?" said Daniel.

"I compiled the information in Edward's file," said Patricia. "You *have* seen the file, haven't you?"

"We only had a chance to flip through that, before the mercenaries turned up," said Tina. "No telling what happened to it, after that."

Patricia looked at her for an uncomfortably long moment. "You lost the file? You really do need looking after. All right, some background. Miss Montague trained me to be her successor, after Edward forced her to retire."

"What did you do before you came here?" Daniel said politely.

"Bad things," said Patricia. "Bad enough that I needed a cause worth fighting for. I thought I'd found it in Jekyll & Hyde Inc., but I should have known anything born of Edward's twisted ambitions would be bound to have the mark of Cain on its brow. It was always going to be all about the killing."

"If he got rid of Miss Montague, why did he bring her back after you left?" said Tina.

"After what he chose to see as my betrayal, he needed someone he thought he could trust."

"Why didn't she find someone else to train?" said Daniel.

"I was a hard act to follow," said Patricia. "Now, before we do anything else . . ."

"Okay, hit the brakes and throw the anchor over the side," said Tina. "What was all that running about in the shadows for?"

"I needed to be sure there was no one else here," said Patricia. "And after everything that happened on the roof tonight, I also needed to be sure you hadn't lost your nerve. That you were still Hydes."

"Count on it," said Daniel.

"I am," said Patricia. "Now . . . being the paranoid and vindictive soul that he was, Edward left some nasty surprises scattered around, to be activated after his death. A few last acts of revenge, on people he hated. And unfortunately, one of them has turned up here. We need to do something about it, before it can destroy the entire armoury."

"Is it a bomb?" said Tina. "Miss Montague had a real fondness for bombs."

"Something much nastier, I fear," said Patricia.

"Where is it?" Daniel said resignedly.

Patricia turned abruptly and strode off into the shadows. Tina made a rude gesture at her departing back, and growled something Daniel pretended not to have heard. He put a warning hand on Tina's arm, and leaned in so he could murmur in her ear.

"Please don't upset the nice new armorer. She could be useful."

Tina scowled. "I hate to admit it, but you're right. With the file and the laptop gone, she's our only source for information on the aliens. Even if she is a snotty, arrogant cow."

"Look on the bright side," said Daniel.

Tina looked at him. "There's a bright side?"

"Things can only get better."

"I have always admired your optimism," said Tina.

Daniel realized that Patricia had got so far ahead she was almost out of sight, and hurried after her. Tina stuck close beside him as he navigated his way through the maze of narrow passageways separating the high shelves. They passed stacks crammed with weird weapons and intriguing devices, including some things that made absolutely no sense at all, and a few that turned in place to watch the

Hydes go by. Nothing was ever labeled or identified, probably because most of it came under the heading of *You really don't want to know.* Daniel's eye was caught by one particularly intriguing item, and he reached out to pick it up. Without even glancing back, Patricia raised her voice.

"Don't touch anything!"

Daniel withdrew his hand, and nodded to Tina. "Just like old times . . ."

"Let's hope not," said Tina. "The last armorer tried to kill us."

"Only because she was in love with Edward Hyde," said Daniel. "I don't think we're going to have that problem this time."

"You got that right," Patricia said loudly.

She suddenly came to a halt. The Hydes almost crashed into her, but had enough sense not to. Patricia indicated a large wooden trunk sitting right in the middle of the aisle.

"I think this is close enough."

"It doesn't look particularly threatening," Daniel said carefully. "What makes you think this is one of Edward's nasty surprises?"

"Because it's not part of the armory's inventory," said Patricia. "And anyway, nothing is ever left out in the aisles, in case someone trips over it and the whole place goes up. I have a very bad feeling about this."

"I have a bad feeling about most of the things here!" said Tina. "In fact, I would have thought bad feelings came as standard."

"She has a point," said Daniel. "The first time I came here, there was a sign over the main entrance saying *Don't Drop Anything.*"

"Miss Montague showed me a black hole in a jam jar!" said Tina.

Patricia looked at her. "I don't suppose you happen to remember where it was? I've always wanted one of those, for my collection."

"You have a collection?" said Daniel.

"Every girl should have a hobby," said Patricia. "Now can we please concentrate on the mysterious trunk that could probably wipe us all out if it felt like it?"

"All I'm seeing is an old-fashioned steamer trunk, held together by leather straps," said Daniel. "I'm not even hearing any ticking . . ."

"Why would Edward would want to destroy his own armory, when he knows we're going to need what's here to fight the aliens?" said Tina.

"He did enjoy his little practical jokes," said Patricia.

"Do you have any idea what's inside?" said Daniel.

"No," said Patricia. "But it looks big enough to contain something that could do an awful lot of damage if it ever got out."

Daniel looked at Tina. He didn't mention the word *rat* because he didn't need to.

"Stand back," said Tina. "I'm going to give it a good kick."

Daniel looked at her. "Why?"

"See if I can wake something up."

"And you think that's a good thing?"

"Wimp," said Tina.

"I can't believe I'm having to say this," said Patricia, "but no one is to kick the potentially very dangerous object!"

"Well," said Tina. "You're no fun."

"Haven't you been blown up enough for one day?" said Patricia.

"It's a Hyde thing," Tina said loftily. "You wouldn't understand."

Daniel cut in quickly, though he was getting just a bit tired of having to do that.

"What can you tell us about this trunk?"

"When the staff of Jekyll & Hyde Inc. left, in something of a hurry thanks to you, they needed a shoulder to cry on," said Patricia. "A number of them sought me out, to unburden themselves about some of the things Edward Hyde made them do—including dropping off a trunk in the armory, that they had been strictly instructed not to look inside."

"Is there anything helpful you can tell us?" said Tina.

"I inspected the trunk earlier, while being very careful not to touch anything or even breathe heavily on it," said Patricia. "The lid is held shut not just by leather straps, but by a solid steel lock you couldn't lever off with a crowbar. I just hope I haven't activated anything by getting too close."

"So whatever happens next, it's all your fault," Tina said happily.

Patricia sighed. "It's like working with children . . ."

"Is this why you saved us?" said Daniel. "Because you need us to deal with this?"

Patricia gave him a long-suffering look. "Try not to be as paranoid as Edward. He needs you to fight the aliens, so there is a good chance this trunk contains special weapons intended for your use. But knowing him, it could also contain some kind of booby trap to protect the contents."

"So it could blow up in our face because it's a defense mechanism . . . or because it's an act of revenge?" said Tina.

"Those are the main possibilities," said Patricia.

Tina looked around. "Isn't there anything here we could use to open the trunk? Or at least blow the lid off?"

Patricia bestowed another of her long-suffering looks. "Do we really want to risk setting off whatever might be in there?"

"I'm still thinking of Dr. Jekyll's test rat," said Daniel.

"You don't need to worry about that," said Patricia. "I found a description of it in the inventory, and since I couldn't see a single good reason to keep something like that alive, I pushed the whole container into the incinerator. And before you ask, no, we are not pushing the potentially very explosive trunk into an incinerator. Particularly when there is still a good chance it might contain something we're going to need to stop the aliens."

Daniel scowled at the trunk. "We need to get in there, so we can see what we're dealing with."

"Do I really need to mention the words *booby trap* again?" said Patricia.

"We could always throw Tina on top of it," said Daniel.

"I want to kick the trunk!" said Tina. "I'm just in the mood to kick something."

"Never knew you when you weren't," said Daniel. He smiled at her. "I don't know where you get your energy from. You went through the same shit I did, and I'm running on fumes."

Tina shrugged. "I've felt worse."

"Must have been one hell of a party," said Daniel. He studied the trunk for a moment. "I say we just open it and see what happens."

"Really?" said Patricia. "That's your solution to the problem?"

"Hydes are very hard to kill," said Daniel. "And we do love a challenge."

"Oh we do," Tina said cheerfully. "Really. You have no idea."

"Even after everything you've been through tonight?" said Patricia.

Daniel gave her his best hard look. "*Because* of what we've been through. Now back off several yards and duck down behind something substantial, while Tina and I walk into the big bad cave and kick the sleeping bear in the nuts."

"Fun time!" said Tina.

"Hydes are weird," said Patricia.

She fell back two steps, and suddenly there was a really big gun in her hand, aimed unwaveringly at the trunk. Daniel didn't see where the gun came from, and couldn't help noticing it looked completely different from the ones she'd had earlier.

"You do what you have to," said Patricia. "But if anything comes out of that trunk that doesn't look one hundred percent friendly, I am going to fill it so full of holes you could use it as a golf course."

"You're thinking of the rat, aren't you?" said Daniel.

"Edward had a very basic sense of humor," said Patricia. "And I didn't actually open the coffin thing, before I pushed it in the incinerator."

Daniel advanced on the trunk, and Tina immediately moved in beside him.

"So," she said lightly. "Do we have anything approaching a plan?"

"Rip off the lock, open the lid, and see what's what," said Daniel. "And then kick the crap out of it, if necessary."

"That does have the virtue of simplicity," said Tina. "But what if there is a bomb? To be honest, I am feeling a bit fragile. I'd rather not be blown up again."

"It has been a hard day's night," said Daniel. "But if there are alien-killing weapons in there, I want them."

They stopped before the trunk. Daniel couldn't help feeling it was looking back at him—and not in a good way.

"Come on," said Tina. "What are the chances of another rat?"

"I was thinking more of a guard dog," said Daniel.

"Let it out," said Tina. "I'm feeling peckish."

Daniel grabbed hold of the heavy steel lock and ripped it off the lid with one great wrench. Nothing happened, so he crushed the lock in his hand and threw it away. He undid the leather straps one at a time, and then threw the lid all the way back. And a massive jack-in-the-box jumped up, grinning like a Mr. Punch who'd gone feral, and brandishing a bloodstained hatchet. Patricia blew its head off with one bullet. The headless puppet collapsed, in a sulky sort of way. Tina shook her head.

"Edward and his sense of humor."

"Makes me wish he was still alive," said Daniel. "So I could kill him all over again."

He hauled the headless Jack out of the trunk, tossed it down the aisle, and stared into the trunk. Tina and Patricia moved in on either side of him. There were no explosives, no booby traps, and no weapons. Just a dozen slim bottles. Daniel fished one out, unscrewed the cap, and took a cautious sniff.

"It's Dr. Jekyll's Elixir."

He handed the bottle to Tina. She took a quick sniff, nodded in agreement, and offered it to Patricia, who really didn't want to know. Tina handed the bottle to Daniel, and he carefully screwed the cap back on, before placing the bottle back in the trunk.

"Aren't you going to taste it, to be sure?" said Patricia.

"One dose changes you into a Hyde, another turns you back," said Daniel. "And I am never going back to what I was."

"I didn't think there was any of the Elixir left," said Tina. "Edward was supposed to have run out."

"But we know he killed all the other Hydes," said Daniel. "He could have recovered the last traces of the Elixir from their bodies."

"That does sound like something he would do," said Patricia.

Daniel searched the trunk carefully, but there were no instructions or letter of intent. Not even a secret compartment, with a clue tucked away.

"Maybe we're supposed to create an army of Hydes," said Tina.

"It only took the two of us to bring down all the monster Clans," said Daniel.

"The monsters didn't have their own private armies to protect them," said Tina. "Maybe it will take an army of Hydes, to overcome an army of mercenaries."

A thought occurred to Daniel, and he turned to Patricia. He started to say something and then stopped, as he realized the gun had disappeared from her hand, with no trace of where it might have gone. That was starting to worry him. He made himself concentrate and started again.

"You told us you compiled the information on aliens that ended up in Edward's file. How did you learn so much about them?"

"Jekyll & Hyde Inc. sent agents out into the field, to gather intelligence," said Patricia. "Edward had them all report to me, because I had to develop new weapons to fight the aliens. It didn't take me long to realize I couldn't learn enough at second hand, so I started sitting in with Edward when he met the aliens' human emissaries. With a gun in my hand. He felt it helped send the right message."

"Why were the aliens so keen to make use of Jekyll & Hyde Inc.?" said Daniel.

"Because Edward was the only one to defy all the monsters and make it stick," said Patricia. "They probably thought they could learn from him. And they really wanted the secret of the Elixir, to make them superior to their fellow aliens."

"Did they respect Edward, as an enemy?" said Tina.

"None of the aliens have any respect for Humanity," Patricia said flatly. "They only want our world. Their only use for Edward was as a resource and a weapon. I never had any doubt that once the monsters were gone, Edward would join the rest of Humanity up against the wall. That's why I stayed with Jekyll & Hyde Inc. as long as I did. Because I knew Edward's war wouldn't end with the end of the monsters."

"You're back now," said Tina, in a not entirely accusing way.

"Edward's dead," said Patricia. "But the aliens are still out there."

Daniel frowned. "Do you think the mercenary soldiers know what the aliens have planned for us?"

"Mercenaries fight for money, not causes," said Patricia.

"Even so," said Daniel, "to fight for creatures whose only purpose is to wipe out Humanity..."

"Mercenaries aren't known for thinking ahead," Patricia said dryly. "They probably think that as long as they keep playing one set of aliens against another, they can have a never-ending payday. They may even believe that as long as they can keep that up, they're actually preventing the invasions."

"Denial isn't just a river in Egypt," said Daniel.

Tina looked hard at Patricia. "You've put a lot of thought into this."

"It's what I do," said Patricia. She scowled at the flasks in the trunk. "I was really hoping for some kind of new and unpleasant weapons. Something to put us on an even footing with the aliens. Sending an assault crew to kill you and blow up the building was just an opening gambit. By removing you from the board, they could concentrate on their real enemies: each other. None of them can begin an invasion until they have control on the ground."

"You've thought about that too," said Tina.

"It's been on my mind for some time," said Patricia.

"So we're all that's left to stop them," said Daniel. "Two Hydes, one armorer, and a blown-up building."

"But the armory is still intact," said Patricia. "I can provide you with everything you need, specially tailored to take advantage of each particular alien's weaknesses. I can even train you on how to use the weapons so you won't blow yourselves up."

Daniel looked at Tina. "Doesn't have a lot of faith in us, does she?"

"She just doesn't know us yet," said Tina. She fixed Patricia with a thoughtful gaze. "If you know where all the weapons are, why didn't you throw some down into the lobby so we could use them against the mercenaries?"

"Because I had more sense than to show myself," said Patricia. "Even the most powerful weapon can't protect you from getting your head blown off by a stray bullet."

"We could have been killed!" said Daniel.

Patricia shrugged. "Better you than me."

"Are you sure you're not a Hyde?" said Tina.

"If we had died, what would have happened to your plans?" said Daniel.

"I was reasonably sure you would survive," said Patricia. "And if you couldn't... then you were no use to me anyway."

"Okay..." said Tina. "Someone just crossed the line. Get out of my way, Daniel, I have my kicking trousers on."

"You can't hurt me," said Patricia.

"Going to give it a damn good try," said Tina.

"You need me," said Patricia. "Or you will, once you've located the alien bases."

Daniel stopped Tina with a raised hand. "Why is that down to us?"

"I have information on the general situation, but nothing specific," Patricia said carefully. "You have to discover where each alien base is, how it's protected, and the best ways to break in.

Edward's people did their best, but you've seen the kind of resources the aliens can call on to protect their secrets."

"So we get to have another crack at the soldier boys," said Tina. She cracked her knuckles loudly. "Payback's a bitch—and you are looking at her."

"Do you know people who can provide you with this sort of information?" said Patricia.

Daniel and Tina shared a look, and nodded slowly.

"We're Hydes," said Daniel.

"We know people," said Tina.

"People talk to Hydes," said Daniel.

"Whether they want to or not," said Tina.

"And while we're gone, Patricia . . ." said Daniel. "Clean up this place. It's a mess."

The look on her face almost made up for everything else.

Daniel and Tina jumped down through the open trapdoor, disdaining the rope ladder. They made their way carefully through the lobby, stepping over the wreckage or kicking it to one side. They were careful to put some distance between themselves and the armory before they said anything, and even then they leaned in close and murmured confidentially.

"Do you trust her?" said Tina.

"Of course not," said Daniel. "She has *hidden agenda* written all over her."

"But we can work with her," said Tina.

"Until we find out what's really going on," said Daniel.

"I'm looking forward to bumping into the mercenaries again," said Tina. "We have so much catching up to do."

"Especially if our new armorer can provide us with some seriously unpleasant firepower," said Daniel. "She can probably advise us on tactics too."

Tina looked at him. "Tactics? Has it really come to that?"

They shared a smile, left the lobby, and went their separate ways.

And all across London important people in places of power shuddered, as they felt two Hydes start to look in their direction.

Chapter Three
MAKING FRIENDS AND INFLUENCING THE HELL OUT OF PEOPLE

✣ ✣ ✣

DANIEL WALKED STEADILY AWAY from what was left of the Jekyll & Hyde Inc. building, and didn't look back once. He strode on through the business area, his footsteps echoing loudly in the deserted street, until finally he began to meet other people coming in the opposite direction. Some were late-working businessmen, striding along in their smart city suits like the uniformed warriors of some very civilised army. striking down the weak and glorying in their plight.

Down the other side of the street came the late-night revelers, loud and cheerful congregations of brightly-colored fun-seekers, stepping it out as they headed from one good time to another. The twilight people, who never saw the sun rise or fall because they only flowered at night. Afraid to step off the carousel, for fear they might not be allowed back on.

Two very different armies of the empty night, never acknowledging each other's presence, but all of them paused to glance at Daniel as he walked by. Partly because he was a Hyde, and prey can always recognize a predator, but mainly because of his charred, bloodstained, bullet-holed clothes. Some people showed concern, others looked round to see where the danger was, but most just fell back to give Daniel plenty of room.

A black taxicab came creeping down the street, hoping to tempt some weary traveler into a swift but expensive ride. Daniel raised an arm to summon the taxi, but the driver took one look at the state of him and immediately speeded up to pass him by. Daniel strode out into the road, right in front of the taxi, and the driver had no choice but to slam on the brakes. The cab screeched to a halt barely a foot short of Daniel, who never flinched for a moment. The driver stared at him with wide shocked eyes, and Daniel smiled easily back. The driver lowered his side window, taking his time because he had a lot to say and wanted to be clearly understood.

"What the hell is wrong with you? I could have killed you!"

"Not on the best day you ever had," said Daniel.

The driver took one look at Daniel's face, and decided he had nothing else to say after all. Daniel pulled open the rear door and settled himself comfortably on the back seat.

"Take me to Thorne and Thorne Tailors, on Savile Row," he said.

"They won't be open," the driver said sullenly. "Not at this time of the night."

"They'll open for me," said Daniel.

Something in his voice told the driver this was no time to argue. He put his foot down hard, and the taxi roared off down the street. The driver had some way to go, and he wanted this particular fare out of his cab as quickly as possible. It felt like he had some kind of wild animal in the back seat. He glanced once at Daniel in his rearview mirror, and quickly decided not to do that again.

But he was, after all, a London taxi driver, and felt like he should say something. It was expected of him.

"Bad night?"

"Like you wouldn't believe," said Daniel.

The driver had one of his rare moments of insight. "I'm not going to get paid for this trip, am I?"

"Get me there in record time and I'll let you live," said Daniel.

"Fair enough," said the driver.

He delivered Daniel to Thorne and Thorne in a time that would have astonished his fellow taxi drivers, but they didn't know what it was to be motivated by a Hyde. It helped that there wasn't much traffic on the roads, but the driver had been quite ready to drive through anything that got in his way. He brought his cab to a halt right outside the tailors, and the moment Daniel's feet hit the sidewalk the cab was haring off down the street as though something was chasing it.

Daniel looked carefully around, but nothing moved in the streetlight and everything seemed quiet and peaceful. Parts of

London never sleep, because there's always a party or illegal gathering going on somewhere, but the business area was always deserted at this hour of the morning. Because no one could be bothered to make an effort when there were no customers to court. The tailors' windows were dark, and Daniel didn't even need to try the front door to know it would be locked. He just kicked it open and strode into the shop.

He turned on the lights, forced the door back into its frame, and then wandered through the racks of elegant and expensive clothes, taking his time as he searched for just the right outfit. It was important he make the right kind of impression, when he met with the man who was going to tell him everything he needed to know. Whether he wanted to or not. Daniel stripped off his ruined suit, parts of which threatened to come to pieces in his hands, and left it lying on the floor. He walked on in his underwear and socks, and took a moment to look himself over for bullet holes and healing wounds. Not entirely to his surprise, he found there weren't any.

Dr. Jekyll's Elixir—the gift that kept on giving.

Daniel finally found just the right outfit, dressed quickly, and moved over to admire himself in a full-length standing mirror. He'd gone for stark black and white, because that suited his mood, but he allowed himself a rich burgundy tie in the hope that would help take the edge off. He'd put his old shoes back on, because they were comfortable and he was used to them. He could always wipe the blood spots off later. He smiled at his dapper reflection, and straightened his tie as the James Bond theme ran through his head.

"I like my enemies shaken, not stirred."

He retrieved his wallet and phone from the remains of his old jacket, tucked them about his person, and strode out of Thorne and Thorne, not bothering to force the door shut behind him. A police car was waiting outside, probably summoned by a silent alarm. Daniel regarded it thoughtfully. Two uniformed police officers got out of the car, and then stopped dead as they took in the hulking figure before them.

"Hello, officers," said Daniel. "I'm a Hyde."

The two cops looked at each other.

"Get back in the car," said the older and more experienced officer. "We're going to need backup."

"Hold it," said Daniel. "I'm going to need that car. Give me the keys."

The younger officer's hand went to his truncheon, but the other put a staying hand on his arm. Because he knew a lost cause when he saw one. He tossed the car keys to Daniel, who snatched them easily out of midair.

"You're giving him our car?" said the younger cop.

"Less painful than having him take it," said the older.

"Now walk away," said Daniel.

The younger cop bristled, but the older man hurried him off down the street, murmuring urgently in his ear. Daniel got into the police car, and settled himself comfortably behind the steering wheel. He'd been wondering exactly who he should approach for information, but his encounter with the police had helped him make up his mind. He knew just the man; not an old friend exactly, but someone who would talk to him. It had been some time since they'd last met, and Daniel wondered what his old colleague would make of the new and improved Daniel. He smiled at the thought, and headed off into the night.

One extremely fast drive across London later, during which he broke every traffic law there was, including a few things that would have been illegal if the authorities had thought anyone was crazy enough to do them, Daniel finally brought the police car shuddering to a halt outside New Scotland Yard. He parked right next to the NO PARKING sign and walked away from the car, which was still twitching from everything he'd put it through. He strode up to the front doors, and they swung quickly back before him, as though afraid of what he might do to them if they didn't. Daniel nodded cheerfully. Start as you mean to go on.

The brightly lit lobby was full of people bustling back and forth, despite the early hour. Daniel came to a halt before the security barriers, and looked meaningfully at the two uniforms on duty. They glanced at each other, and then waved him through without asking to see any ID or authorisation. After all, he couldn't be a terrorist in a suit like that.

Daniel moved quickly across the lobby as though he belonged there, and no one challenged him. He had visited New Scotland Yard before, back when he'd been a very minor plainclothes detective. So long ago it seemed like another person, in another life. He took the elevator up to the top floor, and strode on past an endless series of closed doors, no doubt full of important people doing important things. He finally came to a halt before the very last door, which bore an impressive brass nameplate: COMMISSIONER JONATHAN HART. Daniel stood there for a moment, remembering.

When he started out in basic training, he had been part of a small but select group fast-tracked for success. Five bright-eyed, enthusiastic souls, determined to do well and do good. But somehow success eluded four of them. And then Daniel had ended up crippled and disgraced after his encounter with the Frankenstein Clan, and his three friends had died. The only one to avoid that fate was the only one who'd scaled the dizzy heights of promotion, because he had family connections. Daniel and Johnny had been friends, but that was long ago. They hadn't spoken in years. Daniel smiled. That was about to change. He slammed the door open and marched in like a commanding officer come to inspect the troops.

He had no doubt Johnny would be working, even at this late hour. He'd always been a night owl. He liked to say he got more done then, because there were fewer people around to bother him. He should have known a comment like that would come back to bite him on the arse some day.

Daniel back-heeled the door shut behind him, and made a point of looking down his nose at the comfortably appointed reception area—thick carpets, inoffensive art prints on the walls, and a coffee table with just the right selection of upmarket magazines to read while you waited to be summoned into the inner sanctum. Daniel nodded easily to the secretary behind her desk, but she just stared coldly back at him. One slightly raised eyebrow demanded to know why he was wasting her time. Daniel gave her gaze for gaze, and then checked out the nameplate on her desk: MEERA CHALMONDLEY. He should have known someone as important as Commissioner Hart would be bound to have his own first line of defense.

Meera was a middle-aged Indian woman in a colourful sari, with a round face and dark hair scraped back into a strict bun. Her gaze was all business, and not in the least impressed by the Hyde standing in front of her. Back when he was a mere detective, Daniel used to have all kinds of trouble getting past secretaries; he had moved on since then.

He nodded at the nameplate, and smiled. Meera stared at him coldly.

"It's pronounced *Chumley*."

"I didn't ask," said Daniel. "Hello, Meera. I'm here to see Johnny. Be a dear, and tell him his old friend Danny needs to see him."

The calm and cheerful approach washed right over the secretary, without any noticeable effect.

"Do you have an appointment, Mister . . . ?"

"I don't do appointments," said Daniel.

Meera didn't actually sniff, but looked like she wanted to. "I'm afraid the commissioner doesn't see anybody without an appointment. If you'd like to leave your name and contact details, I'll get back to you as and when an opening occurs. The commissioner is a very busy man."

"He'll see me," said Daniel.

He headed straight for the inner office. Meera slipped quickly out from behind her desk and planted herself right in front of him. Daniel stopped, because it was either that or walk right through her. He towered over Meera, and gave her his best hard stare, but there was nothing in her expression to suggest she gave a damn.

"Leave this office immediately," Meera said flatly, "or I will be forced to summon security, and have you escorted out of the building."

"There isn't enough security in this entire building to do that," said Daniel. "I am here to see Johnny, and nothing is going to stop me."

He started to step around her, and Meera lashed out with a vicious karate blow. Her small but very solid fist slammed into Daniel well below the belt; but he just stood there and took it, entirely unmoved. Meera fell back a step, surprised but still calm and collected. She went for him again, unleashing a flurry of powerful blows and kicks that would have left any lesser man curled up on the floor crying for his mother. Daniel just stood there patiently, letting her get on with it, not giving an inch to even the hardest of impacts, and in the end Meera had no choice but to fall back again. She stared at him, breathing heavily.

"What are you?"

"Determined," said Daniel.

He started forward again, but Meera stood her ground, blocking his way. It was clear to Daniel that he would have to walk right over her to get to the commissioner, and he didn't think he wanted to do that. He admired courage. So he stopped where he was, and looked her over thoughtfully.

"Back in the day, we all knew Johnny was going to get on," he said. "Not just because of who he was related to, but because he was always ready to do whatever it took. Even if it meant trampling over everyone else. I haven't heard anything to suggest he isn't still the complete bastard I remember, so I have to ask: Why are you so ready to defend him?"

"The commissioner does what he has to, to get things done," said Meera. "He is a strong man."

Daniel looked into her eyes and then nodded slowly. "Oh . . . it's like that, is it? Does he know how you feel about him?"

"No," said Meera. "And I can't tell him. He has to see it for himself or it won't mean anything."

Daniel shook his head. "Why do good women fall for bad men? I'll tell you what, Meera: why don't you go back to your desk, pick up the phone, and tell Johnny that Daniel Carter is here. I'm sure he'll want to see me. If only out of curiosity."

Meera looked at him distrustfully.

"I won't move a step," said Daniel. "Scout's honor."

Meera went back to her desk and made the call. Daniel enjoyed the surprise on her face when the commissioner said, *Send him in.* Meera put down the phone, and with a sense of doing something unwise because she didn't have any choice, she hit a control on her desk and the inner door swung open.

"You can go in," she said tonelessly. "The commissioner will see you now."

Daniel looked at her for a moment. "You must know he isn't worthy of you."

Meera shook her head stubbornly. "You don't know him like I do."

"That's just what I was going to say," said Daniel.

He stepped into the office, let the door close itself quietly behind him, and took in Commissioner Jonathan Hart, sitting behind a massive desk that looked like he'd inherited it from a previous century. The great man made no move to stand up and greet his guest, so Daniel took his time arranging himself comfortably on the deliberately stiff-backed visitor's chair. The two men studied each other openly, taking in all the changes the years had made.

Johnny was medium height, but far more than medium weight. His immaculate uniform had to stretch to the breaking point to contain him, though the man's bulk suggested as much muscle as fat. He had a square face, cool steady eyes, and a rapidly receding hairline. The hands resting on top of the desk were large and powerful, with professionally manicured nails. He looked like a very civilized ogre guarding his cave, ready to meet any threats with all necessary violence. Anyone else would probably have found the commissioner's gaze intimidating, so Daniel made a point of sitting back on his chair and crossing his legs casually.

"Hello, Johnny. It's been a while, hasn't it?"

The commissioner didn't actually wince at the familiarity, but he looked like he wanted to.

"Hello, Daniel. Last I heard, you were a basket case."

"I was," said Daniel. "I got over it."

Johnny smiled suddenly. "How did you get past my pet dragon? I know men who'd eat their own head rather than argue with Meera."

"I'm a Hyde," said Daniel.

Johnny nodded slowly. "I know. You've been making a name for yourself, Danny boy—and not a particularly nice one. So . . . what brings you to my neck of the woods, after all these years?"

"I could use your assistance," said Daniel.

"How did you get to be a Hyde?" Johnny said bluntly. "Some kind of super-steroids? You want to be careful with that stuff. You'll end up with wedding tackle so shriveled you could hang them off a charm bracelet."

"There's more to it than that."

"There would have to be," said Johnny. "You look like a man who could eat monsters for breakfast."

Daniel raised an eyebrow. "Have you been keeping an eye on me?"

Johnny looked at him pityingly. "Of course; that's my job. I know all about the Clans, and what you did to them. When we got the good news, everyone on this floor partied for a week. In any sane world we'd give you a medal and a pat on the back, but . . ."

"Yes," said Daniel. "But."

Johnny shrugged, in a *What can you do* sort of way.

"If you and the people like you had done your job, the Clans would never have grown so powerful," said Daniel. "And you wouldn't have needed a monster like me to take them down."

Johnny shook his head slowly. "You know better than that, Danny. We're not here to provide justice, or even to enforce the law of the land. The best we can do with our limited resources is keep the lid on, so the pot doesn't boil over." He stopped, and frowned. "There's a report on my desk about some serious trouble tonight in the middle of London. Were you involved in that?"

"I was there," said Daniel.

"Then I'm amazed you got out alive, never mind in one piece," said Johnny. He opened the file before him and flipped through the pages. "Massed gunfire, helicopters falling out of the sky, explosions so big they rocked every other building in the street; and you walked away untouched?"

"Not really," said Daniel. He uncrossed his legs, leaned forward, and fixed Johnny with his coldest gaze. "Tell me the truth, Johnny. Were you paid to look the other way?"

"Not me personally," Johnny said steadily. "But you can bet certain higher-up personages will be going somewhere really nice for their holidays this year. If you came here to make a fuss about that, forget it. Sometimes you just have to go along, to get along. It's the price of doing business. Speaking of which... would you happen to know what happened to Commissioner Gill? Your onetime boss? She might not have been a particularly good cop, but she did have a certain sentimental value. A lot of people on this floor have been wondering whether you were involved in her sudden disappearance. Given that she was responsible for your sudden plummet from grace. So... is there anything you want to tell me, about what happened to her?"

"The monsters got her," said Daniel. "And when I finally found what was left of Commissioner Gill, killing her was the kindest thing I could do."

Johnny stirred uncomfortably behind his desk, but his gaze never wavered.

"Why are you here, Danny? What can a very busy Commissioner of Police do for a bloody-handed monster-killer?"

"I need you to tell me everything you know about aliens," said Daniel.

Johnny didn't react to the word, just left it hanging there on the air. But finally he nodded briefly.

"Of course—now there's no more monsters left to kill, what's left apart from the aliens . . . ? But I have to ask: Why come to me, Danny? It's not like we're friends anymore; we haven't even exchanged a Christmas card for years. What makes you think I'd open up to you?"

Daniel smiled. "Because I remember how you were always ready to make a deal. You must have figured out by now that even your family connections won't get you any higher. But help me, and after I've stamped on all the aliens and set fire to their bases, I'll make sure the right people hear about it. If you're wondering whether I'm up to the job, you could always ask the monster Clans. Except you can't. Because I killed them all."

Johnny sat back in his chair, and tilted his head back to stare at the ceiling. So he wouldn't have to meet Daniel's gaze.

"Aliens . . . They've been with us for a very long time, like bugs that have burrowed into the skin of our civilization. And we don't have anything powerful enough to dig them out."

"Like the monster Clans," said Daniel.

"Not really," said Johnny. "We came to an accommodation with the Clans long ago, because a war neither side was sure they could win was in no one's best interests. And it helped that the people they were preying on weren't the kind of people we were interested in protecting. But the aliens . . . that's another kettle of nasty. They do whatever they feel like doing, and defy us to do anything about it. Fortunately, they spend most of their time intriguing against each other. And as long as they keep it off the streets, we don't give a damn."

"They're planning to destroy Humanity," said Daniel. "And you just let them get on with it."

"Because there isn't a damned thing we can do to stop them!" said Johnny. And then he paused, and looked thoughtfully at Daniel. "Or at least, that used to be the case. Maybe things have changed, now you're here. What exactly is it you want from me, Danny?"

"Information. Before I can do anything, I need to know where to find them."

Johnny was already shaking his head. "Their secret bases? You'll need someone a lot higher up the food chain than me to get a straight answer to that one."

"You could find out for me," said Daniel.

"I could," said Johnny. "But what's in it for me?"

"Your life," said Daniel.

He stood up, and brought one fist slamming down on the massive wooden desk. It split in two, with a great rending of wood, and he tore the desk apart and threw the pieces aside. He grabbed Johnny by the throat with one hand, and lifted him out of his chair and into the air. Johnny clutched desperately at Daniel's wrist with both hands, but couldn't even loosen the grip. His eyes bulged and his face grew flushed as he fought for air. Daniel pulled Johnny in close, until they were eye to eye.

"Just because we're having a nice polite conversation, don't make the mistake of thinking we're still chums. I was left broken and disgraced, and kicked out of the force, and you did nothing for me. Not even a Get Well Soon card."

He released his hold, and dropped Johnny back into his chair. The commissioner tore open his collar with trembling hands, and fought to get his breathing back under control, looking at Daniel like a fox caught in the headlights. Daniel sat down again, and now that there was no desk to separate them, Johnny actually flinched away from him. He had looked into Daniel's eyes and seen his own death staring back at him.

"I need information on all the different kinds of alien," said Daniel. "Where they've hidden themselves, and what kind of defenses they have. Help me out and I'll see the knowledge is put to good use. Give me a hard time, or stitch me up with misleading information, and the second thing I'll do is find someone else to make a deal with. You know there's always someone who'll make a deal."

"What's the first thing?" Johnny said hoarsely.

Daniel smiled. "Guess."

Johnny sat up straight, and somehow found the strength to glare at Daniel.

"I let them throw you to the wolves, because you wouldn't do the sensible thing and shut up about the monsters! Preserving the status quo was always going to be more important than one lost lamb with a bit of a limp. You want a deal, Danny boy? Fine; how about this? From what I've been hearing, what's left of Jekyll & Hyde Inc. is just a busted flush, floating facedown in the water. There's just you, and that nasty girlfriend of yours. And if you knew what's in her file, you'd run a mile. You haven't a hope in hell of taking on the aliens without the power and resources of an established organization to back you up. Which means it's time for you to return to the police force, Danny boy."

Daniel sat up straight. "You have got to be joking..."

"Not at all," said Johnny. He let his smile spread slowly, so Daniel could see the triumph in it. "Come back to the fold, Danny. Back to where you belong. I can get you reinstated, all sins forgotten if not forgiven. Work for me, and I'll see you get all the intelligence, weapons, and manpower you'll need, to get the job done."

Daniel shook his head. "Nice try, Johnny, but I've moved on. I don't work for anyone, anymore. Least of all someone like you, with your deals, and your status quo, and all the people you've thrown to the wolves as the price of doing business. I don't need anything you have to offer. Jekyll & Hyde Inc. is still a going concern, and we have weapons and resources beyond your worst nightmares."

Johnny levered himself up out of his chair, and moved away to stare down at one half of his desk.

"Look what you've done.... That desk was a genuine antique."

He bent down, pulled open a drawer, and took out a gun. He turned quickly to point it at Daniel.

"You don't understand the nature of the deal I'm offering you, Danny boy. You don't have a choice. Either you come back into the force voluntarily, or you'll be dragged back, kicking and screaming all the way. You might be a Hyde, but you're still only one man." Johnny shook his head sadly. "You shouldn't have walked into the lion's den, Danny, because these days I have really big teeth."

And then he stopped, because Daniel was smiling. He was still smiling when he rose to his feet and advanced steadily on Johnny, who backed away despite himself. He aimed his gun steadily between Daniel's eyes.

"One step farther and I'll blow your brains out the back of your head."

"You can try," said Daniel. "Remember that report on your desk? Helicopters and soldiers and machine guns, oh my. Put the gun away, Johnny. I am really not in the mood."

The commissioner shot Daniel between the eyes; but Daniel's hand snapped up and caught the bullet in midair. He held it out before Johnny's shocked eyes, and then smeared the bullet flat between his fingertips, before letting it drop to the floor. Johnny made a shrill disbelieving sound, and fired his gun again and again. Daniel slapped the bullets aside before they could reach him, and then grabbed the gun out of Johnny's hand. He crushed it into pieces, and let them fall to the floor. Johnny retreated quickly, making desperate *Go away* motions with his hands.

"You're not human!"

"No," said Daniel. "I'm a Hyde."

Johnny kept backing up until he hit the rear wall, and made a small helpless sound as he realized there was nowhere left to go.

"Get access to all the alien files, and pass them on to me," said Daniel. "And then you'll never have to see me again. Won't that be nice?"

The door behind them slammed open. Daniel looked round, to find Meera pointing a machine pistol at him. He nodded resignedly.

"I should have known you'd come running to save him, once you heard the gunfire. But not to worry, he's perfectly fine. Might need to change his trousers at some point, but . . ."

"Don't you ever stop talking?" said Meera.

Her hand was perfectly steady as she opened fire. Daniel ducked under the stream of bullets, surged forward, and snatched the gun out of her hand. He straightened up, crumpled the machine pistol into so much scrap metal, and dropped it on the rich carpeting.

"Why is everyone shooting at me today?" he said, just a bit plaintively.

"Because they know you?" said Johnny.

Daniel glanced back at him. "Don't push your luck. I have had a really bad day, and I could use someone to take it out on."

"Don't you dare touch him!"

Daniel looked at Meera, sighed quietly, and stepped out of her way. "He's all yours."

Meera rushed past him, and took Johnny in her arms as his legs finally gave way. He slid slowly down the wall, his weight carrying her with him, and they ended up sitting together on the floor, holding onto each other. Meera was smiling happily. Daniel shook his head, and left them to it.

Out in the reception area, a dozen security men were waiting for him. Large brutal men, armed with Tasers, pepper sprays, and truncheons. Presumably because only commissioners and their secretaries were allowed easy access to guns. Daniel looked them over, and shook his head.

"Run away now; and I won't chase you."

Two of the men tased him. The barbs dug into Daniel's shirtfront, and the long wires trembled as heavy current poured through them. The two men held the triggers down for a lot longer than was recommended, but Daniel just stood there and smiled at them. The two men stared at him, unable to believe what was happening. Daniel grabbed the dangling wires, ripped them away from his shirt, and then yanked the Tasers out of the men's hands with one good tug. He cracked the cheap plastic things in his hand, and threw them away.

"Can't we be civilized about this?" he said reasonably. "I've had a very tiring day."

"Take him down!" said a man at the back, who apparently fancied himself as officer material. "Stamp him into the ground. And make it hurt."

One man stepped forward and blasted pepper spray right into Daniel's face. Daniel grinned, enjoying the sensation, and the man backed away in confusion. And then the man playacting commanding officer started shouting orders and they all charged forward, raining down blows with their truncheons. Daniel took those away from them, broke them in two, and threw the pieces away. The security men continued their assault anyway, punching and kicking with increasing desperation. Daniel sent them flying with casual sweeps of his arms, and in just a few moments the fight was over. Daniel nodded cheerfully at the quietly groaning figures.

"That's what you get for being rude," he said. "But thanks for the workout. Very bracing."

He'd been careful not to use his full strength, because if he'd killed any of them Johnny wouldn't have been able to help him. He glanced back at the open inner office door, and raised his voice.

"You know where to find me, Johnny! Don't make me have to come back here. Hope the office romance works out."

He left the office, and walked unhurriedly down the corridor. People peered at him from half-open office doors, like frightened animals peering out of their holes, and all the way to the elevators he could hear them whispering the word *Hyde*. And the awe and terror in their voices was all the validation he needed.

When Tina left the Jekyll & Hyde Inc. building, she deliberately strode off in a different direction from Daniel. It wouldn't do to let him think she needed him. She rounded the corner just in time to see a taxi pulling up for a refined gentleman in a smart city suit. She raised her voice as she hurried forward.

"Hold that cab!"

The businessman took one look at her torn and blood-soaked clothes, and pulled a face as though he'd just stepped in some dog muck.

"Keep your distance, please. If you will insist on picking up rough trade, you have no one to blame but yourself. And no, I am not interested in sharing a cab with you. Just piss off back to whatever gutter you crawled out of, and don't bother your betters again."

By that point Tina was standing right in front of him. She grabbed a handful of his shirtfront, and slammed him against the cab so hard it rocked on its wheels. The businessman's eyes rolled up, and his legs buckled. Tina dropped him on the pavement, briskly removed his wallet, and got into the back of the taxi. The big black driver gave a big black laugh as he turned round in his seat to grin at her.

"Always happy to see the city gents get what's coming to them. There's not one of them ever gave me a decent tip. Where to, lady?"

Tina gave him the address of her favorite fashion house, and then busied herself investigating the wallet's contents as the black cab moved smoothly off into the night.

"What happened to your clothes, lady?" said the driver.

"Hell of a party."

"Been there, done that thing, lady."

When they finally arrived at their destination, Tina paid the driver with a wad of newly acquired cash, and he chuckled happily.

"Want me to wait, lady?"

"Why not?" said Tina.

She went over to MADAME RENE'S—WHERE TALL WOMEN ARE A WONDER OF THE WORLD. It was closed, and all the lights were out, but the locked door opened easily enough when she leaned on it. An alarm bell set just inside the door immediately set up a loud and spiteful racket, but Tina just ripped it off the wall and crushed it until it gave up the ghost. She turned on the lights, pulled down the blinds, and then went strolling through the shop, stripping off what was left of her clothes and letting the pieces lie where they fell.

She wandered through the forest of attractive displays in her underwear and sensible shoes, picking things out and then tossing them aside, until finally she found an electric-blue dress that had slits all the way to the hips, and clung like a coat of paint. She topped it off with a smart creamy fedora, and then kicked off her sensible shoes and replaced them with knee-length white leather boots. She admired her new look in a tall standing mirror, and tipped herself a wink. She retrieved her phone from the remains of her jacket, dropped the businessman's credit cards on the counter by way of payment, and went back outside.

The driver was sitting slumped in his seat, enjoying a large hand-rolled. He smiled cheerfully as Tina opened the rear door.

"Is that the latest style, lady?"

"It is now," said Tina. The driver laughed loudly, and fired up the engine.

"Where to next, lady? My cab is yours. For as long as the money holds out."

"Wait," said Tina.

She got out her phone and called a number that didn't officially exist. A voice answered on the second ring.

"We need to talk," said Tina. "Right now."

"The usual place," said the voice. "As soon as you can get there." And then he hung up.

Tina gave the driver the address of a very exclusive restaurant in one of the most upmarket areas of London, and put the phone away. She'd chosen this particular contact at least partly because she knew he would insist on meeting at the restaurant. The evening's exercise had left her with a very definite appetite.

✣ ✣ ✣

When they arrived at their destination, bright light was blazing out of the restaurant's windows like an oasis of hospitality in the long night. The front door stood invitingly open, despite the early hour. Anyone would think it was a trap. Tina smiled. She got out of the taxi, took a moment to smooth down her nice new dress, and then gave the driver all the remaining cash in the wallet. He laughed his big laugh again.

"For this I'll wait around all night, lady."

"No," said Tina. "You can go now. And for your own sake, never talk about this."

"Forgetting you already, lady."

The cab roared off into the night. Tina looked carefully up and down the street, but there didn't seem to be anyone else around, and all the other establishments were closed. She smiled quietly to herself, cracked her knuckles in anticipation, and then walked into the restaurant as though she didn't have a suspicion in the world.

The place was packed with customers, whole groups of them around every table; happy smiling people chatting away. Which was just a bit odd, at this hour in the morning. Uniformed staff bustled back and forth, bearing steaming plates of the very best cuisine, all of them cheerful and smiling and full of energy. Which was also just a bit odd. Tina had no trouble spotting her contact, sitting at a rear table with his back to the wall, so no one could sneak up on him. She made her way through the maze of crowded tables, and no one so much as glanced at her. Even the staff just dodged around her, busy being busy. And that was more than a bit odd. People might stare at a Hyde, or run away, but no one ever ignored one.

Tina pulled out the waiting chair and sat down opposite her contact. Alan Diment nodded easily to her; he was a pleasant, middle-aged man in a shabby suit, with an unremarkable face under a mop of floppy blond hair. His eyes were a faded blue, and his smile had an apologetic air, as though he couldn't help but see the funny side. He looked Tina over carefully.

"Well, my dear, it's good to have the pleasure of your company once again. Though you have changed a bit, since we last saw each other."

"Hello yourself, spyman," said Tina. "You've changed too. You got old."

"At least I did it honestly," said Alan. "You must tell me, dear heart: what's it like being a Hyde?"

Tina smiled happily. "Exhilarating."

"I am consumed with jealousy," said Alan. "I have to ask: Why don't we do this more often?"

"Because ours is a strictly business relationship," said Tina. "And don't you ever forget it."

"You wound me, dear lady, you really do."

Tina shrugged. "If I ever wound you, it'll wipe that professional smile right off your face."

Alan just nodded. "Direct as ever, old thing. I do hope you have a really good reason for summoning me here at this ungodly hour. I am of an age where one's beauty sleep becomes vitally important."

"I knew you'd show up," said Tina. "You'd heard I'd become a Hyde, because you hear everything, but you had to see it for yourself."

"How well you know me, my sweet. Can we now discuss the reason for this delightful reunion?"

"I need to know things," said Tina. "And you are famously the man who knows things."

"That has always been my raison d'être," said Alan. "Which part of my extensive repertoire do you feel the need to consult? Though I feel I should remind you that everything I know comes with a price tag. Or, at the very least, with strings attached."

"What?" said Tina. "No discount, for old times' sake?"

"As you have already pointed out, we were never friends," said Alan. "Just two people who make use of each other, when it suits us."

"Trust me," said Tina, "you'll do very well out of this particular give-and-take."

"I'm not so sure, my sweet," said Alan. "I take my payment in information and the promise of future favors, and since Jekyll & Hyde Incorporated no longer exists after that unfortunate business tonight . . . I have to wonder what you could possibly offer me."

"We'll come to that," said Tina. "It might just surprise you."

Alan raised an eyebrow. "Really, old thing? You do intrigue me." He offered her a large embossed menu. "Do feel free to order something. You have a lean and hungry look."

Tina realized a uniformed waitress was already hovering at her elbow, pad poised to take her order. Given how busy the rest of the staff seemed to be, Tina added that to her list of odd things. She thrust the menu into the waitress' hands.

"Bring me one of everything, starting at the top and working your way down. And don't stint on anything—he's paying."

Alan nodded to the waitress. "I'll have my usual."

The waitress smiled quickly and then scurried away to disappear through the kitchen door. Alan looked thoughtfully at Tina.

"It has been some time since you honored me with your illustrious company, my sweet. Though to be fair, prior to this you have been monstrously busy."

"Of course you'd know about the monsters," said Tina. "You probably know more about what I've been involved in than I do."

"That is my job," said Alan. "Everyone in British Security has been absolutely fascinated by your exploits. All the monster Clans brought down, left dead and broken in the ruins of their dreams! There has been much discussion among my dear little boy and girl spies as to whether we should have a whip round and send you some flowers. But then, you've never been a flowers sort of person, have you? You'd probably just eat them. Still, given the current state of the Jekyll & Hyde Incorporated building, I'm frankly bewildered as to what you plan to do next. I'm actually astonished you're still here."

Tina smiled easily. "Hydes are hard to kill."

Alan sat back in his chair and looked her over.

"You do appear to be in splendid form, my dear. You've come such a long way since we first met."

Tina's eyes narrowed. "You sure you want to go there?"

Alan smiled. "Oh I must, my dear. I really must."

At which point the waitress returned, bearing food. Tina fell ravenously on a plate full of spaghetti and meatballs, shoveling it in with her bare hands while making loud appreciative noises. Alan toyed with his salad and tried not to look too obviously appalled.

"Cannelloni to follow?" said the hovering waitress.

"Bring it on," said Tina, indistinctly.

The waitress hurried back to the kitchens. Tina grinned at Alan with several strands of spaghetti dangling from her mouth.

"This is refueling. I've had a busy night."

Alan nodded. "You always were famous for your appetites, old thing."

By the time Tina had finished her first course the waitress was back, whipping away the empty plate and slapping a new one into place. Tina took a moment to savor the aroma, before getting stuck in again. She felt a little easier now she'd taken the edge off.

"It has been a long time since we first met," she said. "Back when we were both well-known faces on the party scene. I was a wild child with no restraints, while you hung around the edges looking for people you could bribe or blackmail into working for your very unofficial department."

Alan nodded easily. "Broken people always make the best spies, because they have nothing to lose."

"I lived to party, back then," said Tina. "Because that was all I had. But serious pleasures are seriously expensive, so I took your money to be your eyes and ears. Telling you who was doing what, and why, and pointing out useful people. I thought I was just helping you make the right connections, but you were using the information I provided to pressure people. Putting them in danger so you could go after bigger fish. Some people got hurt, some died, and finally I told you to go to hell." She smiled briefly. "And then you tried to pressure me, so I kicked you down a flight of stairs."

"I hadn't forgotten," Alan said dryly. "What a field agent you would have made, my dear girl."

"I doubt it," said Tina. "I never was one for following orders."

"We all have to serve someone," said Alan.

Tina looked at him. "I don't. I'm a Hyde."

"Well, quite, old thing." Alan pushed his plate away from him, and looked at her steadily. "I can't say I was all that surprised when I heard you'd become one of Edward Hyde's creatures. You always were so much larger than life."

"Of course you knew," said Tina. "You know everything." She gestured around the restaurant with her knife and fork. "Are you sure you feel safe, meeting with me in such a public place?"

"Of course," said Alan. "Because everyone here is one of my people."

Tina looked around her. All the customers and staff had given up any pretense of being ordinary people, and held themselves ready for action as they stared at her unblinkingly. Tina smiled at them, and most flinched away from what they saw in her eyes. Satisfied, Tina turned back to Alan.

"You really think they'll make any difference, if I decide you've annoyed me?"

"Let an old spy cling to the illusions of his profession," Alan said smoothly. "Now, what is it you want to talk about, my sweet?"

Tina pushed her empty plate aside, and stared at him steadily. "Aliens."

Alan just nodded.

"I knew you'd know all about them," said Tina. "Which is more than I ever did. I was busy concentrating on the monsters. Still, after bringing the Clans down, going head-to-head with a few invaders from beyond should make a nice change."

"I wouldn't count on that, old thing," said Alan. "The aliens are the biggest monsters of all. Let us begin with the Martians, the Bug-Eyed Monsters, the Reptiloids, and the Greys."

"Is that all of them?"

"Hardly. They're just the main movers and shakers. But take care of them, and you can be sure the minor players will keep their heads down and behave themselves."

"How long have there been aliens on Earth?" said Tina.

Alan shrugged. "As long as there have been monsters. The shadows at the edge of civilization are deep and dark, and contain more surprises than most people will ever realize."

Tina nodded. "Start with the most dangerous."

"Currently, that would be the Martians."

"Are they really from Mars?"

"Oh yes. They have massive cities hidden away in caverns deep under the surface of their planet. You must remember that Mars is much older than the Earth. Entire civilizations have risen and fallen under the two moons and then crumbled back into the Martian dust, before Humanity first appeared on Earth. What we now call Martians are just the latest in a long line of creatures to claim the title."

"Did they ever actually invade us?"

"More like they sneaked in, when no one was looking."

"But if they've got the technology to bring them all the way here, why not start a war of the worlds? Kick our arses and get it over and done with?"

"Because they need a new world to replace their worn-out home," Alan said patiently. "And they don't want to risk destroying everything, by fighting over it. They work on the edges, conspiring to drag us down. They're an old species; they can afford to take the long view."

"Any chance of finding a middle ground?" said Tina.

"Bargaining is something that only takes place between equals," said Alan. "As far as the Martians are concerned, we're just something to be wiped out before they take possession."

"What about the other aliens?" said Tina.

"Next, we have the Bug-Eyed Monsters."

Tina looked at him sternly. "That can't be what they call themselves."

"We have no idea. We have no language in common. Basically, they're big insecty things. Horrid, relentless, utterly inhuman."

"Which planet are they from?" said Tina.

"We have no idea. Like the Martians, all they're interested in is territory. And wiping us out, for being in their way. Then there's the Reptiloids. Nasty big-lizardy humanoids. We can't talk to them either; I'm not sure we even have concepts in common.

"Finally, we come to the most disturbing of the alien threats to all we hold dear: the Greys. They look exactly like you'd think—except for when they don't. Because the Greys are shape-shifters. When they want to, they can look like us."

Tina stared at him. "Really?"

"There could be a dozen Greys in this restaurant, right now," Alan said calmly, "and we'd only know if they chose to reveal themselves. All of which has played merry havoc with the usual spy games."

"What are your people doing to stop the aliens?" said Tina. "Tell me you're doing something."

"We manage our little victories, from time to time," said Alan. "But we don't have the resources to drive any of them away."

"You never did anything to stop the monster Clans either," said Tina. Not actually accusing, just letting the comment lie there.

Alan met her gaze steadily. "You must understand that there are people in very high positions who want this all kept swept under the carpet. Any government forced to admit it couldn't protect its people wouldn't last five minutes. Which is why my superiors were so very pleased when you and your young man finally freed us from the monsters. Are you intending to do the same to the aliens?"

"That is the plan," said Tina. "Are you prepared to help?"

"What is it you need?"

"Information," said Tina. "Starting with where the alien bases are. What kind of protections they have. And any suggestions as to what the aliens' weaknesses might be."

"I can provide most of that," said Alan. "But we now come to the unfortunate matter of the reckoning. In return for our under-the-counter assistance, you must agree to turn over to us all alien weapons and technology you might happen across along the way."

"No problem," said Tina. "We don't need it anyway."

"I'm afraid there's more," said Alan.

"Of course there is," said Tina.

Alan leaned forward across the table, and fixed Tina with an icy blue stare. "I was given very firm instructions by my superiors, before I was allowed to come here and meet with you. It's important you understand that your destruction of the monster Clans led to extreme nervousness in high places. They decided that Jekyll & Hyde Incorporated could not be allowed to become a power base in its own right, and a threat to the established power structures. Basically, they were afraid you might become the new monsters. And now here you are, going after the aliens . . . It has therefore been decided that you and Daniel can only be allowed to operate under the direct control of my department."

Tina looked at him. "You want me and Daniel to work for you?"

"I'm afraid so, dear old thing." Alan shrugged apologetically. "It's time for both of you to come in from the cold, and warm your hands at the communal fire. You've had a good run as independents, but now Edward and his organization are no long around to protect you . . ."

Tina rose up, overturned the table, grabbed Alan by the throat with one hand, and lifted him out of his chair. Everyone else in the restaurant jumped to their feet and aimed a whole bunch of really big guns at her. Tina smiled around her, and dropped Alan back into his seat, where he sat slumped and gasping for breath.

"Excuse me for a moment," Tina said sweetly.

And then she went raging through the restaurant, too quickly for any of Alan's people to draw a bead on her. She slapped guns out of hands, picked up tables and used them to slam whole groups of people against the walls. She darted back and forth, dodging increasingly inaccurate shots and lashing out with devastating punches and kicks. Alan's highly trained agents went flying in all directions. Tina's waitress appeared, and fired her gun directly into Tina's face, but she just ducked under it and headbutted the waitress in the midriff. She bent over, and Tina straightened up, driving the top of her head into the waitress's chin. She fell backward, but Tina was already moving on in search of new enemies before the waitress hit the floor.

Tina stormed through the remaining agents, easily dodging the last of the gunfire, and putting the hard word on anyone still standing. She had been through a lot for one night, and was grateful for a chance to take out her mood on someone deserving.

Two customers reared up from behind an overturned table and threw a heavy steel mesh over Tina. She tore it to pieces with her bare hands, punched out the customers, and pressed on. A waiter stabbed her in the back with an electric cattle prod. A shower of sparks rose up from between Tina's shoulder blades. She turned around and looked at the waiter, and he dropped the cattle prod and ran for his life. Tina nailed him with a thrown table before he managed three yards. The last of Alan's people came at Tina with every kind of weapon and dirty trick they had left, even throwing themselves at her in groups in the hope their sheer weight might be enough to bring her down. But none of it worked.

Because they were just secret agents. And she was a Hyde.

In the end, Tina stood alone in the middle of a wrecked restaurant, surrounded by the broken but not actually deceased bodies of the fallen. She knew that if she killed any of Alan's people, he would never agree to help her. The odd figure groaned here and there, or sat slumped against walls pressing handkerchiefs to their bloody faces. One man reached for a dropped gun. Tina stamped on his hand, and smiled coldly at the man as he whimpered.

"Really not in the mood to be messed with."

"I got that," said the agent, cradling his broken hand to his chest. "Would it be okay if I crawled away and hid now?"

"Don't let me stop you."

Tina took a good look round what was left of the restaurant, to make sure she hadn't missed anything . . . and so she could savor her achievements. After getting her arse handed to her by the mercenaries, it felt good to be back in the saddle again. She went back to Alan, picked up a chair, and sat down facing him.

"I told my superiors this would never work," said Alan. "Thank you for your restraint, old thing, in not killing any of my people. You wouldn't believe the paperwork I have to fill out these days..."

Something in his eyes warned Tina. She darted quickly to one side, and a bullet slammed through the air where her head had been. A uniformed chef was aiming a gun at her from the kitchen door. He fired again, and Tina snatched the bullet out of midair. She threw it back at the chef with such force it punched right through his shoulder. He cried out, and fell backward into his kitchen. Tina waited hopefully to see if he'd try again, and when he didn't she looked at Alan again.

"There's always one, isn't there?"

"At least," said Alan.

"Thanks for the warning."

"I'm sure I have no idea what you're referring to."

"Of course you don't," said Tina. "Now, we can negotiate in better faith... or I can make a hole in the wall with your head and go find someone else to make a deal with."

"What kind of perfectly reasonable understanding did you have in mind, dear heart?" said Alan.

"Tell me where to find the alien bases, and you can have what's left inside them afterward."

"Deal."

"Daniel and I will remain entirely independent," said Tina. "You and your bosses do not get to give us orders, or get involved. In return, we agree to wipe out all the aliens we find."

"Deal," said Alan. "And as a sign of good will, allow me to present you with a map showing the location of the Martian base in London."

He reached inside his jacket, being very careful not to look like he was going for a weapon, and produced a buff envelope. He presented it to Tina, who rolled it up and stuffed it into her cleavage. Alan then offered her a card.

"My private number. Feel free to call any time."

Tina had to laugh. "You wish."

But she tucked the card into her cleavage as well—just in case. And then she leaned forward, kissed Alan breathless, laughed again, and walked out of the ruins of the restaurant.

Chapter Four
MARS IS HELL

✣ ✣ ✣

DANIEL EMERGED FROM New Scotland Yard with a distinct feeling of unfriendly eyes digging holes in his back. So he stopped quite deliberately at the top of the steps to look around him, quietly enjoying the thought that behind him people were probably ducking and hiding in case he turned and went back in again. They were probably also trying to find someone brave enough to come out and ask him to move on; part of him hoped they would, because he was just in the mood for a little more light exercise. But no one came out to challenge him. Probably because they were still clearing up the mess he'd made on the top floor, and trying to put the security men back together again.

Daniel's phone rang, and he sighed resignedly. It had to be Tina, because she was the only one who had his number. He didn't like to be bothered, when he was out and about.

"I know where the Martian base is," said Tina. As usual, not wasting any breath on a *Hello* or a *How are you?* "It's right here in London, at Horse Leigh Common. See you there."

She rang off before Daniel could ask where the hell Horse Leigh Common was. He had a good working knowledge of the high crime areas, but had never seen any reason to bother with tourist hotspots. He glared at his phone, just on general principles, put it away, and hurried down the steps to his very illegally parked car. He'd been hoping someone would have clamped it by now, so he could have the fun of ripping the nasty thing off and throwing it through the windscreen of a car belonging to someone important. But apparently word about him had got around, because no one had bothered it.

When he got back behind the wheel, he was relieved to discover the car came with satnav. He didn't like to think what it would have done to his Hyde dignity, if he'd had to go back inside New Scotland Yard and ask for directions.

Daniel accelerated through the nighttime streets, putting the wind up what traffic there was and occasionally driving on the pavement just for the hell of it. Because he had a reputation to live down to. He finally slammed to a halt right outside the main entrance to Horse Leigh Common: towering Victorian gates composed mostly of black iron bars. Daniel got out of the car, patted it fondly on the bonnet, and looked around for Tina. He could hear her sneaking up behind him, but sportingly pretended not to notice until she tapped him on the shoulder. He turned to smile at her, and she threw her arms around him in a fierce embrace that would have crushed any normal man's ribs. Daniel hugged her back, and she laughed happily as he lifted her feet off the ground. Though neither of them would have admitted it, they were both still getting over nearly dying on the rooftop. They finally stepped back and nodded easily to each other.

"Miss me?" said Tina.

"Always," said Daniel. "How did you get here?"

"I got this really neat new car from my contact."

Daniel raised an eyebrow. "Should I be jealous?"

"Not really," said Tina. "He probably hasn't noticed it's missing yet. Well . . . it was just standing around, and hardly locked at all. What's a girl to do?"

Before Daniel could suggest an answer, she reached into her cleavage, pulled out an envelope, and removed a map. Daniel considered raising another eyebrow, but it felt like too much of an effort. Tina held the map out before her, and they studied it carefully in the pleasant golden glow from the streetlamps. Daniel didn't actually think much of the map, and was ready to sniff disparagingly, but given that Tina had a map and he didn't, he rose above the impulse. It was just a hand-drawn outline of the Common, with a few useful landmarks and a big red cross to mark the Martian base. Tina peered through the gate, and pointed decisively.

"Just follow the main path. Easy peasy, lemon squeezy."

"If you say so," said Daniel. "I never was very good with maps. All the details confuse me."

Tina thrust the map into Daniel's hands, and he folded it neatly before slipping it into his pocket. The gate was held shut with lengths of steel chain and an industrial-strength padlock. Daniel ripped the lock away, and the chains promptly fell to the ground, as though they knew there wasn't any point in putting up a fuss. Tina kicked the gates open, and they flew smoothly back as though they'd been specially oiled for the occasion. Daniel shot them a suspicious look, and then led the way onto Horse Leigh Common.

The open ground was calm and quiet, under a star-speckled sky. The faint breeze barely had enough energy to move the cool night air around. A murmur of far-off traffic was frequently drowned out by the cry of some nightbird or other. The Hydes' footsteps were the loudest sound on the Common, crunching crisply on the gravel path. Daniel kept a watchful eye on his surroundings, but there didn't seem to be anyone else about.

"How did you get on with your contact?" said Daniel, quite casually.

"Oh, Alan was delighted to see me," Tina said lightly. "Couldn't do enough for me. How about you?"

"I had a very productive meeting with an old colleague," said Daniel. And then he couldn't hold his grin back any longer. "How many people did you beat up?"

"Lots and lots," Tina said happily. "You?"

"Not as many as that. But mine were professional bastards. I almost broke a sweat."

They laughed easily, and walked on. Glancing surreptitiously at each other's new outfits. Tina weakened first, and raised her voice.

"Well? What do you think of my new look?"

"It's very you," said Daniel. "But possibly just a bit draughty round the sides, for a nighttime stroll?"

"It's a style thing," Tina said loftily. "You wouldn't understand."

"Probably not," said Daniel.

"I like your new tie," Tina said sweetly. "It's very colorful."

They both knew there was something they weren't talking about, and in the end Daniel shot Tina a sideways glance.

"Did you feel as uncomfortable as I did, having to reach out to an old acquaintance for help?"

Tina shot him a quick smile, clearly glad he'd raised the subject so she didn't have to.

"We all have people in our past we thought we'd put behind us. Unfortunately, needs must when the devil has his teeth buried in your throat."

"It worries me, that we might have made deals with the devil," said Daniel.

Tina laughed. "We're Hydes! Which makes us a match for any devil."

Daniel would have liked to laugh with her, but that felt too much like whistling past a graveyard. He looked out over the Common so he wouldn't have to look at Tina.

"We don't have the Jekyll & Hyde Inc. organization to back us up anymore."

"We have a new armorer," said Tina. "Which means really big guns and spectacularly nasty devices are back on the menu."

"But how much can we trust her?"

"About as far as we can throw her."

Daniel smiled. "We can throw people pretty far."

"Hydes don't do the trust thing," Tina said firmly. "We'll just have to take advantage of her, while she thinks she's taking advantage of us."

Daniel nodded thoughtfully. "Do you think we should have found the time to pay the armorer a visit before we came here?"

"It's just a bunch of aliens making trouble in the shadows," said Tina. "How hard can it be?"

Daniel shook his head. "You had to say that, didn't you?"

The path led them through pools of golden lamplight, ornate flower gardens that had been laid out to within an inch of their lives, and the occasional copse of trees still burdened with heavy greenery. Wherever they went, it was all very quiet, like the hush before the curtain goes up and the play begins. Daniel was quietly pondering what a Martian base would look like when Tina spotted something up ahead, and made an impatient sound.

"Of course! I should have guessed!"

"What?" said Daniel.

Tina nodded to an archaeological dig set right on the edge of the Common, and steered Daniel into the deep dark shadows of a nearby copse of trees. The dig was surrounded by tall temporary walls with just the one entrance, guarded by uniformed men with really big guns. Daniel felt an eyebrow rising as he realized they were wearing the same uniform he'd seen on the rooftop earlier. More armed guards patroled the perimeter, studying the Common with experienced eyes. Daniel cleared his throat.

"Tina, why are we hiding in the trees?"

She shot him an impatient look. "Hello? Really big guns alert!"

"Your usual response to that is to charge straight at them," said Daniel. "It's not like you to be cautious."

Tina scowled. "When a fleet of attack helicopters and an army of mercenaries get together to kick your arse, it's time to take the hint."

Daniel wisely switched his attention back to the dig.

"How long has that been there?"

"Oh, come on," said Tina. "It's been all over the news for the past month. No one has been allowed inside, but supposedly they're uncovering the biggest Roman mosaic ever found. But that would make perfect cover, for access to an underground base."

"It's a bit public, isn't it?" said Daniel.

Tina shrugged, and then shot Daniel a knowing look. "Good thing my contact was able to provide us with the exact location; wasn't it?"

"My contact provided me with lots of useful information," said Daniel, just a bit defensively. "And should be able to get me even more, in the future."

"But right now I have a map," said Tina. "You don't have a map."

"Actually, I do," said Daniel. "I have your map, in my pocket. It's good to share." He looked carefully at the dig, checking out the possible approach routes. "Though I would feel just a bit happier if our map provided at least some information on the kind of protections and defenses we'll be facing."

"We're Hydes!" said Tina. "We can cope, whatever they throw at us."

"And that doesn't sound at all like the kind of remark that will come back to haunt us," said Daniel.

Tina glared at him. "Since when are you so superstitious?"

"Since Lady Luck vomited on my blue suede shoes earlier tonight."

Tina sniffed loudly, and gave her full attention to the dig. "Does it feel a bit odd to you, that the Martian base should turn out to be right in the middle of London?"

"Not necessarily," said Daniel. "All the monster Clans held their big gatherings in the city."

"Maybe London really is the center of the world," said Tina. "Okay . . . the Martian base is right ahead of us, and I feel a definite need to kick some Martian arse."

"Always assuming they have any," said Daniel.

"Well, whatever they've got I'm going to kick it," said Tina.

"After we get past the armed guards," said Daniel. "There's a lot of open ground to cross, before we could get anywhere near them. If they all opened fire at once . . ."

"We survived the machine-gun fire on the roof," said Tina.

"Good to know you've got your confidence back," said Daniel. "But I don't feel like putting what's left of our luck to the test. And besides, if the guards see us coming they could sound an alarm. Alert the Martians, and give them time to put all kinds of special protections in place. We need a distraction. Something loud and dramatic, to hold the guards' attention."

"I'm all for loud and dramatic," said Tina. "What did you have in mind?"

Daniel considered the nearest tree. It was tall and broad, the branches weighed down with lots of greenery. He gave the trunk an introductory shove, and the branches barely bobbed. Daniel grinned, and put his shoulder to the trunk.

"This tree . . . is going down."

He dug his feet into the earth, and threw all his strength against the trunk, but even though the tree tilted right over, its branches waving madly, deep-set roots held the tree firmly in place. Daniel heaved and strained, but the tree would not be moved—until Tina put her shoulder next to Daniel's. Gnarled roots burst up out of the ground, sending clods of earth flying in all directions, and the tree slammed all the way over. The crash was deafeningly loud, and all the guards' heads snapped round. It probably helped that the top of the tree protruded a good yard or more outside the perimeter of the copse, so they really couldn't miss it.

Daniel and Tina retreated back into the shadows and stood very still—just two more shapes in the gloom. They watched carefully as half a dozen guards came together at the entrance to the dig, and consulted with each other. There was a lot of shrugging and headshaking, before one of them gestured angrily and started toward the copse. The others hurried after him.

"There's always one," said Daniel.

"How does this help us?" said Tina.

"We wait for the guards to venture into this nicely gloomy setting," said Daniel, "and then we take them down one at a time, steal their uniforms, and walk into the dig through the front entrance."

Tina nodded. "That should work."

"Just keep it quiet," said Daniel. "We don't want to alarm the other guards."

Tina glowered at him. "I have done this before, you know."

They eased out of sight behind two of the more substantial trees, and waited for their enemies to come to them. The guards stopped right at the edge of the copse, looked at the fallen tree, and then stared suspiciously into the gloom before slowly moving forward. The one in charge gestured urgently for the others to spread out, and Daniel smiled. It did help when the enemy made things that little bit easier for you. He waited for the first guard to pass him by, and then moved silently in behind him, clapped a hand over his mouth, and snapped his neck. He'd had enough of soldiers for hire for one day, particularly those who served invading aliens.

The Hydes took down three more guards in swift succession. The two remaining guards seemed to have some sense that they might not be alone in the trees. They looked quickly about them, sweeping their guns back and forth. Daniel concentrated on the guard nearest him, waited until the man was pointing his gun in entirely the wrong direction, and then moved quickly forward. Only to stop dead as the other guard turned suddenly to face him. His gun rose up, and Tina struck the man down from behind. The final guard heard the body crash to the ground, and spun round to find Daniel and Tina already looming over him. He started to lift his gun, and Daniel hit the man in the face so hard his head ended up pointing in the wrong direction.

Daniel and Tina shared a satisfied nod. After everything they'd been through earlier, even a small payback felt good. They looked over the fallen bodies, selected the two largest, and stripped them of their uniforms.

Tina picked up one of the guns, and waggled it hopefully. "Pretty please?"

"Too noisy, and anyway, relying on guns makes you predictable," Daniel said sternly. "Better to stick to our Hyde strength and speed. The Martians won't be expecting that."

Tina tossed the gun aside. "Hand-to-hand vengeance has always been the most satisfying."

"It's the Hyde way," said Daniel.

Tina started to pull off her dress, and then stopped. "Hold everything; I see a problem . . ."

Daniel looked at her. "What?"

"I can't just leave my nice new dress here!"

"Hang it over a branch," said Daniel. "We can come back for our clothes later."

"What if someone comes along and steals my nice new dress?" said Tina.

"Like who?" said Daniel. "The fashion police? Or do you think one of the guards will come in here looking for his colleagues, and then get distracted by your dress?"

"You never know," Tina said darkly. "You hear funny things, about some of these soldiers of fortune . . ."

"Put on the uniform," said Daniel.

They hung their clothes carefully over nearby branches, and then discovered that the guards' uniforms weren't nearly large enough to accommodate a Hyde's dimensions. Daniel had to struggle just to get into the trousers, and the jacket's shoulders groaned warningly as he slipped it on. When he tried to pull the sides together to do up the buttons, the jacket split resoundingly all the way up the back.

Tina would have laughed, but she wasn't doing much better. The trousers stretched dangerously tight across her rear, and when she pulled on the jacket she only had to look down at her bosom to know that buttoning it up was not going to be an option. She looked at Daniel, who shrugged helplessly.

"It's night," he said. "The guards should accept anyone who comes walking out of the trees in the right uniform. Just walk confidently, and none of them will give us a second glance."

"What if someone does notice something?" said Tina.

Daniel grinned. "Flash your cleavage. And while they're standing there stunned, move in quick and batter the life out of them."

Tina grinned. "I like the way you think."

They strode out of the trees and across the open space. Daniel held his head high and did his best to look like he didn't have a care in the world. Tina strode along as though hoping someone would do something she could object to. The other guards accepted this as perfectly normal behavior, and didn't spare them a second glance. Daniel and Tina headed straight for the main entrance.

"What if someone asks us for a password?" said Tina.

"Punch them out," said Daniel. "But quietly."

"I can do that."

But when they stepped through the entrance, there was no one there. Just a great hole in the ground, with rough earth walls falling away. A long spiraling stairway had been cut into the inner wall. Daniel moved to the top of the steps and peered down into a darkness that seemed to fall away forever. Electric lamps had been strung along the inner wall, but their light didn't travel far. Tina moved in beside Daniel.

"No way this is anything to do with uncovering a Roman mosaic," she said. "It looks more like someone has been mining here."

"I can't tell how far down this hole goes," Daniel said slowly, "but I'm guessing pretty deep."

"Maybe the Martians need that, to feel secure," said Tina. "Like moles."

"I'd hate it if the Martians turned out to be giant moles," said Daniel. "Those things have always freaked me out, with their weird noses and little hands."

"Just pretend we're weasels, come to seize Toad Hall for the masses," Tina said briskly. She peered down into the hole. "The stairs would seem to suggest people come and go on a regular basis, so . . . when we get to the bottom, do we have anything like a plan?"

"Kill everything that moves that isn't us," said Daniel. "We need to send a message to Mars: coming to Earth can be seriously dangerous to your health."

"Good plan," said Tina.

Daniel started down the narrow stairs, with Tina tucked in close behind him, and step by step they descended into the Martian underworld.

There was no handrail, so Daniel and Tina had to press their shoulders against the earth wall to make sure they didn't stray too close to the open edge and the long drop. After a while Tina put a hand on Daniel's shoulder, to guide herself and reassure him.

"I'm not hearing anyone coming up," she said.

"I shouldn't think the soldiers are allowed down here," said Daniel. "They just guard the entrance."

"Then who uses these stairs?" said Tina. "Unless the Martians look like us."

"I seriously doubt that," said Daniel.

"Moles . . ." said Tina, in her best sepulchral voice.

"Stop it," said Daniel.

They continued on down, listening carefully, but the only sounds were the scuff of their feet on the rough steps. Daniel turned once, to look back up the way they'd come, and found the entrance of the hole was no longer visible. Tina's hand tightened reassuringly on his shoulder, and he started down again. The descent went on so long that Daniel's leg muscles actually started to ache, but finally the stairs came to an end, and the Hydes found themselves confronted by a great open chamber, lined with gleaming metal walls. There was something disturbing about the color of the metal, as though it had soured and gone off. Daniel and Tina stood close together, and their reflections stared silently back at them, distorted and strangely ghostly, as though seen through a heat haze.

A number of large circular openings gave access to tunnels heading off into the earth, like a maze, or a warren. All of the tunnels were brightly lit, though Daniel was damned if he could see how.

"I'm not seeing any signs, or instructions," he said finally. "I guess we just choose a tunnel at random and see where it takes us. The base can't be that big. Maybe we'll bump into someone along the way who can give us directions."

Tina started to say something cutting and then broke off to cough harshly and spit on the floor.

"There's something bad about this air."

Daniel took a deep breath, and shook his head. "Could just be that new Martian base smell." He pointed at the nearest opening. "This looks promising."

"It'll do," said Tina.

As they made their way along the tunnel, their weird reflections floated serenely along with them, like watchful spirits. Daniel frowned as his feet clanged loudly on the metal floor, sending a warning that intruders were on their way. The light in the tunnel grew bright enough to blind a normal human, but Daniel just squinted into it and kept going. It worried him that he still couldn't work out where the illumination was coming from.

The tunnel branched repeatedly, and Daniel felt the first faint stirrings of unease as he was forced to choose each new direction at random.

"We should have brought a compass," he said.

"Or a ball of thread," said Tina. "How are we going to find our way back?"

"I'm memorizing the route," said Daniel.

"Of course you are," said Tina.

And quite suddenly they emerged into a cavern the size of a cathedral. The huge open space was so wide the distant walls had no discernible details, and the roof was so high it gave Daniel a strange sense of vertigo. The sudden change in scale made him feel like a mouse that had just emerged from the skirting board. The Hydes moved in close together, for mutual support and protection, but it seemed they had the whole place to themselves. Massive stalactites thrust down from the high ceiling, encrusted with moving parts and flickering lights, and the closest metal walls were pitted and scarred, as though eaten away by some disfiguring disease. The cavern floor was split into separate areas by curving stone walls that rose and fell like frozen tides. Tendrils of alien technology spread across the rough stone, crawling and seething in a slow, deliberate way that made Daniel think they must have been grown as much as made. Shimmering lights pulsed up and down the tendrils, like thoughts chasing each other back and forth.

"What is that stuff?" said Tina.

"Connective tissues," Daniel said absently. "Nerves in a gigantic brain, passing information to where it's needed."

Tina looked at him sharply. "How the hell could you know that?"

Daniel looked slowly around him. "There's an underlying pattern to everything here, and it speaks to me, on some level I don't understand. Aren't you picking up any of this?"

"I'm getting something," Tina said carefully. "Like picking up radio shows on your fillings. But I think we need to be very cautious about what we let into our heads, Daniel."

He nodded briefly, and then started forward into the cavern, treading his way through the maze of stone walls as though following a path that was obvious to him. Tina stuck close behind, watching him cautiously. The light was painfully harsh now, and both Hydes had to breathe deeply to keep from coughing on the increasingly unpleasant air. The heat was so intense that sweat ran down their faces and dripped off their chins.

"Conditions are getting worse," said Tina. "I'm not sure any normal human could survive this. It's like being on another planet."

"Exactly," said Daniel. "All of this is for the benefit of the Martians. So they can feel at home."

Tina looked at him sharply. "You mean they're recreating how things are on Mars?"

"That's why we haven't encountered any guards or workers down here," said Daniel. "Breathing this air would kill them. Luckily, we're made of sterner stuff."

"Good to be a Hyde," said Tina.

"At least we can be sure we won't find anything down here but Martians," said Daniel.

And then he stopped and looked round, as something that sounded very much like human footsteps echoed out of a side tunnel. Tina raised her fists, but Daniel gestured urgently for her to join him in ducking down behind the nearest stone wall. She scowled, but went with him. As they crouched down, one of the metallic tendrils twitched and stirred, as though disturbed by their presence. It slowly detached itself from the stone wall, reached out like some metallic snake, and then closed and tightened suddenly around Daniel's throat.

For a moment he couldn't breathe, and then he braced his neck muscles to hold off the awful pressure. He dragged in a lungful of air, forced his fingers under the tendril, and broke its hold. He tore the struggling thing from his neck, and it twisted horribly in his grasp, fighting to break free. Daniel ripped the whole tendril away from the wall with one great heave. It twisted and whipped around with nightmarish strength and malevolence, and tried to wrap itself around his hands and arms, but Daniel just tore the whole thing to pieces and threw them on the floor. And then he and Tina took turns stamping on them till they stopped moving.

More tendrils stirred dangerously on the stone walls, but when Tina glared around her, hands opening and closing with dangerous intent, the tendrils grew still.

"It would appear they're capable of learning," said Daniel.

"Listen!" said Tina. "Those footsteps are getting really close now. Maybe those things summoned the night watchman."

They turned quickly back to face the side tunnel. A tall humanoid figure stepped out, and then stood very still. It appeared to be fashioned from the same metal as the walls, and its form was all smooth curves with no joints or sections. Like a statue that had come alive in the night and gone looking for its creator. The face was blank, apart from a single light glowing in the center of its forehead. The figure turned its head slowly, as though scanning the chamber.

"Some sort of robot?" Tina said quietly.

Daniel nodded. "This must be what the Martians use when there's hard labor to be done."

"Why would Martians make a robot in human shape?"

"Because this form works best on Earth?"

"You're just guessing now," said Tina.

"Do you have a better idea?"

"I haven't a clue," said Tina. "This place is blowing all my fuses." She scowled around the chamber. "I hate not understanding things."

"You'll feel better when we find something to hit," said Daniel.

The robot turned abruptly, and went back into the tunnel. Daniel gestured quickly to Tina and they set off after it, at a discreet distance. The robot led them through several twisting tunnels and then out into an even larger chamber. The massive underground cavern was full of machines the size of buildings, with slowly moving parts and flaring lights that came and went. The shapes of the machines were constantly changing, their edges and boundaries slumping and reforming. Daniel tried to force some sense into what he was seeing, and only then took in the dozens of humanoid robots moving purposefully around the bases of the machines.

"I can't even guess what this as all for," he said.

"Probably something only a Martian could hope to understand," said Tina. "Just looking at all of this makes my head ache."

"The robots are here to keep the machines running smoothly," said Daniel. "Like worker drones in a hive."

Tina started to say something, and then broke into loud hacking coughs. Daniel thumped her hard on the back, trying to clear her lungs before the robots noticed. Tina finally twisted out from under Daniel's hand.

"It's not me, it's the air! It's getting worse." She shook her head hard, and glowered around her. "Where are the Martians? Why haven't we seen anything but machines and robots?"

"The air, the heat, and the light seem to be building toward full Martian conditions," Daniel said slowly. "But the gravity is still Earth normal. Maybe the Martians can't change that without drawing unwanted attention to themselves. And since they can't function properly in our greater gravity, they have to rely on robots to get things done."

He broke off as a robot stamped right past their hiding place. Daniel stood up suddenly and gave the robot a friendly wave, but it didn't even glance in his direction. Tina slapped Daniel hard on the shoulder, but when he moved out into the open she went with him. Daniel waved both arms around and shouted at the robots, but not one of them reacted.

"I think we're invisible to them, as long as we don't interfere with their work," said Daniel.

"At some point we may have to," said Tina.

Daniel smiled at her. "And that's when you get to hit something."

Two of the huge machines lurched forward and slammed together, like rutting deer banging foreheads. The noise was deafening, and their whole structures trembled. Both machines put out jagged metal protrusions and thrust them into each other, locking themselves together. Daniel gestured for Tina to back away, in case one of the giant structures lost its balance. But instead the two machines seemed to fall into each other, merging and melding until finally there was just one quite different machine.

"It's like they're alive . . ." said Tina.

"Maybe they are, on some level," said Daniel. "Remember the tendril that tried to strangle me?"

Something on the edge of his vision caught his attention, and he tapped Tina on the arm. She followed his gaze, and stood very still. In the metal wall beside them, the Hydes' distorted reflections were moving independently, their arms waving slowly in unfamiliar gestures.

"They're trying to communicate," said Daniel. "Or whatever's behind them is."

Tina pulled him away. "Never talk to strangers. Especially in an underground base created by aliens intent on wiping out Humanity."

"I was just curious about what they were trying to tell us," said Daniel.

"I doubt it's anything we'd want to hear," said Tina. "But you're missing the point: this means something knows we're here. We need to concentrate on finding the Martians, so we can kill them."

"Why can't we all be friends?" said Daniel, just a bit wistfully.

"Please," said Tina. "Remember you're a Hyde."

And then she started coughing again, great hacking spasms that racked her whole body. That started Daniel off, and they ended up leaning on each other as they struggled to control their breathing. The sweat from their exertions soaked into their uniforms.

"Things got worse when we came in here," Tina said finally, mopping at her face with her sleeve. "It must be down to these machines. We were coping well enough before."

"Of course!" said Daniel. "The machines are recreating conditions on Mars as part of a terraforming process, so the Martians can wipe out Humanity and just move in. What need is there for a war, when you can change the whole world enough that it will wipe out the local population for you?"

Tina grabbed Daniel by the shoulder and gave him a good shake. "You can't let these things get inside your head! Stop listening to them!"

"I'm not," said Daniel, calmly removing her hand. "It's just common sense. This must be the trial run, to see if the machines can do what's necessary."

"We have to find the Martians," Tina said stubbornly. "Slaughter every one of them, burn down the base, and then piss on the ashes."

"Sounds like a plan to me," said Daniel. "Only . . . where are the Martians?"

And then his eyes went to a series of thick pipes that emerged from one of the machines, ran along the base of the wall, and out of the chamber. He moved quickly over to the wall, knelt down, and listened carefully.

"These pipes are carrying the newly manufactured air to another part of the base. And since the Martians would need the purest form of that air, all we have to do is follow the pipes and they'll take us straight to them."

"I had better get to hit something soon," Tina said darkly.

Daniel trotted along beside the pipes, and when they took a sudden turn and shot off down a side tunnel, Daniel hurried after them. He could hear Tina muttering behind him. He glanced at the metal wall, and suddenly realized that the distorted reflections had disappeared. He didn't think he'd mention that to Tina. The tunnel branched again and again, but Daniel just kept following the pipes.

"This base is a lot bigger than I expected," said Tina.

"Not to worry," said Daniel. "We're Hydes. There's nothing so big that we can't break it."

Tina beamed at him. "You always know the right thing to say."

Daniel stopped suddenly. Tina looked around sharply.

"What?"

"I can smell something," Daniel said slowly. "Something bad."

Tina sniffed at the air, and pulled a face. "Spoiled meat and spilled blood. Have the Martians been killing things?"

"They must eat," said Daniel.

"How would they smuggle animals down here?"

"Maybe there are other entrances."

Tina looked at him steadily. "You don't think it's livestock, do you?"

"No," said Daniel. "I think we need to find out where this is coming from."

He turned his back on the pipes, and followed his nose through several tunnels until the way was blocked by a featureless metal slab that sealed off the whole tunnel. Tina stepped forward and studied the slab carefully.

"I'm not seeing any handle, or lock mechanism."

Daniel tried waving his arms, just in case it was motion activated, but the slab ignored him. Tina tried forcing it, but couldn't get a grip on anything to give her some traction. In the end, Daniel stiffened his fingers and slammed them into the metal. It hurt like hell, but he was able to force his fingers all the way in to the second joint. He braced himself, and threw his whole weight against the slab. For a long moment he stood like a statue, straining every muscle. The slab creaked and groaned, started to edge sideways, and then slammed back into place. Tina thrust her fingers into the metal beside Daniel's, and together the two of them forced the door sideways, inch by inch. A terrible stench burst out of the opening, and the Hydes had to turn their faces away. The metal slab ground to a halt, and refused to move any further. Daniel and Tina let go of the slab, ready to grab it again if it started moving, but the slab stayed where it was. Daniel forced himself through the narrow opening, with Tina right behind him. The smell hit them like a fist in the face, as they stepped into the bloody chamber.

The intense heat of the Martian base was immediately replaced by a bitter cold. Then the room reacted to their presence and turned on the lights, revealing hundreds of corpses hanging on rows of hooks like an abattoir of human meat. A forest of dangling bodies: men, women, and children who'd been torn open from chin to crotch, and all the internal organs torn out. Blood had streamed down the dangling legs and dripped onto the floor. The stench of death and horror was almost unbearable.

"Daniel," said Tina, "given how tight the seal on that metal slab was, how were we able to smell this out in the corridor?"

"I don't think we did," said Daniel. "It was just more information, picked up by our minds. Something wanted us to see what's here."

He had to stop talking. His stomach was churning, not just from the awful sight but because he was flashing back to memories of a cellar where the Frankenstein Clan had butchered people for their organs, for use in illegal transplants. Three of Daniel's friends had been killed in that cellar, while he was left for dead. Dr. Jekyll's Elixir repaired his broken body, but his mind had never fully healed. He suddenly couldn't get his breath, and his legs started to give way. Tina was quickly there to throw an arm around him, as much for comfort as to hold him up.

"Don't let this get to you," she said fiercely. "We can't save these people, but we can make the Martians pay for what they've done. And the things we'll do to those bastards will make this seem like nothing."

Daniel nodded, and stood up straight again. Hate made a Hyde strong. Tina stepped back to give him some room, and nodded at the hanging bodies.

"I wonder who they were."

"Homeless people, sleeping rough on the Common," said Daniel. "Or maybe just anyone who visited the Common at night. Get too close to the dig, and they'd be grabbed and dragged down the steps."

Tina looked at him sharply. "You think the guards . . . ?"

"More likely the robots. This is why the Martians made their robots in human shapes. Because at night people wouldn't see them as a threat until it was too late. And why the Martians needed a new base, with a new inviting entrance. So they could acquire human bodies without anyone noticing."

"But why would they want human bodies?" said Tina.

"According to Edward's file," Daniel said slowly, "Martians have a taste for human flesh. They even drink the blood. But why keep so many bodies in storage?"

"Because they're expecting company?" said Tina.

Daniel looked at her sharply. "It's the invasion! The Martians are finally coming in force, to take possession of their new home. We have to stop the terraforming process."

He turned to leave, only to find the door had silently closed behind them. Daniel hit it several times, but it wouldn't budge. Tina lowered a shoulder and charged the door, but couldn't even dent it. She stumbled back, rubbing at her shoulder.

"Now what?"

Daniel peered through the forest of hanging corpses, and narrowed his eyes.

"I can just make out what might be another door, on the far side of the chamber."

"What if that won't open either?" said Tina.

"At least it's a chance."

Tina looked at him steadily. "We'll have to force our way through the bodies. Are you up to that?"

"They're dead," said Daniel. "They can't hurt us."

"Very good," said Tina. "Now try saying it like you mean it."

It took Daniel a moment before he could make himself move forward. He had to turn sideways, and ease himself between the tightly packed bodies. His skin crawled from the contact, and he quickly learned to keep his gaze fixed on the floor, so he wouldn't have to look at the staring eyes and silently screaming mouths. Tina stuck close behind him, one hand resting on his shoulder, as much to reassure him she was still with him as to make sure she didn't get left behind. Sometimes Daniel would bump into a body and set it swinging, and then it would set another moving, until a whole row was swaying back and forth in a horrible imitation of life.

He kept thinking he'd get used to the stench, but somehow he never did. He breathed through his mouth as much as possible, and his breath steamed thickly on the freezing air. More and more bodies, row after row with hooks thrust through their shoulders and upper chests . . . Daniel could feel a scream building deep inside him, but he fought it down. Because if he let it out he wasn't sure he'd ever be able to stop. Finally the bodies fell away before him, and revealed the far door.

"All right," said Tina, moving quickly in beside him. "We're here. Now what?"

Daniel closed his eyes, and concentrated. Ever since he'd entered the Martian base he'd been aware of what was going on around him. He knew things he shouldn't know, as though he was tapping into a stream of hidden communications. He frowned, as he made a fleeting contact with . . . not a living thing, definitely not a Martian . . . one of the machines. It had been built to connect everything around it; but no one had ever thought to instruct it not to talk to strangers.

"Let us out," said Daniel.

"Daniel?" said Tina. "Who are you talking to?"

"I don't know," said Daniel. "I just hope it's listening."

He walked steadily forward, and the door slid sideways. He stepped out into a metal corridor, and Tina hurried after him. The moment they were out, the door closed behind them. Daniel and Tina both stumbled and almost fell, as the bitter cold of the abattoir was replaced by the intense heat of the Martian atmosphere. But at least the stench of the dead was gone. Daniel smiled briefly at Tina.

"It seems we have an ally. Apparently the Martians never taught their machines the value of loyalty."

"You always were good at making friends," said Tina.

Daniel pointed suddenly at the opposite wall. "I see pipes!"

"Good for you," said Tina. "Now let's go find the Martians, before they discover their machines have been speaking out of turn."

Following the pipes led them to the biggest chamber yet: a cavern deep in the earth large enough to land a plane in. The ceiling was hidden behind layers of shimmering mist, and the walls were so far off they were just a suggestion in the distance. The air was so foul Daniel and Tina had to struggle to get their breath, the heat was so intense it baked the sweat right off them, and the light was so dazzling they had to peer around through half-closed eyes.

"We're not on Earth anymore," said Daniel. "This is Mars."

"Minus several thousand on Tripadvisor," growled Tina.

There were no giant machines; the great open space was divided by a maze of stone walls, rising and falling in stationary waves. Their layout suggested a meaning without ever collapsing into one, hinting at purposes too alien for any human mind to cope with. Daniel felt Tina's hand nestle into his, and without looking down he squeezed it reassuringly. They moved slowly forward into the cavern, like children who'd wandered into a dark wood.

Long strands of red weed hung down through the ceiling mists, like an upside-down forest. Thick and bloated and crusted with bulbous nodes, the red weed pulsed with slow malevolent life. The strands twitched sluggishly as Daniel and Tina approached, and started to reach out to them, only to pull back at the last moment, as though repulsed by the Hydes' very nature.

Daniel investigated one walled-off section after another. The rough stone walls were beaded with something very like sweat, and when Daniel put a hand on the stone he felt something like a pulse of life. The walls were aware, and quite possibly dreaming; he didn't think he wanted to know what was on their minds. Whatever had been speaking to Daniel had nothing to say, leaving him to wander without a guide in an alien landscape. He led Tina carefully around strange dark pools that seethed and bubbled, like tarns full of liquid night. Every now and again one would blast a geyser of frothing liquids high into the air. The heat that radiated from these explosions was enough to send both Hydes staggering, and the falling drops would smart fiercely when they hit their bare skin.

Mars, thought Daniel. *This is Mars. So where are the Martians?* His hands clenched into fists so tight they ached, and it was only then that he realized he'd let go of Tina's hand. He looked quickly round, and found she'd dropped back a way, glaring around her with almost feral malevolence. Daniel started to say something and then stopped, as he made out a huge dark shape up ahead. He called out to Tina and she turned on him, her lips drawn back in a vicious snarl. He pointed steadily at the thing before them, and Tina's face slowly cleared. She nodded quickly, to tell him she was back, and moved forward to stand beside him.

"I don't know what that is," said Daniel, "but it's alive."

"A Martian, at last," said Tina. Her voice was heavy, almost drugged with hate. "Let's go introduce ourselves."

"Slowly," said Daniel. "We don't want to trigger any alarms."

"Revenge is a dish best savored slow," said Tina.

They moved cautiously forward, weaving their way round the stone walls surrounding the shape, until finally they had a clear view of the Martian. Huge and round, some twenty feet in diameter, it looked like nothing so much as a giant brain. Its crimson surface was mottled with dark throbbing veins, and from its base sprouted dozens of churning tentacles, punctuated with vicious barbs. A single great eye stared unblinkingly, set above a huge serrated beak like a cuttlefish. The Martian was feeding on a human corpse, tearing the meat off the bones with its tentacles and then stuffing the bloody morsels into the gaping beak. The Martian heaved slowly as it fed, making deep grunting sounds like a pig in its sty.

"I have never wanted to kill anything as much as I want to kill that thing," said Tina. "I want to tear it to pieces with my bare hands and laugh as it screams."

"Not yet," said Daniel. "I want it dead as much as you, but first we have to make sure it's the only one here."

Tina looked quickly about her. "I'm not seeing any more, and something that size would tend to stand out."

"But why would there be only one?" said Daniel.

Tina frowned. "The robots do all the hard work. Maybe it only takes one Martian to run the machines, and make sure there's enough food in the larder for when the rest of them arrive."

Daniel nodded. "Makes sense. Okay, let's do this. It's time to send the Martians a message they'll never forget."

"Finally!" said Tina.

She jumped up onto a low stone wall and shouted obscenities at the giant brain, and the huge eye rolled wetly round to stare at her. The Martian dropped the half-eaten corpse, and swiveled on its base until it was facing the Hydes. Its nest of tentacles roiled and churned, and then rose up like dozens of angry snakes.

"You're going to die," Daniel said to the Martian. "For everything you've done, and planned to do."

"You think it can understand you?" said Tina.

Daniel shrugged. "It needed saying."

And then the Martian spoke, in great bass booming sounds that reverberated through Daniel's and Tina's bodies. They staggered and almost fell, beaten back by sounds like blows. The Martian paused, as though to judge the effect of its words, and Daniel grabbed a nearby stone wall with both hands, broke off a large piece, and threw it with all his strength. The jagged-edged stone smashed right through the Martian's unblinking eye, and buried itself deep inside the giant brain. Frothing liquid exploded from the ruptured eye, and the Martian swayed back and forth on its base and screamed like a wounded god. Tina howled with a pure and malicious joy and ran at the Martian, her fists raised.

A dozen tentacles shot out to intercept her. They snapped around Tina and brought her to a sudden halt, before lifting her effortlessly into the air. Vicious barbs sank deep into her flesh, and her blood rained down onto the giant brain. Tina struggled to break free, throwing all her Hyde strength against the tentacles, until they all contracted at once and crushed the breath out of her. She slumped in their grasp, her head lolling, and the tentacles pushed her toward the snapping cuttlefish beak.

They stuffed her limp body in—and that was when Tina's eyes shot open. She got a hand on each half of the beak, and forced them apart. The Martian rocked back and forth, its ruptured eye rolling madly. And Tina forced the two parts of the beak so far apart, she broke it. The two halves sagged separately, dark blood spurted, and the Martian howled its deep bass scream.

Tentacles dropped on Tina like the wrath of a lesser god, but this time she was waiting for them. She grabbed them in midair and tore them apart, one after another, laughing out loud as she crippled the Martian. Until one tentacle snapped around her throat and squeezed until her eyes bulged. She tore at the tentacle with both hands, her fingers sinking deep into the crimson flesh, and a dozen tentacles fell on her from different directions.

Daniel should have been fighting at her side, but he was working on something. He'd spotted a high stone wall protruding out over the Martian, and set about climbing it. He smashed holes in the stone so he could use them as footholds, and scrambled all the way up to the curving top, and only then did he stop and look down, to where Tina was struggling for her life. Without any hesitation he launched himself out over the long drop. He plummeted down and slammed headfirst into the screaming Martian brain; the sheer impact of his weight forced him all the way in.

Violent spasms tore through the Martian. Its bass scream was so loud the vibrations buffeted Daniel back and forth. He thrashed around, trying to find some purchase in the crimson haze of half-liquid Martian flesh. And then he saw something ahead of him: a complicated pulsing shape that he just knew had to be important. He forced his way through the shuddering crimson veils, took hold of the shape with both hands, and crushed it to a pulp.

The Martian's scream broke off. Its tentacles spasmed, and threw Tina away. She hit the ground hard, rolling over and over in a flurry of blood. Daniel dropped what he was holding and let it sink to the bottom, and then stamped on it hard. Just to make sure. After that, it was the easiest thing in the world to walk through the giant brain and tear a gap in its outer layers. He took a great shuddering breath of the foul air, and brushed away shreds of Martian flesh to leave a uniform soaked in gore. Behind him, the crimson brain was slowly collapsing, like a ruptured basketball. He moved forward to help Tina to her feet. She grabbed his arm with both hands, until she could get her feet under her and make herself stand up straight. She was bleeding profusely from dozens of wounds, her uniform almost as badly soaked in gore as his, but she still managed a smile for him.

"I did all the hard work, and you just fell on it?"

"I couldn't have done it without you," said Daniel.

He took her in his arms. They clung together for a long moment, and then pushed each other away. Because they were Hydes, and there was still work to be done.

"Now what?" said Tina. She was so tired she was swaying on her feet, but her gaze was perfectly clear.

"We have to destroy the terraforming equipment," said Daniel. "Sabotage it, so the whole base will explode. That should send a message to Mars, as well as put an end to their invasion."

"Good," said Tina. "Do you have any idea how to get us out of here, before the whole place goes up?"

"Of course," said Daniel. "I memorized the route on the way in."

"Show-off," said Tina.

Daniel looked around, thinking hard. Tina was almost out on her feet, and he was so exhausted it was all he could do to stand up straight. They had no weapons, no explosives, and no help. Except, just maybe, they had an ally. Daniel concentrated, reaching out to the machine presence he'd contacted earlier. And just like that, an idea came to him. He smiled at Tina.

"Rejoice! For I have a plan."

"Does it mean we can blow this place to shit and go home?"

"Oh yes."

"Then I love this plan and want to have its babies. What do we do?"

"Follow the pipes," said Daniel.

It took them a while, staggering on through endless metal corridors while holding each other up, but finally they made their way back to the chamber where the massive machines were manufacturing Martian atmosphere. And then all Daniel and Tina had to do was punch the hell out of the pipes until they collapsed in on themselves, blocking the flow of Martian air. Immediately the pressure began to build, and with the Martian dead there was no one to tell the machine to stop production. Daniel was confident that once the pressure built high enough, explosions would tear the pipes apart, and then one by one the great machines would go up too, in a chain reaction powerful enough to blow the whole base apart. The little voice in his head seemed quite sure about that. Daniel tried to say thank you, but wasn't sure it understood the concept.

He still had to get Tina out of the base before everything blew. He pulled her arm over his shoulder, and got her moving in the right direction—only to find the humanoid robots had formed a solid wall to block their way. Daniel gave Tina a good shake, and her head came up.

"What? I thought we were done?"

"One last job before we leave," said Daniel. "How would you like to beat up a whole bunch of robots that probably dragged lots of innocent people down here to die?"

Tina smiled slowly. She stood up straight, and pushed Daniel away from her.

"Better than flowers and chocolates."

Daniel and Tina gathered up the last of their strength, and went to meet the robots. The metal figures surged forward, flailing their arms with inhuman strength. Daniel struck down one robot after another as they came within reach, tearing their arms off and using them as clubs to beat their heads in. Tina kicked the robots' legs out from under them, and then stamped on their heads till they stopped moving. But no matter how many the Hydes destroyed, it seemed like there were always more robots waiting to replace them. And Daniel couldn't shake the feeling that somewhere a clock was counting down.

He finally discovered that one good punch to the glowing eye in the middle of a robot's head would drop it like a stone. He passed this on to Tina, and one short but very satisfying onslaught later, there was nothing left for them to hit. They looked around at the scattered robot bodies and nodded, satisfied.

And then, leaning heavily on each other because even Hyde strength has its limits, they headed for the exit. Exhausted, broken, and bloodied, they staggered through the metal tunnels until they reached the entrance chamber, and then made their way back up the steps and into the dig. They lurched out of the main entrance, and found themselves facing a whole bunch of startled guards with guns. And that was when the first underground explosion rocked the whole dig and toppled half the temporary walls. Daniel glared at the soldiers.

"Run!"

The guards took one look at the blood-soaked figures before them and didn't stop to argue, just turned and ran. Explosions, one after the other in swift succession, shook the ground hard enough to throw some of the mercenaries off their feet. Daniel and Tina plunged on into the nearby copse, grabbed a tree each, and hugged it tightly. The ground rose and fell in an endless earthquake. The trees flexed and groaned, but didn't fall.

Finally, the explosions stopped, and a blissful peace fell over Horse Leigh Common. Daniel and Tina relaxed their grip on the trees, and looked out at the great open space. It was covered with fallen mercenaries, some of whom were groaning loudly. Beyond them, the whole dig had disappeared. Not a trace of it remained—just a huge ragged hole in the ground with steam coming out of it. Daniel smiled at Tina.

"You can usually tell where Hydes have been."

"Why did you warn the guards?" said Tina.

"Because it was possible they genuinely didn't know what was going on, down below."

Tina shook her head. "I'm going to have to toughen you up."

"Looking forward to it," said Daniel.

They moved back into the trees, to retrieve their good clothes.

Chapter Five
THE HORROR OF THE INSECT NATION

✣ ✣ ✣

IT TOOK DANIEL AND Tina some time to walk back across the Common, because every step hurt. As Hydes they were used to soaking up punishment and then bouncing right back, but it had been a really hard night. Daniel was starting to wonder if Dr. Jekyll's marvelous Elixir had its limits. He'd mopped most of the blood from his face and Tina's, but the exhaustion felt like it was there for the duration. Their clothes had survived intact in the copse, but bloodstains were already starting to appear, here and there. All in all, a high price to pay for killing one alien. Tina leaned heavily on Daniel as they made their way slowly along the gravel path, and Daniel was quietly grateful there was no one around to see the state they were in. His pride would have been hurt, if everything else hadn't hurt worse. He felt like he'd been hung out to dry and then beaten with sticks, while Tina looked like she'd been tossed off a mountain and then had rocks thrown at her. She wasn't complaining, and that worried Daniel the most. It wasn't like her.

They finally trudged through the open Victorian gates, and Daniel half carried Tina to his car. It was a sign of just how tired she was, that she didn't object to his help. He tucked her into the passenger seat, and she just sat slumped bonelessly with her head hanging down. Daniel settled himself carefully behind the steering wheel, trying not to wince as every movement sent stabs of pain racing through him. He sat for a while, getting his breath back, and finally managed a small smile for Tina.

"You look as bad as I feel," he said, struggling to keep his voice light.

"Then you must feel really bad," said Tina, not raising her head. "I wish that Martian was still alive, so I could kill it all over again."

"Good thing we heal fast," said Daniel.

"Not fast enough," said Tina. "Drive this piece of junk to the nearest bar. I feel a real need to get outside of a whole bunch of drinks."

"Good plan," said Daniel.

His phone rang. Daniel took it out and stared at it.

"Well it's obviously not me," said Tina. "Aren't you going to answer it?"

"I don't know," said Daniel. "I'm thinking about it. There's no way this is going to be good news."

"When is it ever?" said Tina.

Daniel growled at his phone. "Yes?"

"This is Patricia. Your armorer."

"I hadn't forgotten," said Daniel. "How did you get this number?"

"I'm the armorer. I know everything."

"That isn't as reassuring an answer as you seem to think," said Daniel.

Patricia was already talking over him. "You need to return to Jekyll & Hyde Inc. immediately. I have important information for you."

She terminated the call before Daniel could even start to tell her how he and Tina had killed a Martian and blown up its base. Tina raised her head just enough to shoot him an accusing glance as he put his phone away.

"Are we really going to jump to do her bidding, every time she gives us an order?"

"Do you know where to look for the next alien base?" said Daniel.

Tina scowled. "Not as such. Not yet."

"Then we need to talk with Patricia," said Daniel.

Tina started to shake her head, and then stopped because it hurt too much. "She'll look at us. And make comments."

"By the time we get back, we'll look like Hydes again."

"God, I hope so," said Tina. "The only way I could feel worse is if I was twins."

"We won," said Daniel. "And that is all that matters."

"You know," said Tina, "there will come a time when we won't need Patricia."

"You see?" said Daniel. "Something to look forward to."

"Drive," said Tina.

Daniel made his way carefully through the nighttime streets, giving a wide berth to whatever traffic dared to share a road with him. Not because he'd developed a new respect for the traffic laws, but because he was feeling so fragile he didn't feel up to any sudden changes in direction. He did still ignore the traffic lights, because stopping and starting took too much out of him. Tina remained slumped in her seat, making low unhappy noises every time Daniel changed gear.

He finally eased the police car to a halt outside the Jekyll & Hyde Inc. building, and turned off the engine with a sense of relief. There had been times when he'd wondered if he'd make it this far. He had to yell at Tina to wake her up, and then they both took their time getting out of the car, while being careful not to comment on each other's groans and bad language. Tina glowered at the car, and sniffed loudly.

"I can't believe we drove halfway across London in a stolen police car. We couldn't have attracted more attention if you'd chosen a shocking pink Rolls Royce."

"That is next on my list," said Daniel. "I know you've always wanted one."

Tina smiled briefly. "Lady Penelope rules."

"I loved the Thunderbirds show too; but I am not wearing a chauffeur's outfit," said Daniel.

"I'll let you wear the peaked cap in bed," said Tina.

They put their backs to the car so they could lean on it for support, and looked the building over. All the fires had gone out, apparently without any assistance from the fire brigade, but smoke was still drifting up from what remained of the roof. There wasn't a light on anywhere, least of all in the shattered-glass, broken-doored lobby—which couldn't have shouted *There's no one here!* any louder if someone had given it a megaphone.

"Nobody home, and no one to put the kettle on," said Daniel. "I thought Patricia would at least have the decency to show up and welcome us back. Are we going to have to climb that bloody rope ladder into the armory again?"

Tina sighed, in an *I'm not exasperated, just quietly disappointed* sort of way, and pointed a reasonably steady finger at a sign taped to the front door. Daniel leaned in for a closer look, winced as his back creaked loudly, and read the neatly handwritten words *Jekyll & Hyde Inc. Has Moved to New Premises. Three Doors Down, to Your Right.*

"We've moved?" said Daniel.

"Apparently," said Tina. "Quick work, given that we haven't been gone ten minutes."

"Our new armorer is starting to get on my nerves," said Daniel. "Just how efficient can someone be, before they start feeling creepy?"

"I am getting extremely tired of her dragging us around on a leash," said Tina.

"But she could still be very useful to us," said Daniel.

Tina glowered at him. "Do you have to be so reasonable?"

"We need someone to run the organization," said Daniel. "Someone with people skills. Unless you want to deal with all the day-to-day problems?"

"I'd rather stab myself in the eye with a chain saw," said Tina. "I didn't become a Hyde to sit behind a desk and be reasonable to people who haven't got the sense to sort things out for themselves."

"I'll take that as a no," said Daniel. "And since I feel even less qualified than you to hold the position, let's just be grateful that Patricia volunteered."

"Don't you even hint to her we feel that way," said Tina.

"Wouldn't dream of it," said Daniel. "Come on, let's go see what the new Jekyll & Hyde Inc. building looks like. Maybe there'll be bunting."

Tina sighed. "Don't try to make me smile. I don't feel strong enough."

They set off down the street, leaning on each other just a little, for company as much as support. Daniel counted off the doors until finally they found themselves in front of an old-fashioned business building with the usual marble and frosted-glass exterior. Very like the one they'd left behind, except that here lights blazed from every window. A signwriter in paint-smeared dungarees was kneeling in front of the main door, carefully applying the name *Jekyll & Hyde Inc.* in tasteful gold-leaf lettering. Daniel and Tina stared at the half-finished sign until the signwriter became uncomfortable enough to acknowledge their presence.

"You won't get better for the money, you know. That's craftsmanship, that is. You can't hurry craftsmanship."

"Get on with it," said Tina.

The signwriter quickly returned his attention to the lettering.

"It's a bit up front, isn't it?" Daniel said critically. "Do we really want everyone to know our business, and where to find us? Particularly after tonight's unexpected visitors."

"I like it," said Tina. "It sends a message: We're back, despite everything that's been thrown at us. It also tells everyone that even blowing up a building isn't enough to slow us down."

Daniel called up his inner reserves, straightened his back and lifted his chin, and headed straight for the door, with Tina stepping it out at his side as though this was just another night. The signwriter scrambled to get out of their way. Daniel slammed the door open and strode into the lobby, while Tina snarled around her like an attack dog with attitude. The wide-open space was packed with people hurrying back and forth, and doing everything they could to give the impression that they hadn't noticed the arrival of two battered and bloodstained Hydes.

Daniel watched interestedly as people pushed stylish new furniture into position, or hung tasteful art prints on the walls, or fussed over the very impressive new reception desk. Everything today's smart new business needed, to make a good first impression. There was a sense of worker bees buzzing around a new hive, making sure everything was just right.

Daniel was sure he recognized some of the employees as having worked for the old organization, under Edward Hyde—until he and Tina had no choice but to kick their arses and scatter them sobbing to the four winds. Daniel was amazed Patricia had been able to track them down so quickly, never mind lure them back to work.

And then everyone bustling away before him seemed to suddenly fall back, revealing Patricia holding court at the rear of the lobby. Tall and stately in her outfit of basic black, she seemed perfectly cool and serene, and apparently unmoved by having to deal with a sea of troubles. People kept running up to her with questions, requests, and important pieces of paperwork, and she handled them all like a dominatrix debating whether or not to withhold the whip. Daniel and Tina exchanged a glance, and headed straight for her.

The few employees still in their way immediately discovered pressing reasons to be somewhere else, but Patricia didn't even glance at the Hydes until they planted themselves right in front of her. Daniel was pretty sure Patricia had known exactly where they were from the moment they'd entered the lobby, but she still took her own sweet time before deciding to acknowledge them. She looked Daniel and Tina over like a headmistress trying to decide which punishment would be most appropriate, and Daniel glared right back at her, to make it clear he really wasn't in the mood. Tina growled.

"Well, well, look what the night dragged in," said Patricia, entirely unmoved. "Who the hell happened to you?"

"We've been working," said Daniel.

"Right," said Tina. "Martians nil, Hydes won."

Patricia just nodded, as though no other outcome had crossed her mind.

"Reports have been coming in from Horse Leigh Common," she said, "concerning massive underground explosions, traumatized security officers running weeping for the horizon, and a really big hole in the ground."

"It made the news already?" said Daniel.

"I have my own sources," said Patricia. "It sounds like you did a good job. In your own highly destructive way."

"There used to be a Martian base," said Daniel. "Now there isn't. What more do you want?"

"An assurance that none of the Martians made it out alive," said Patricia. "I'd hate to have to send you back, to mop up any survivors."

"There was only the one Martian," said Tina. "I hit it a lot, and Daniel jumped on it. The Martian was very thoroughly dead, before we blew the place up."

Daniel nodded. "I could have brought you its eye back as proof, if you'd said."

Patricia shook her head. "You need to get back to work immediately. Time is not on our side."

Daniel folded his arms and gave her his best *I'm not going anywhere* look. "A thank-you would be nice."

"We are not going after any more aliens until we've had a serious time-out," Tina said firmly. "And just possibly a complete change of blood, followed by a whole bunch of drinks with an Adrenalin chaser."

Patricia nodded slowly. "I suppose we can't have you going around looking like that."

"Like what?" Daniel said ominously.

"The clothes will do," said Patricia. "The occasional bloodstain comes as standard, where Hydes are concerned. But you both look like you're running on fumes, and could use a really good pick-me-up." She reached inside her jacket and produced a large pressure-spray hypo. "This is the good stuff, guaranteed to meet all your current health needs. It will turbo-charge your immune system, repair all damage down to the cellular level, put the bounce back in your step and a twinkle in your eye. Lean forward and bare your necks."

Daniel and Tina just looked at her. Patricia raised an eyebrow.

"Is there a problem?"

"Tina and I have trust issues, when it comes to allowing unknown substances into our bodies," said Daniel.

"Right," said Tina. "Let's see you shoot some of that shit into your own neck first."

Patricia sighed loudly, like a busy mother being forced to deal with unreasonably recalcitrant children, and then jammed the hypo against her neck. There was a quiet sigh as the hypo did its business, and then the armorer pulled it away and looked meaningfully at Daniel and Tina. They kept her waiting for a moment, ostensibly looking for side effects but actually just to make a point, and then bared their necks. Daniel did his best not to flinch, even though it felt like being blasted with freezing cold birdshot. Tina just took it in her stride. She'd indulged in much worse in her time.

And then both Hydes stood up straight so suddenly their spines cracked, and grinned broadly as all their pain and fatigue vanished in a moment. Daniel laughed out loud, grabbed Tina by the hips, and threw her so high into the air the top of her head brushed against the ceiling. She whooped loudly as she fell back, and threw her arms around Daniel. She bent him over in a full dip, and kissed him resoundingly before planting him back on his feet. Some of the staff applauded.

"We're back!" Daniel said loudly.

"Let all the worlds there are beware!" said Tina.

Daniel looked at Patricia. "What the hell did you just give us?"

"My very own personal blend of herbs and spices," said the armorer. "Absolutely guaranteed to jump-start your well-being. Maybe next time you'll trust me, when I tell you I have your best interests at heart."

"I wouldn't put money on it," said Daniel.

Tina grinned. "What he said. Only with even more cynicism."

Daniel looked round at the staff, who were busy being busy again. "How did you persuade all these people to come back?"

"Doubled their wages, gave them stock in the company, and promised to kick their arses if they didn't," said Patricia.

Tina nodded. "That would do it."

"I couldn't help noticing that they seem as intimidated by you as they were by Edward," said Daniel. "I am not a big fan of bullying in the workplace."

"Unless we're doing it," said Tina.

"Remember the doubled pay?" said Patricia. "Everyone in this building is here because they want to be. I just make sure they earn that pay."

Daniel decided to leave it at that, for the time being. "How were you able to acquire this building so quickly?"

Patricia nodded approvingly, as though he'd finally asked a sensible question.

"Put up enough cash and you'd be surprised how fast a deal can go through. I wasn't just Edward's armorer, back in the day; I did all kinds of things for him that he couldn't be bothered to do himself. Fortunately, he never did get around to changing the passwords on his accounts."

"Have you transferred the old armory here yet?" said Tina.

"Not yet," said Patricia. "A lot of what's in there will have to be handled with extreme care, if we want most of this street to still be here in the near future. The armory is safe enough in the old building. Nothing can get out, and anyone who gets in deserves every truly appalling thing that will happen to them. And, of course, after what happened on the roof, everyone is giving the old building plenty of room anyway."

"What's the official line on that?" said Daniel.

"Terrorist attack," said Patricia. "A very useful catch-all phrase. We don't need to worry about the authorities, they have a long history of turning a blind eye where Jekyll & Hyde Inc. is concerned. I've no doubt polite queries are already being drafted, and by the time they arrive here I should have people in place to send back properly worded answers. You have to use the correct official phrases when you tell important people to go to hell, or they sulk."

She looked steadily at Daniel and Tina. "Leave the everyday problems to me. You just concentrate on the alien bases. I've been receiving reports that suggest some of the aliens are actively preparing for invasion."

Daniel nodded. "The Martians were getting pretty close."

"Hold it," said Tina, giving Patricia her best hard look. "Who is giving you these reports?"

"I have my own people, out in the field," said Patricia.

And then she just stood there and stared at them, defying them to get anything else out of her.

"So," said Tina. "Jekyll & Hyde Inc. is still a going concern?"

"As far as the world is concerned, we never went away," said Patricia. "Our official motto is still *Be afraid. Be very afraid.* Now, Daniel, I have something for you."

She produced a very official-looking envelope, and presented it formally to Daniel.

"This arrived, addressed to you, courtesy of a messenger from New Scotland Yard. A personal communication from Commissioner Jonathan Hart."

"My old friend and ally," said Daniel.

"Really?" said Tina.

"No," said Daniel. "But he can have the job until I can find someone better. And he does know things."

The envelope contained a single sheet of paper, on which was written "*Woolwich Docks. BEM.*"

"That's the location for the next alien base?" said Tina.

"The East London docks would make an excellent place to conceal a secret base," said Daniel. "There's always enough coming and going to disguise any secret business."

"BEM," said Tina, grinning broadly. "Bug-Eyed Monsters! Cool!"

Daniel nodded to Patricia. "Anything useful you can tell us, about these particular aliens?"

"Not really," said the armorer. "There's no shortage of information out there, but not a lot you can depend on. The general feeling is that the Bug-Eyed Monsters are a race of superintelligent insects from outside our solar system."

"Any advice?" said Daniel.

"Get them before they get you."

Daniel gave Patricia a hard look. "We could use some help, in your capacity as armorer."

"Guns!" said Tina, bouncing happily on her feet. "Big shooty things, to really ruin a superintelligent insect's day."

"Because you only get one chance to make a real first impression," said Daniel.

"I thought you might ask," said Patricia, "so I looked this out for you."

She snapped her fingers, and a young woman came hurrying forward. She deposited a briefcase at Patricia's feet, like a priestess delivering an offering to her goddess, smiled bashfully at Daniel and Tina, and then hurried away. The armorer opened the briefcase, took out a small metal box, and presented it ceremoniously to Daniel. The box had no details and no controls, just a large red button on top.

"This is an explosive device," said Patricia. "Of quite extraordinary malevolence."

"It's not very big," said Tina.

"Size isn't everything."

Tina scowled at the armorer. "Why do you always hand everything to Daniel, and never to me?"

"Because he's less likely to drop it," said Patricia. "Or break it."

Daniel offered Tina the box. "You can hold the nasty blowy-uppy thing, if you want."

Tina didn't actually back away, but looked like she wanted to. "I was just making a point."

Patricia fixed her attention on Daniel. "Hit the button, and you've got a ten-minute delay before you're off to the races. I recommend throwing it and then running like hell, because that bomb doesn't mess about."

"Best kind," said Daniel.

He slipped the box into his jacket pocket, being careful not to let his fingers stray anywhere near the button. Patricia shook her head.

"You have to hit the button really hard to trigger it. It's a standard safety feature."

"Good to know," said Daniel.

"Bombs are all very well," said Tina, with the casual air of someone who'd blown up a great many things in her time. "I'm all for bringing a major explosion to the party—loud noises and mass destruction, what's not to like? But we could still use some guns, this time. Heavy-duty big-bang things, with attitude. I felt a real need for something long range, when we were down in the Martian base. Daniel and I had to get seriously hands-on with the Martian, which didn't turn out to be nearly as much fun as I'd hoped."

"According to my predecessor's records," said Patricia, "you two don't do subtle. And given that you're going to be breaking into an alien base with no idea of what you'll be walking into, I think it would be better if you took the time to think your way through whatever problems you encounter."

"No guns?" said Tina.

"You'll do better without them," said Patricia.

Daniel gave her his best scowl. "You don't get to make decisions like that."

"As long as I'm in charge of the armory, I do."

Tina smiled at Daniel. "Want me to punch her head through a wall?"

Daniel sighed. "Come away, Tina. She's not worth it."

Tina sniffed. "I could always make an exception, in her case."

Even in the early hours of the morning, there was a lot of traffic moving in and out of Woolwich Dockyard, carrying all kinds of goods that might or might not have the proper documentation. Daniel and Tina strolled casually up to the main entrance, wearing their best *Don't mess with me, I have a perfect right to be here* expressions. And while there were quite a few people hanging around the dock gates, discussing important matters in hushed voices, they all moved quickly to get out of the way when Tina looked at them.

Hundreds of huge steel shipping containers stood side by side in long rows, off-loaded from the nearby ships, waiting to be emptied out and put to use again. Large muscular men in heavy jackets and brightly colored hard hats swarmed around the containers like bees in a hive. There was a lot of noise, and even more bustle, and no one paid any attention at all to Daniel and Tina.

"Who do they think we are?" Tina said quietly.

"They don't care," said Daniel, "as long as we're not the authorities. Which is why I parked the police car so far away. Smile at the nice dockworkers, Tina—that should really unnerve them."

"You say the nicest things," said Tina.

They strolled back and forth, covering each section of the docks in turn, checking out row after row of containers big enough to hold entire buildings, if they'd been laid on their side. The doors were usually left open, showing off goods and produce from every corner of the earth.

"What are we looking for?" said Tina.

"Anything that doesn't belong," said Daniel.

Tina glowered around her. "That covers a really wide area. Why couldn't your friend have been more specific?"

"We were lucky to get this much out of him," said Daniel.

"I thought you said he knew things?"

"He does. But Woolwich Docks is its own private world, and even the people who work here don't know everything that goes on."

They strolled up and down the narrow aisles between the containers, peering into open doors and studying everything with great interest. Some of the large gentlemen standing guard over certain containers tensed visibly when Daniel and Tina leaned in for a look, but as long as they just checked things out and moved on, the security guards wisely kept themselves to themselves.

Daniel and Tina finally stopped to consider a warehouse right next to the waters. It was the biggest warehouse in the whole area, long and broad with a high roof. It caught Daniel's attention because he hadn't seen anyone go in or come out, and the dockworkers seemed to be going out of their way to give it plenty of room. As he got closer, Daniel noticed that all the windows had been blacked out, and the only entrance was being guarded by half a dozen very well-armed men, in very familiar uniforms. Daniel eased Tina into the shadows between two hulking containers, so they could study the warehouse without being noticed.

"It's those damned mercenaries again," said Tina.

"Just like the guards at the Martian base," said Daniel. "Maybe there's one big company that specializes in providing security for aliens."

"I am getting really tired of bumping into these guys," said Tina. "We need to take them down hard. Send a message."

"I think it's time for another distraction," said Daniel. "Something to draw the guards away from those doors."

"I don't see any trees," said Tina.

"We can still bring the loud and dramatic," said Daniel.

He indicated the container to their left, whose open doors showed it had been emptied out. Tina nodded happily. The Hydes pressed their shoulders against the corrugated metal, braced themselves, and started the container rocking slowly from side to side. They worked at it, building the momentum, until finally the container passed the point of no return and slammed over onto its side. The deafening crash reverberated all across the docks.

Daniel and Tina retreated farther back into the shadows, and watched happily as dockworkers came running from every direction. Everyone wanted to see what had happened—except the guards at the warehouse doors. They kept a watchful eye on the proceedings, but didn't budge an inch.

"Oh, that is so not fair," said Tina. "How can they not react to something like that? What's wrong with them?"

"They've probably been given specific orders, after what happened at the Martian base," said Daniel.

The dockers crowded around the overturned container, chatting cheerfully about what might have caused it. They didn't really give a damn; it was just a legitimate excuse to take a break. A few bosses wandered over to call them back to work, only to get caught up in the discussion, which blamed everything from earthquakes to metal fatigue, and finally divine intervention. After a while the bosses decided they really didn't care either, and browbeat everyone into going back to work. Daniel and Tina took advantage of the commotion to move silently forward again, until they were as close to the warehouse as they were going to get without being noticed.

Tina glowered at the guards. "Now what? It's just like Horse Leigh Common—lots of open space between us and them, and no cover."

"I doubt that's a coincidence," said Daniel.

"We should have insisted Patricia issue us some guns," said Tina.

"No," said Daniel. "If we opened fire on the guards, it would tell everyone we were here. Including the aliens."

"Then what are we supposed to do?" said Tina. "Throw things?"

Daniel smiled suddenly. "You have the best ideas."

He produced a handful of small change from his pockets, and shared some with Tina. She looked at the coins, and then at Daniel.

"What am I supposed to do with these? Bribe the guards?"

"Think how fast and hard coins could travel, when backed by Hyde muscle," said Daniel. "How's your aim?"

Tina grinned suddenly. "If I can see it, I can hit it."

"Go for the eyes," said Daniel.

They took up positions right at the edge of the shadows, and took careful aim. Daniel's first coin flashed through the air, drilled through a guard's eye, and punched out the back of his skull. He was still crumpling to the ground when Tina's coin struck home, taking out the guard next to him. The others barely had time to react before a flurry of coins slammed through their heads—and just like that there was no one left to guard the warehouse door.

Daniel and Tina raced across the open ground, and crouched down before the door. They performed a quick check on the motionless guards, to make sure all of them were dead, and then Tina did a quick search of the ground.

"What are you doing?" said Daniel.

"Gathering up the coins," said Tina.

"Leave them," said Daniel, with great patience.

"You might be grateful for it one day," said Tina.

They dragged the dead bodies away from the warehouse, and disposed of them silently in the dark waters. Daniel looked quickly around, but the general noise and bustle of the docks had kept anyone from noticing. He moved back to the warehouse door, and examined the lock. It wasn't any make he was familiar with, so he just drew back his fist and punched the lock through the door and out the other side. It made a dull thud as it landed on the inside floor, and he froze . . . but there was no reaction. He pushed the door open, stepped quietly inside with Tina right beside him, and then pulled it shut.

✣ ✣ ✣

A sudden and dramatic drop in temperature stopped the Hydes dead in their tracks, and left them shaking and shuddering. Tina huddled up against Daniel, and they leaned together for a moment, sharing their warmth. Their breath steamed thickly on the air.

"Okay . . ." said Tina. "This is seriously cold. Even worse than the Martian slaughterhouse."

"Cold enough to stop anyone who wasn't a Hyde," said Daniel.

"I swear there are icicles hanging off my tits," said Tina.

"I've definitely got icicles hanging off something," said Daniel.

The warehouse stretched away before them, packed full of things that made no sense at all to human eyes. They might have been machines, or living things, or something for which Earth had no equivalent. The centerpiece appeared to be a single massive honeycomb structure, composed of pulsing yellow flesh. Strange dark shapes peered out from the hexagonal cells. Weird latticeworks of metal rods covered all of one wall, arranged in patterns incomprehensible to the human mind. Cobwebs hung down in long gray streamers that twitched constantly even though there wasn't even a hint of a breeze. The light was painfully harsh, even to Hyde eyes, but Daniel was already adjusting.

A thought struck him, and he bounced up and down on his feet. "You know, I'd swear the gravity in here is less than it should be."

"Wonderful," said Tina. "More complications. You think it's another attempt at terraforming?"

"Another home away from home, for aliens," said Daniel.

And then they both stopped talking, to give their full attention to what they'd come there for. The warehouse interior was overrun with giant insects. Nine to ten feet long, with dark gleaming carapaces, horned heads, and bristling antennae. Bulging compound eyes glowed with phosphorescent fire, giving the creatures their name: Bug-Eyed Monsters. Constantly twitching mouth parts nestled inside heavy mandibles that slammed together like living mantraps. The huge thoraxes had far too many legs, with too many joints, ending in claws so sharp they scratched the warehouse floor with every step.

The giant insects scuttled lightly back and forth, the spindly legs tap-tapping in intricate rhythms. Some skittered up the walls and ran along the ceiling. They moved in sudden darts and pounces, pausing here and there to manipulate pieces of alien machinery, most of which appeared to have disturbingly organic components. Daniel had to struggle to follow the insects as they shot back and forth, moving far too quickly for anything that size.

"Actual Bug-Eyed Monsters," Daniel said quietly. "Proper aliens."

"Ugly bastards," said Tina. "At least they don't seem to be paying us any attention."

"Just the sight of them is really freaking me out," said Daniel. "Insects shouldn't be that big. It's just wrong. They're more horrible than any of the monsters we fought, because even vampires and werewolves had a human element we could relate to."

"It's not just the size that makes them dangerous," said Tina. "Insects have no emotions, and no restraint. They do appalling things because they can, following biological imperatives designed to keep them alive at the expense of everything else. Like laying their eggs inside other creatures, so the larvae can eat their way out. William Burroughs said it's only the mercy of scale that saves us from the tyranny of the insect nation."

"You've been watching those nature documentaries again," said Daniel. "Even though you know they give you nightmares."

"Know your enemy," said Tina.

Daniel slipped a hand into his pocket, so he could check the bomb was still there.

"I say hit the button, throw the bomb, and get the hell out of here."

"That might not be enough," Tina said carefully. "Look at the size of this warehouse. We need to find just the right place to set the bomb, to make sure it does maximum damage."

Daniel tried a small smile, but couldn't bring it off. "How freaked out am I, that you have to be the practical one?"

Tina spoke slowly and carefully, in an *I'm going to be calm and collected about this because one of us has to be and it clearly isn't going to be you* sort of voice. "We can't let any of these things survive. But we have to make sure we don't miss anything important. We understood what the Martian was up to, but I haven't a clue what the Bug-Eyed Monsters are doing here."

"Practical and sensible," said Daniel. "What is the world coming to? All right, let's take a look around, figure out what we can, find the best place to plant the bomb . . . and then get the hell out of here.

But I'm warning you: if just one of those insects touches me, I think I'm going to scream."

"Could be worse," said Tina. "There could be spiders."

Daniel glared at her. "You just had to go there, didn't you?"

"Concentrate on how we are eventually going to blow all of this to shit," Tina said comfortingly. "You know that'll make you feel better."

Daniel nodded stiffly, and made himself move forward. Tina stuck more than usually close beside him. Daniel didn't look at her, in case she was smiling. Being a big bad Hyde was usually enough to cope with most situations, but everyone has their pressure points. And ten-foot insects were really hitting his buttons. He found the going hard at first, because the lesser gravity made him want to hop and jump rather than walk, but he quickly adapted. It made him wonder whether he and Tina had ever really investigated what the Hyde package could do. When this was all over, they owed it to themselves to discover what those limits might be. It could save their lives one day. He knew he was only thinking about that because it was better than being freaked out by the Bug-Eyed Monsters, but he still thought it was an important point.

He glanced at Tina. For all her confidence she looked as jumpy as he felt, but it didn't seem to be bothering her as much. She seemed genuinely fascinated by the alien world they were moving through. Daniel let her concentrate on the weird stuff, while he kept a watchful eye on the Bug-Eyed Monsters, who seemed so intent on their own unfathomable business they hadn't even realized they had trespassers in their territory. Either they relied on the guards to keep people out, or they just couldn't conceive that anyone could break in.

Tina stopped, and gestured urgently to Daniel. He joined her before a particularly odd piece of alien technology. A jagged collection of metal shapes and shimmering crystals, the towering structure rose all the way up to the roof, held together by weird arrangements of yellowed bones and stringy tendons. They didn't look like anything you'd expect to find inside a giant insect, and Daniel quickly realized he was looking at human bones and tissues.

And then he made a small shocked noise, as a row of implanted human eyes turned to follow him. Tina put a hand on his arm to get his attention, and pointed at a human heart, pumping fast as a hummingbird as it forced some strange shimmering liquid through lengths of crystal tubing. Tina didn't look fascinated anymore. She looked angry.

"Every machine I've seen has human components," she said quietly.

"The insects must have been abducting people, so they could harvest the bits they needed," said Daniel. "Taking them apart, to build their machines."

"I told you we needed to know what they were doing," said Tina.

"The aliens couldn't have gone out and snatched these people themselves," said Daniel. "They must have used human agents."

"The mercenaries," said Tina. "But why would they agree to be a part of something like this?"

"As an ex-cop, I can tell you some people will do anything for money," said Daniel.

"Then they're bigger monsters than the aliens," said Tina.

Daniel nodded grimly. "We have to destroy everything in this place." He looked quickly around, and then gestured at a closed-off section of the warehouse, half hidden behind thick curtains of grey cobwebs. "What could be so bad that the insects felt they had to hide it?"

"You want to go in there and find out?" said Tina.

"I don't think *want* is quite the word I had in mind," said Daniel, "but we need to know."

"Then we're going to need another distraction," said Tina.

She looked at him expectantly, because plans were his area of expertise. Daniel thought quickly.

"If the alien technology is based on alien principles," he said finally, "maybe introducing a human element will disrupt things."

"Sounds logical," said Tina. "What did you have in mind?"

Daniel smiled briefly. "Sometimes, you just have to take the piss."

He moved over to stand before the giant honeycomb, unzipped his fly, and pissed all over the fleshy yellow cells. His urine steamed on the chill air, and then more steam rose up in billowing clouds as the urine ate into the yellow cells like acid. Daniel zipped up and moved quickly back to rejoin Tina, who had both hands pressed hard over her mouth to hold in her laughter.

Bug-Eyed Monsters came skittering forward from all directions as they realized something was wrong with their honeycomb, and while they were preoccupied, Daniel and Tina forced their way through the cobweb curtains protecting the sealed-off area. The room beyond was full of low slabs, covered in disassembled human bodies. These people hadn't just been dissected, they'd been reduced to their component parts. The tables were splashed with dried blood, and more had run down to stain the floor. Daniel shuddered as he remembered the Frankenstein cellar, but wouldn't let the flashback paralyze him. He had to remain in control, because there was work that needed doing.

Tina didn't say anything, but she leaned in close so she could press her shoulder against Daniel's. He barely noticed. He was too angry.

All kinds of organs, separated according to function, had been neatly set out, just waiting to be plugged into whatever alien mechanism needed them. Human bones had been assembled into shapes and structures that made no sense. Rows of faces had been pinned to the far wall. Their eyes moved to follow Daniel and Tina.

All through the room there was a horrible sense of things kept alive, long after they should have been dead.

"This is worse than the Martian slaughterhouse," Daniel said finally. "At least their suffering ended after they were killed."

"You think those faces are still aware?" said Tina.

"I'm not taking any chances," said Daniel, as much to the faces as to her. "It's not about sending a message anymore. It's about payback."

"It's bomb time," said Tina. "Because this is what the Bug-Eyed Monsters would do to all of us, once they invade."

The Hydes turned their backs on the wall of staring faces, and left the room.

Outside the cobweb curtains, the way was blocked by rank upon rank of Bug-Eyed Monsters, standing poised and waiting. Here and there heavy mandibles snapped together with enough force to take off an arm or a leg, but otherwise the insects held themselves unnaturally still, their protruding glowing eyes fixed on the Hydes.

"Okay . . ." said Tina. "What do we do now?"

"I suppose we could jump up and run across their backs," said Daniel. "But I don't think we'd get very far."

"You should have let me take the guards' guns," said Tina.

"Next time, I'll listen to you."

Tina shot him a smile. "It's sweet that you think there'll be a next time. We are seriously outnumbered here."

"But they're just insects," said Daniel. "We're Hydes."

"I'm glad you're over your little panic attack," said Tina.

Daniel scowled. "I'm just too furious to be freaked out."

"Go with what works," said Tina. "Tell me you have a plan, Daniel."

"We need another distraction," said Daniel.

"You're not going to whip your dick out again, are you?" said Tina.

"I thought I'd trigger the bomb, and throw it into the honeycomb," said Daniel. "And when some of the insects go to investigate, we plow through the ones that are left and then exit the premises before the really nasty explosive device turns this warehouse and everything in it into a pile of ashes."

"Not the best plan you've come up with," said Tina. "But for want of anything better, let's do it."

Daniel started to put his hand in his pocket, and all the insects surged forward. They crossed the ground inhumanly quickly, propelled by their many-jointed legs, while their bulging compound eyes burned with cold malevolence. Daniel thought briefly about retreating into the sealed-off area, in the hope the insects wouldn't want to fight in their own supply room... but he was too angry to back away. All he could think of was how badly he needed to punish the Bug-Eyed Monsters for what they'd done.

"You should never have come here," he said, and went to meet them with Tina at his side.

The lesser gravity made the huge insects so light they jumped onto the Hydes and swarmed all over them. Daniel and Tina struck and elbowed them away, and trampled them underfoot when they fell. The Bug-Eyed Monsters tried to drag the Hydes down by brute force, and clutched at them with their many-jointed legs. Heavy claws tore through clothes to savage the flesh beneath, while the legs' serrated edges cut into the Hydes like the teeth on a buzzsaw. Horned heads thrust forward like battering rams, their razor-sharp mandibles lunging in to tear off Daniel's and Tina's faces. The Hydes stood their ground and lashed out at everything that came within reach, refusing to be brought down.

Daniel plunged his fists deep into brittle insect thoraxes, grabbed pulsing alien organs, and ripped them out through the hole he'd made, in flurries of sickly green blood. He punched in devil-mask faces, and slammed huge alien forms into the floor. Insect after insect died at his hand, only to be immediately replaced by more.

Tina ripped the heads off Bug-Eyed Monsters and threw them at approaching insect faces, laughing out loud when the bulging eyes exploded. Sometimes the headless bodies would just keep pressing forward, serrated legs still reaching out to enfold her. She just snapped off the legs until the insect body collapsed or fell over, and moved on to the next target. She barreled past insects with great sweeps of her arms, and thrust her fists into glowing compound eyes, forcing her hands in deep to crush the brains.

The vicious struggle took on an awful nightmarish quality, and Daniel couldn't see an end to it. Bug-Eyed Monsters kept rearing up before him—devil masks with unfeeling eyes, and claws that came at him too quickly to avoid, not slowed for a moment by all the terrible things the Hydes had done to other insects. They just kept swarming forward, driven on by the implacable need to protect their territory at all costs. Daniel ached all over, as much from fatigue as all the damage he'd taken. It had been a terribly long day, and it seemed the armorer's pick-me-up could only do so much. But still he fought on, even as the floor beneath his feet became slippery from all the blood he'd lost. All he had to do was remember a row of faces pinned to a wall, and it seemed like he would never grow tired of killing.

Daniel and Tina ended up fighting back to back, as the Bug-Eyed Monsters came at them from all sides. The huge insects swarmed all over them, pressed so thickly together now that Daniel couldn't even see the warehouse anymore. He grabbed up an insect body with its legs still kicking, and used it to bludgeon other insects. He flailed wildly around him, sending body parts flying, and hammered the deteriorating body into one insect after another until the battered thorax finally came apart in his hands.

Tina punched in devil face after devil face, puncturing bulging eyes and crushing skulls, not laughing anymore because she didn't have the breath. Heavy claws and serrated legs had ripped half her dress off and blood ran steadily down her heaving sides. Every punch hurt her hands, but she wouldn't let that stop her. She tore off a spiked leg and thrust it deep into a glowing eye. Thick green blood spattered all over her, and she wore it like a badge of honor.

The Hydes had one advantage: there were so many Bug-Eyed Monsters they kept getting in each other's way.

The aliens came at Daniel again and again, cutting him with their saw-toothed legs, and thrusting their clacking mandibles forward to tear off his face. Blood was already dripping down his chin and onto his chest from too many near misses. He was so tired his muscles screamed with every effort, and fresh pains struck through him as he reopened old wounds. He could feel blood running down his sides, and the last of his strength going out of him. He had to struggle not to cry out every time the insects hurt him, but somehow he held it back. He didn't want Tina to know how badly injured he was. It didn't even occur to him that she might be doing the same. He could feel her back slamming against his as they fought, hear her grunts of exertion and the occasional obscenity, so he just assumed she was busy being Tina and making her enemies fear her.

Daniel fought on, with increasingly leaden arms and too many wounds to count. His legs trembled from the strain, but he had enough hate left in him to kick in an insect's thorax if it got too close. He punched and back-elbowed and headbutted the Bug-Eyed Monsters as they came within reach, and never tired of smashing his aching fists into their horrid faces. Fighting not for himself, but for all the victims who could no longer fight. Blood covered one side of his face from where a flailing mandible had opened up a deep gash on his forehead, and he had to keep blinking blood out of his eye.

The giant insects ran up the walls and onto the ceiling, so they could drop down from above. Daniel and Tina took it in turns to slap them out of midair. More and more the Hydes were reduced to fighting like machines, little more than brute strength and instinct with no sense of strategy.

Daniel could tell he was slowing down, because the snapping mandibles were getting closer to his face. He flailed around him with a torn-off insect head to open up some space, and pulled the bomb out of his pocket. He knew he'd never get to the door in time, but he was past caring. All that mattered was revenge, for the insects' victims. But even as he reached for the big red button a horned head surged forward and its razor-sharp mandibles clamped down viciously on his forearm. Daniel's hand spasmed and flew open, dropping the bomb. It hit the floor, and Daniel's heart ached as an insect stamped on the metal case until it broke apart. He punched the insect holding him until its skull shattered, and jerked the mandibles out of his arm. His blood flew on the air as he kicked the flailing body away from him. He looked at where the bomb had been, and wondered what to do next.

"I saw that!" Tina said behind him. Her voice sounded raw and hoarse. "Now what?"

"Stay alive long enough to think of something else," said Daniel.

He could still put on a good face for her, even if he couldn't believe it himself. He wondered vaguely how many more Bug-Eyed Monsters were left in the warehouse—and how many he could get his hands on before they dragged him down. And then he noticed that his punches seemed to be landing harder, and doing more damage, while the insects grew increasingly slower and more sluggish. It took him a while to realize that the gravity in the warehouse was getting heavier, returning to Earth normal, as though whatever alien machine had interfered with the force of gravity was failing.

Daniel struggled to make sense of the weary thoughts lurching through his head. He remembered alien machines with human parts. Eyes that moved to follow him. That meant something. He remembered finding an unexpected ally among the living machines in the Martian base, and wondered if something in this base that had once been human had seen him fighting the Bug-Eyed Monsters, and was trying to help. He spat out a mouthful of blood and raised his voice.

"If you can hear me, tell me what to do!"

A small but very human voice whispered in his ear. "I was made a machine, to control their gravity, but I still remember who I was."

"Which machine?" said Daniel, staring blearily around him. "Where are you?"

A light started blinking on a many-sided machine clinging to the side of the great honeycomb.

"Finish me," said the voice, "and you finish the monsters."

Daniel turned his head. "Tina! We are breaking out—right now! Follow me! I've got a plan!"

"Well, it's about time!" said Tina.

Daniel plunged forward, plowing through the insects, drawing on the last of his resources to keep him moving. The Bug-Eyed Monsters scattered as Daniel headed for the machine. He didn't need to look round to know Tina was right there beside him; he could hear her cursing with every step. He kicked his way through piled-up insect bodies scattered across the floor. He only wished there were more of them.

His legs trembled with every step, but he wouldn't let them betray him. Faces on a wall were depending on him. He hurt everywhere, blood spilling from too many wounds to count, but he wouldn't give in to them. He glanced once at Tina, and his heart ached as he realized she was as badly hurt as he was. He gestured at the machine, and Tina nodded grimly. She lurched to a halt, and turned around to face the Bug-Eyed Monsters coming after them.

"Do it, Daniel. Do whatever you have to. I've got your back."

"Do it," said the small voice in his ear. "Set me free."

Daniel didn't hesitate, just lurched forward and smashed his fist into the heart of the machine, driving his arm in deep even as jagged broken metal tore at his flesh; and then the machine fell apart. And just like that, Earth gravity was back. Daniel jerked his arm out of the wreckage and turned to see giant insects scrabbling helplessly on the floor, unable to raise themselves. A great cry went up from the Bug-Eyed Monsters—the first noise Daniel had heard from them. It sounded like despair, and that warmed his heart.

He grabbed Tina by the arm and steered her toward the exit. Leaning heavily on each other, staggering along, they kicked their way through struggling insect bodies until they reached the door. Daniel glanced back, to see a whirlpool of strange energies forming around the machine he'd smashed. He'd let something loose: a cold, implacable pull that was already dragging the nearest Bug-Eyed Monsters toward it. One by one they slid across the floor and disappeared into the sucking pit. A quiet but still very human voice spoke in Daniel's ear, saying "Thank you." It faded away before Daniel could say anything in return.

He turned back to the warehouse door. Tina was leaning heavily against it, her face a mess of blood and bruises just like his. Together they hauled the door open, and staggered out into the night.

✣ ✣ ✣

For a while, all Daniel could think of was getting Tina away from the warehouse. He helped her along, step by step and foot by foot, his head full of pain. People ran toward them, pointing and shouting. Daniel looked behind him one last time, and saw the warehouse disappear. It simply blinked out and was gone, with nothing left to show it had ever been there. The dockworkers cried out in shock, and skidded to a halt. Tina raised her battered head and looked blearily at Daniel.

"What the hell just happened?"

"A machine that remembered it was human turned itself into a black hole to destroy the alien base," said Daniel.

Tina considered the matter carefully, her face slack with pain and exhaustion.

"That makes no sense at all."

Daniel managed a small smile. "Bug-Eyed Monster science."

"Let's get out of here," said Tina. "I need to lie down for a while."

"We're done here," said Daniel. "We sent a message."

"Bloody loud one too," said Tina.

Crowds of dockworkers stared at where the warehouse had been and babbled questions at each other. They looked at the two Hydes, took in the state of them, and wisely decided not to bother them. Daniel and Tina trudged slowly out of the Woolwich Docks, leaving a bloody trail behind them.

"Can we go home now?" Tina said drowsily into Daniel's shoulder.

"Sure," said Daniel. "Maybe the armorer will have some more of that *Feel Better Real Fast* stuff."

"Next mission," Tina said determinedly, "make her give us guns. Really big guns."

"Damn right," said Daniel.

Chapter Six
MAKING A DEAL WITH SOMETHING OLDER THAN THE DEVIL

✣ ✣ ✣

DANIEL DROVE SLOWLY THROUGH the London streets, and anyone else on the road with any sense got the hell out of his way. Daniel was so tired he could barely see where he was going, and Tina was so tired she didn't care. One of Daniel's eyes was stuck shut with dried blood, and he could barely feel the steering wheel under his hands or the pedals under his feet. His whole body was one great pulse of pain. All through the long nightmare drive, Daniel could never give his full attention to the road ahead because he had to keep concentrating on Tina's harsh breathing at his side. In case it stopped.

Eventually the new Jekyll & Hyde Inc. building loomed up before him, and he hauled the steering wheel all the way over and slammed on the brakes. The engine stuttered and stalled, and Daniel's hands dropped onto his lap, their work done. Tina rocked limply in the seat beside him, only held in place by her seat belt.

Daniel just sat there for a while, breathing harshly, and then he remembered why he'd fought so hard to get where he was. He snapped his seat belt in two when his numb hands couldn't work the clasp, and shouldered his door open. He hauled himself out of the car, coughed painfully, and spat a mouthful of blood onto the sidewalk. It felt like more than one thing inside him was broken. The world swayed sickly around him as he worked his way around the front of the car, forcing himself on despite everything his injuries could do to slow him. Because Tina needed him. He managed to open her door, but had to rip her seat belt away when it wouldn't cooperate. He eased her out as gently as he could, but he must have hurt her anyway because she cried out and tried to fight him. Her eyes were half open, but she didn't seem to see him.

Daniel got his feet planted firmly under him to make sure he could support her weight, and then got her moving. Tina's feet dragged as she lurched along, and he was half carrying her by the time they reached the lobby doors. He caught a brief glimpse of their reflection in the lobby windows: two half-dead scarecrows in ragged clothes soaked with blood. Wounded bodies with torn faces. He snarled defiantly back, hit the lobby door with a lowered shoulder, and staggered inside.

Everyone stopped what they were doing to stare in horror at the new arrivals. Battered and bloodied, beaten and broken in every way there was, Daniel had made it back. He stood like a hounded beast brought to bay, his blood pattering steadily onto the polished floor. His determination had brought him this far, because he had to save Tina, but now his strength just ran away, like the last sand in an hourglass. He couldn't force out another step. Tina hung limply at his side, her head hanging down, only on her feet because Daniel was damned if he would let her go. He peered blearily around the lobby with his one good eye, and when he raised his voice it sounded like the howl of some tortured animal.

"Armorer! Armorer!"

Some of the people in the lobby started forward to help, jolted out of their shock by the anguish in his voice, only to stop immediately when Patricia yelled at them to get out of her way. She came striding through the lobby, and Daniel focused on the gleaming hypo in her hand. The one thing he'd been concentrating on, all the way across London. He allowed himself to feel the first faint stirrings of hope. Patricia came to a halt before him.

"Tina," said Daniel, forcing the words out. "Help her."

"Of course," said Patricia. "That's why I'm here."

The armorer blasted Tina in the neck with the hypo, and then moved quickly on to dose Daniel. Lighting surged through his broken body, scouring out all the pain and weakness. His back slowly straightened and his head came up, as the pick-me-up put him back together again. Dried blood cracked and split apart as his eye forced itself open, and the first thing Daniel did was look at Tina. Her legs were slowly firming beneath her, and her breathing deepened and steadied as the light came back into her eyes. She pushed herself away from Daniel, so she could stand on her own. They looked at each other, taking in their tattered state and healed wounds; and then they both laughed—a wild and savage sound, of survival and triumph over everything that had tried so hard to kill them.

Daniel felt like he could punch out a charging bull, and then rip its head off and eat it raw. He flexed his arms and stamped his feet, savoring the feel of a body back in full working order. And yet a small part of him couldn't help realizing that the healing had taken longer than it had the first time—either because he and Tina had been hurt so very badly, or because they were getting used to the stuff. Daniel hadn't realized how much he'd come to depend on the Hail Mary hypo, until it was all he could think of on his desperate trip across London. Now he was thinking clearly again, he knew he should have relied on Hyde strength and resources to see them through. He and Tina had been hurt far worse on the rooftop, and they'd come back from that without any outside help.

Daniel nodded his thanks to Patricia, even as he quietly decided he and Tina couldn't afford to rely on the armorer's magic pick-me-up. It made them far too dependent on her. He had to wonder whether that had been Patricia's plan all along, to give her control over him and Tina.

His thoughts were interrupted when Tina whooped loudly, and slapped him so hard on the back he rocked on his feet.

"Damn, I feel good!" she said cheerfully. "How did we get here?" And then she stopped, and looked accusingly at Daniel. "Were you carrying me?"

"Only for a while," he said. He could tell he was grinning all over his face, and didn't give a damn.

Tina reached out a hand and brushed away the dried blood on his face, and he did the same for her.

"How are you both feeling?" said Patricia, businesslike as ever.

"Fine!" Tina said immediately. "Couldn't be better!" Because she could never admit weakness to anyone.

Patricia took a good look at the ragged remains of Tina's dress, and shook her head.

"I don't have anything in a hypo that could put that right."

Tina frowned. "What are you talking about?"

"Aren't you finding it just a bit drafty?" said Daniel, trying for tact. "It's only the dried blood that's holding what's left of your dress together. In fact, I would have to say there is rather a lot of you on open display, just at the moment."

Tina looked down at herself, and then flashed Daniel a smile. "You say that like it's a bad thing."

She threw back her shoulders and took a deep breath, and her bosom thrust itself through the front of her dress. Several young men, and a few young women, blushed fiercely and had to turn away.

"We need to get you both decently covered," said Patricia. "This is a respectable organization."

"Since when?" said Tina. She looked at Patricia, still wearing the same black blouse over black slacks, and sniffed loudly. "Like you're in any position to hand out fashion advice. You're just feeling outclassed."

"Let's try to talk nicely to the woman who just saved our lives," said Daniel.

Tina tried to pull the rags and tatters of her dress together, and swore loudly as it almost fell apart in her hands. "This was the best outfit I've had in ages! Look what those oversized insects have done to it! I want to go back there and kill every one of them all over again!"

Patricia sighed quietly, raised a hand, and snapped her fingers imperiously.

"Joyce!"

A young woman in basic T-shirt and jeans came hurrying forward to stand quivering at Patricia's side, eager to be put to use.

"Take them to the tailors," said Patricia. She turned back to the Hydes, and gave them her best long-suffering look. "Once you've been kitted out in something suitable, you can come and see me in my office on the top floor."

"You have an office?" said Daniel. "Already?"

"How else am I going to get things done?" said Patricia. "Now get out of here, and stop cluttering up my nice new lobby."

She spun on her heel and went straight back to work, firing orders at anyone who didn't get out of her way fast enough.

"A hard woman to dislike," said Daniel, "but worth the effort."

"Trust me," said Tina, "it's no effort at all."

Daniel turned to the young woman standing before them.

"Joyce, isn't it?"

"Yes sir. Joyce Harper. At your service."

"Take us to the tailors," said Daniel, "before we have to start charging people for the free show."

"They should feel privileged," said Tina, taking a deep breath and making several people walk into each other.

Joyce sprinted for the elevators at the rear of the lobby. She was almost halfway there before she realized Daniel and Tina weren't following her. She stumbled to a halt and looked back, confused at being prevented from carrying out the armorer's orders as quickly as possible. Daniel gestured for her to return and she did so, just a bit reluctantly.

"It's not a race, Joyce," Daniel said kindly. "And Tina and I don't feel like one anyway, after the day we've had. Just lead the way at a steady pace, and we'll bring up the rear in our own time."

Tina glared at him. "I feel fine! I do not need to be treated like an invalid!"

"We're making a point," Daniel said calmly. "First, that it might be wise to pace ourselves for a while, and second; that we don't run anywhere at the armorer's orders."

"Why would we need to pace ourselves?" said Tina. "We're Hydes!"

"We have no idea what's in the stuff the armorer has been giving us," Daniel said quietly. "Or how long its effects will last."

Tina nodded reluctantly. That answer appealed to her natural paranoia.

Joyce had been listening in with such concentration she was actually leaning forward. When she picked up on the implications of what Daniel was saying, she appeared genuinely shocked that anyone would even think of questioning whatever the armorer proposed.

"Is there a problem?" said Daniel.

"You can trust Patricia!" said Joyce. "She's the armorer!"

"So?" said Tina.

"She brought us all back together!" said Joyce, bouncing on her toes in her eagerness to get the point across. "She gave us a purpose, and made us feel good about ourselves again!"

"So you worked here before," said Daniel. "When Edward was in charge."

Joyce nodded quickly. "You wouldn't remember me. I was very minor."

"But you remember us," said Tina.

Joyce brightened immediately. "Oh yes! We all thought you were so glamorous! Being Hydes, and going off on missions, and fighting monsters! We all wanted to be you!"

"Well," said Tina, sounding just a little mollified. "That's more like it."

"Take us to the tailors, Joyce," said Daniel. "At a civilized speed."

Joyce nodded quickly and set off again for the elevators, occasionally glancing back over her shoulder to make sure she wasn't going too fast. Daniel and Tina strolled after her, smiling graciously on the little people toiling industriously around them. No one smiled back.

"I'm not seeing much hero worship in the general population," Daniel said quietly to Tina.

"They just need to get to know us better," said Tina.

"They'd have nightmares," said Daniel.

"Good," said Tina.

Normally the Hydes would have sprinted up the back stairs and arrived at the first floor not even out of breath, but Daniel felt like being cautious for a while. He and Tina might have bounced back from the horrific beating they'd taken, but couldn't help feeling that at some point a price would have to be paid. And it worried him that he had no idea what that might be. There was a certain tension in the elevator, as they all stood quietly thinking their separate thoughts, and then Joyce led the Hydes along an eerily quiet and deserted first floor to the door marked TAILORS. Daniel nodded to her graciously.

"Thank you for your assistance, Joyce. We can take it from here."

Joyce's head bobbed, and then she was off and running back to the elevator, so she could hurry back down to the lobby and be ordered around some more by the armorer.

"I think our little friend has a crush on Patricia," said Tina.

"Let's hope that's all it is," said Daniel. "For all we know Patricia has been dosing the workforce with her very own happy-happy, joy-joy stuff. She does seem to have taken charge around here surprisingly quickly."

Tina shrugged. "If she wants to do all the hard work, let her."

Daniel looked at the door before them, and then glanced up and down the corridor.

"You know, the tailors appear to be in exactly the same position as they used to be in the old building."

"That's odd," said Tina. "Why would Patricia arrange for everything to be exactly as it was before?"

"We must make a point of asking her that," said Daniel. "When we visit her in her nice new office."

He barged through the tailors' door without knocking, and found himself facing familiar rows of ready-made clothes, in every size and style. Blank-faced dummies showed off all manner of colorful bits and pieces, like guests at some very informal party. Long shelves were stuffed with hats and gloves and every fashionable accessory under the sun, while foam heads modeled a wide variety of wigs. The tailors offered clothes, outfits, and designs for every conceivable occasion, because you never know who you might be sent out to kill.

Daniel and Tina were suddenly ambushed by two very familiar figures: the same grim-faced types who used to work for Edward, still wearing the old-fashioned mourning outfits that always made Daniel think of undertakers. They swarmed all over Daniel and Tina with flailing tape measures, and then ripped off the remains of their clothes with brisk impersonal motions. The tailors dropped the bloody remnants into disposal bags with professional distaste, and then disappeared with them into the shadows, leaving Daniel and Tina standing in their underwear.

Daniel stared after them, turned to say something to Tina, and then stopped. She stood there tall and splendid, and apparently not in the least discommoded, like Diana the Huntress in designer black underwear. Wide-shouldered and richly curved, she looked like a goddess come down to slum it with mortals, just for the hell of it.

Tina looked Daniel over, tall and broad and muscular, in his white jockies and gray socks. Daniel instinctively started to pull in his stomach, and then remembered he didn't have to. He was a Hyde now.

Tina smiled suddenly. "Not tonight, dear. I have an all-over ache."

"Same here," said Daniel. "Our wounds may have healed, but I'm not sure my body believes it. You know, we are lucky to be alive."

"Of course I know," said Tina. "I was there. But we're fine now. Aren't we?"

"Patricia's pick-me-up did its usual excellent job," said Daniel. "But at some point we need to find out what's in it, and where Patricia gets it from."

"At some point," Tina agreed. "But for now, don't look a gift armorer in the mouth."

Daniel started to say something, but she stopped him with a look.

"Change the subject."

"Given that the Bug-Eyed Monsters reduced our old outfits to so many bits and pieces," Daniel said carefully, "I'm amazed your underwear was able to survive entirely unscathed."

"I have them specially made," said Tina. "Because a girl can't be too careful, when she's a Hyde."

The two tailors suddenly appeared out of nowhere, thrust bundles of new clothes into the Hydes' arms, and disappeared back into the shadows before they could be asked any questions.

"Why do they always do that?" said Tina.

"Maybe they're shy," said Daniel.

"Maybe they're not entirely human."

"Wouldn't surprise me," said Daniel. "Jekyll & Hyde Inc. has always been an equal opportunity employer."

He put on the new pair of baggy gray slacks, starched white shirt, tweed jacket, some freshly polished black shoes, and a spotted bow tie—though in the end Tina had to tie that properly for him.

"Fumble fingers," she said, not unkindly.

"It was all clip-ons, when I was younger," said Daniel. "But, bow ties are cool. The Traveling Doctor said so."

Tina slipped into a gleaming white pants suit, lavender blouse, and studded black leather choker. She looked at the pair of sneakers she'd been given, and then threw them the length of the room with such force they slammed into the far wall.

"Sneakers?" she said loudly. "Hydes don't do sneakers!"

There was barely a pause before a pair of white plastic stilettos sailed out of the shadows to land at her feet.

"Well," said Tina. "That's more like it."

She put them on, pointed her toes this way and that to judge the effect, and then nodded briskly. She moved over to a tall standing mirror to admire her new look, and Daniel moved in beside her.

"I'm not sure this is really me," Daniel said finally.

"Or me," said Tina. "But needs must when an alien hoard stamps you into the ground."

"We could always think of our new outfits as disguises," said Daniel.

"I will if you will," said Tina.

They took the elevator to the top floor, trying not to wince as it played an easy listening version of Motörhead's "Ace of Spades" all the way up. The Hydes' footsteps sounded loud and confident as they strode along the empty corridor, but even though Daniel kept his eyes and ears open he didn't pick up anything to suggest anyone else had taken up residence on the top floor. He located the armorer's office easily enough, because it had a big brass plaque on the door, saying ARMORER. He looked at it thoughtfully.

"I'm pretty sure this is in exactly the same place as Edward's office, in the old building. Is Patricia trying to send some kind of message? *Meet the new boss, same as the old boss?*"

"I'm more concerned with where she got the nerve to put up a brass plaque," said Tina. "Because there's nothing that says *I'm in charge and don't you forget it* like a brass plaque on a door."

"I told you she had her own agenda," said Daniel.

"You think that about everyone," said Tina.

"And I'm usually right. Come, my dear, let us favor our armorer with the pleasure of our company."

"Let's," said Tina, grinning like a wolf.

They didn't bother to knock. Tina just kicked the door open, and they strode in. The door rather spoiled the effect by easing to a halt and then closing itself quietly behind them. The armorer's office was packed with sinfully luxurious furniture and fittings, the carpeting was thick enough to muffle even the most determined of footsteps, and the art on the walls gave every appearance of being the real thing—in a dull and unadventurous sort of way. Daniel didn't even want to think how much all of this must have cost. Patricia sat behind a sturdy office desk and stared calmly at her visitors, apparently entirely unmoved by their sudden appearance. Daniel arranged himself as comfortably as possible on a visitor's chair, while Tina slumped down beside him, not even trying to look interested in why they were there.

The first thing that caught Daniel's eye was the big steel safe he and Tina had dug out of the wall of Edward's office, in the old building. It had been set down right next to Patricia's desk, with the door left hanging open—as though to make it clear the safe and all its secrets now belonged to Patricia. Daniel considered it thoughtfully. The only thing of value he'd found in the safe was Edward's file on the aliens, but given that Patricia had felt the safe important enough to have it transferred to her office, Daniel had to wonder if he might have missed something. Unless that was what he was supposed to think, to keep him distracted and off-balance.

"I like the new outfits," said Patricia.

Tina scowled at her. "Tell me you didn't choose them."

"I never interfere in other departments' decisions," said Patricia.

"Yeah, right," said Tina.

"Play nicely, ladies," said Daniel, and then stopped talking when they both looked at him.

He sat back in his chair and let them try to out-glare each other, while he gave some thought to the situation. Could Patricia be using the Hydes as her personal foot soldiers, to establish her authority in the eyes of the world? And if that was the case, he had to wonder what would happen when Patricia decided she didn't need her pet Hydes anymore. He suddenly realized it had gone very quiet in the office, and looked up to find Tina and Patricia staring at him.

"Whatever the question was, I missed it," he said easily. "Not that it matters. I don't do questions."

"We were talking about how an entire warehouse could disappear from Woolwich Docks," Patricia said coldly. "You were sent to deal with the Bug-Eyed Monsters base, not create a whole new talking point for the conspiracy theorists."

"We dealt with the insects," said Daniel. "They are dead and gone and won't be coming back."

"But was it really necessary to be so ostentatious?" said Patricia.

Tina bristled. "Things got complicated, all right? All that matters is we kicked major Bug-Eyed Monster arse, and the whole base has gone bye-bye. Game over, and a big tick in the *Screw you, aliens* column."

Daniel cleared his throat loudly, to bring Patricia's attention back to him.

"Since you have all these agents out in the field, informing you on everything that's going on, perhaps you can tell us where to look for the next alien base."

Patricia raised an elegant eyebrow. "Are you sure you're ready to go back to work? You have been through a lot."

"We're Hydes," said Daniel. "We don't break, no matter how hard the world hits us."

"I did see the extent of your injuries, before my little pick-me-up did its work," said Patricia.

"We would have bounced back," said Daniel. "It's what we do."

"And you are the one who keeps telling us that time is not on our side," said Tina.

"It really isn't," said Patricia. "But . . ."

"Put the buts on hold," said Daniel. "We have work to do."

"Who's next?" Tina said briskly. "Greys or Reptiloids? I vote Reptiloids. I could use a new set of luggage."

Patricia opened a drawer in her desk, brought out a very familiar-looking file, and leafed slowly through it.

"I've been studying the information Edward left behind. Did you get as far as the section on the Elder Ones?"

"We didn't have much time with the file, before we were violently interrupted," said Daniel.

"Who are the Elder Ones?" said Tina, frowning. "More aliens?"

"The Earth has been visited many times, by many different species," said Patricia. "So often I sometimes wonder if we're just one stop on a coach tour. The Big Four are simply the most dangerous new arrivals. The Elder Ones came here long before any of the others. Also known as Lords of the Outer Dark, the Forbidden Ones, and the Unfolding Terror. I'm guessing they didn't choose those names themselves."

"When did they arrive here?" said Tina.

"Before human history had even stuck its first toe in the water," said Patricia. She tapped the page before her with a thoughtful fingertip. "There's not much actual information here—it's mostly ancient legends from people trying to get their heads around something that was always going to be too much for them. Basically, the Elder Ones came here from beyond the stars, and possibly from another reality. So huge and powerful our ancestors worshipped them as gods... until finally the Elder Ones fell or were forced from power. They're supposed to be sleeping deep in the Earth, like ancient unexploded bombs. But if they could be safely awakened, they might make useful allies against our current alien threats."

"The Elder Ones don't sound like something we should disturb," said Daniel. "If they're as powerful as you say, they could pose a greater threat to Humanity than all the Big Four put together."

"Right," said Tina. "Once you've been worshipped as gods, it must be hard to settle for anything less. And anyway, do we really need allies? Daniel and I shut down two alien bases all on our own."

"And nearly died doing it," said Patricia.

"Hydes don't die," said Tina. "We just regroup in Hell and come out fighting for the second half."

"There's more to it than that," said Daniel. "It's not enough to just destroy the alien bases. We have to scare them enough that they won't even think about coming back." He switched his gaze to Patricia, and looked at her meaningfully. "Of course, it would help if we had some decent weapons from the armory."

"Trust me," said Patricia, "we don't have anything that could affect the Elder Ones."

"Something must have prised their grip off the Earth," said Daniel.

Patricia nodded, accepting the point. "I'll do some research."

"In the meantime," said Tina, "we want weapons that will kick Grey and Reptiloid arse."

"Guns," said Daniel. "Something so appallingly powerful and devastatingly nasty that they will wipe the smile off any alien face."

"When you get back, we'll take a stroll through the armory," said Patricia. "And you can help yourselves to whatever takes your fancy."

"Hold it," said Tina. "When we get back from where?"

Patricia folded her hands together on the file and leaned forward across her desk. "Like it or not... We can't hope to kick the Big Four off Earth completely, without the help of the Elder Ones."

Daniel looked at her narrowly. "Are you saying you know where to look for these sleeping ancient alien god things?"

"No," said Patricia. "But according to Edward's file, there are people who know, and can arrange contact."

"Renfields," said Tina.

"Exactly," said Patricia. "However, I'm afraid all the file has to offer is an address in London."

"Of course," said Daniel. "It would have to be London."

"How are we supposed to get these Renfields on our side?" said Tina.

"Make them see it's in their best interests to send the Big Four home, crying their eyes out," said Patricia. "If being reasonable doesn't work, feel free to try bribes, blackmail, and threats."

"That is the Hyde way," said Tina.

"Offer them anything you think they might want," said Patricia. "We can decide afterward whether we're going to deliver it."

Daniel scowled. "I'm not good at lying to people."

"That's all right," said Tina. "I am."

The armorer slid a card across the table to Daniel. "This is an address for the oldest gentleman's club in London: the Albion." Patricia paused thoughtfully. "I can't tell you who's in charge these days. They've gone to great pains to stay off the radar. And if my people can't dig out the truth, they must be good."

"We are going to have to have a talk about these people of yours, at some point," said Daniel.

"At some point," said Patricia.

Tina scowled at her. "Why are you so determined to keep secrets from us?"

"Because not all my secrets are mine to share," said Patricia.

"We are the heads of Jekyll & Hyde Inc.," said Daniel. "By right of having killed the previous head."

"You are the cutting edge of the organization," said Patricia. "The part that gets things done. I represent the support structure, that makes what you do possible."

"But you still won't tell us what we need to know," said Tina.

"Because you don't need to know," said Patricia.

Daniel and Tina looked at each other, and then rose to their feet. They each took a firm hold on different ends of Patricia's desk and then tore it in two, with a great screeching of rending wood. They then threw the separate halves at opposite walls with such force they cracked the plaster before falling to the floor. Patricia sat perfectly still in her chair.

Tina cracked her knuckles so loudly even Daniel winced, and then smiled brightly at Patricia.

"You work for us, armorer. Not the other way round."

Patricia looked at her steadily. "Why can't you just trust me?"

"We have trust issues, when it comes to authority figures," said Daniel.

Tina took a step toward Patricia, and then stopped as the armorer held up a strange device that appeared in her hand out of nowhere.

"My hypo put you together," said Patricia. "This can take you apart."

"And that, right there, is why we have trust issues," said Daniel.

While Patricia was looking at him, Tina's hand snapped forward with inhuman speed and snatched the device away from the armorer. She grinned cheerfully at Patricia.

"Want to watch me crush this into pieces?"

Patricia rose quickly to her feet. "That would be a really bad idea. You could turn everything on this floor into ashes."

"Cool!" said Tina, examining the device interestedly. "Just what we need." She put the device in her pocket.

"I *am* on your side," said Patricia.

"You have an odd way of showing it," said Daniel.

"We all want to see the big, bad aliens kicked off the Earth," said Patricia. "I can help make that happen. Any other issues we might have . . . we can work on."

Daniel and Tina shared a look, shrugged pretty much in unison, and sat down again. Patricia sat down facing them, and everyone ignored the fact that they didn't have a desk between them anymore.

"There is something you need to know," said Daniel.

"I'm listening," said Patricia.

Slowly and carefully, Daniel made a full report on what the Bug-Eyed Monsters had been doing in their base: the human abductions, and what the insects had done with the bodies. Sometimes his voice failed him, and then Tina would fill in until Daniel felt able to continue. When they were done, Patricia nodded.

"I'll have my people track down the human support structures, and put an end to them."

"Kill them all," said Tina.

"That is the plan," said Patricia.

"I don't see that we have any further business," said Daniel. "It's time we were going."

"Things to meet, people to do," said Tina. "You know how it is."

The Hydes rose to their feet. Daniel gave Patricia one final look.

"I won't make any deal with the Albion that I'm not happy with. And when we get back, either you supply us with the weapons we need, or Tina and I will break into the armory and take them for ourselves."

"What he said," said Tina. "Only with a lot more menace."

They turned their backs on the armorer and strode out of the office, shutting the door firmly behind them. They then walked a fair way down the corridor before either of them said anything.

"I suppose that went as well as could be expected," said Daniel. "Do you think she was intimidated, or impressed?"

"Not even a little bit," said Tina. "We'll just have to try harder."

"Her reaction was very interesting," said Daniel. "Any sane person would have filled their trousers with two Hydes openly threatening them."

"We do need to get to the bottom of our new armorer," said Tina.

"When we've run out of aliens to kill," said Daniel.

"Well, that goes without saying," said Tina. "Are we off to the Albion Club now?"

"Not just yet," said Daniel. "I think we need to know a little more about what we're getting into, before we put our heads into the lion's mouth. I thought I might have a word with my police contact, and see what he can dig up."

"He'd have to get permission from his superiors just to ask the right questions," said Tina. "But I know someone who'll know all there is to know about the Albion, because that's what he does. Wait till we're outside the building, and none of Patricia's people can hear us, and I'll call him."

Daniel looked at her admiringly. "You don't trust anyone, do you?"

"No," said Tina. "Except you, of course."

"Nice save," said Daniel.

✣ ✣ ✣

After they'd walked some distance down the street, Tina took out her phone and punched in a number that didn't officially exist.

"Who is your contact?" said Daniel.

"Alan Diment," said Tina. "The spy's spy. Ah—Alan! This is Tina!" She listened for a moment, and then talked right over him. "Yes, of course I know what time it is, and no I don't care that I woke you up because Daniel and I haven't been to sleep at all. Now stir your stumps out of bed, because we need to meet as soon as humanly possible. If you don't I will come and kick your door in, and after that things will only get worse. This is important. I need information about the Albion Club." She stopped and listened, smiled briefly, and put the phone away.

"Well?" said Daniel.

"Alan will meet us at a particular bench in Hyde Park," said Tina.

"Where he will tell us what we need to know?"

"He will if he knows what's good for him," Tina said cheerfully.

"It's good to have friends," said Daniel.

"I wouldn't say friend, exactly," said Tina.

"But you trust him."

"Not really, no."

"Then why are we meeting him?" said Daniel.

"Because Alan knows things no one else knows," said Tina. "That's his job."

"Oh," said Daniel. "One of those. Which department does he work for?"

"Haven't a clue."

"Hold everything," said Daniel. "Why are we meeting at *Hyde* Park? Is he having a laugh?"

"Alan is not famous for his sense of humor," said Tina. "Come on—let's go back and pick up your not-at-all-conspicuous stolen police car, so we can be on our way."

"Don't be rude about my car," said Daniel. "I'm almost sure it drove us back here, when I wasn't in any condition to."

"Okay," said Tina. "That isn't in any way worrying."

One reasonably sedate drive across London later—because even though they'd never admit it both Hydes were feeling just a little bit fragile—they ended up outside the main entrance to Hyde Park. Daniel parked the car extremely carelessly, and they went inside.

By now the sun had come up, and it was officially morning. Daniel and Tina strolled along, enjoying the wide-open space and the warm sunshine. The air was rich with the scent of grass and flowers, and it seemed like every bird in London was singing its little heart out.

"I was starting to think the night would never end," said Daniel.

"It did rather outstay its welcome," said Tina. "And it is nice to be out and about in the sunlight. We spend too much of our life in the dark."

"Comes with the job," said Daniel. "Speaking of which . . . take a look around. Notice anything interesting?"

Tina let her gaze switch back and forth without turning her head. "Rather a lot of people about, for this early in the day."

"Notice how they have a tendency to drift together, talk quietly for a while, and then break apart and form new groups with other people."

"All right," said Tina. "Clearly you know something. Who are these people?"

"Spies, assassins, and all the other twilight souls interested in peddling information," said Daniel. "Hyde Park has always been a meeting place for people connected to the intelligence game. Because all this space and open air makes it harder to overhear or record conversations. Think of Hyde Park as a clearinghouse for hot secrets and unauthorized gossip, where agents of all kinds can come together to trade insider knowledge. Money and favors change hands, the fate of nations is decided, and everyone gets some healthy exercise."

"That's why Alan chose this as our meeting place," said Tina.

"Wouldn't surprise me in the least," said Daniel.

They found the designated bench easily enough, right next to a statue of Peter Pan dueling with Captain Hook. The Hydes sat down and leaned companionably together, as though they were just another couple taking a morning break.

"Where is this friend of yours?" said Daniel, after a while.

"Probably checking us out from a distance," said Tina. "To make sure we weren't followed, and haven't brought anyone with us that he didn't agree to."

"You mean he doesn't trust us?" said Daniel.

"I know," said Tina. "Shocking, isn't it?"

Alan Diment finally appeared strolling casually down the path toward them, just another middle-aged man in a smart city suit, enjoying a walk in the park on his way to work. He sat down next to Daniel and Tina and looked out over the view, smiling easily as though he didn't have a care in the world.

"This had better be important," he said, without even glancing at the Hydes. "A man my age needs his downtime."

"You look sharp enough," said Tina, "for someone who's just been hauled out of his bed."

"I am never off duty," said Alan. "I have to say, you're both looking very well, considering what happened to you in the Martian and Bug-Eyed Monster bases. After the reports I read, I'm surprised you're even up and about."

Tina looked at him narrowly. "Have you got people watching us?"

"Always," said Alan.

Tina smiled at him. "I'm amazed you have anyone left who'll agree to go anywhere near me, after what I did to the last batch."

"I do have to offer them danger money," Alan admitted.

Tina nodded, satisfied.

"I am very pleased to meet you at last, Daniel," said Alan. "The man who changed everything!"

Daniel wasn't sure how to take that. "What did I do?"

"My dear fellow!" said Alan. "You are responsible for the destruction of the monster Clans, and the death of Edward Hyde! You really must tell me how you managed that last one, when you have the time."

"I was there too," said Tina, just a bit dangerously.

"Of course you were, my dear," Alan said quickly. "An invaluable part of everything that happened, I'm sure. My point is that when Daniel appeared on the scene, he knocked over so many dominoes he changed the whole established balance of power."

"We're not here to talk about me," said Daniel.

"We want to know everything you know about the Albion Club," said Tina.

Alan shot her an admiring glance. "You do pick the most dangerous things to get involved in."

"Talk," said Tina.

"Unfortunately, that won't take long," said Alan. He crossed his legs casually, and took on a lecturer's tone. "The Albion was founded during the reign of Elizabeth I, by her Court magician and head spy, Dr. John Dee. The first organized intelligence center in the civilized world. It spent centuries stamping out all kinds of unnatural business, only to find itself left behind in recent years, because of its refusal to embrace the technological advantages of the twentieth century, never mind the twenty-first. These days the Albion is just a watering hole for old spies—somewhere they can sit around and gossip about the good old days."

"Who runs the Albion now?" said Daniel.

"A very interesting question, my dear Hyde," said Alan. "The current head is William Dee, latest in a very long line of Dees who have always run the club. Except . . . this particular Dee has been in place for so long many of us believe it's merely a code name for a number of people with very good reasons for not wanting to be identified." He paused, and then looked directly at Daniel and Tina. "There's only one reason why anyone would want to visit the Albion, and that's because you're looking to make contact with the Elder Ones. Something else I know far too little about for my own comfort. There's never been any solid information on the Elder Ones . . . but if they are still sleeping in the deep, dark places of the earth, the general feeling is that they should be left alone. Children shouldn't play with gods they don't believe in."

"But what are they, really?" said Daniel. "Aliens, supernatural beings, entities that have downloaded themselves from a higher dimension?"

"The truth is probably in there somewhere," said Alan. "There are many stories about amazing and incredible and appallingly scary things these creatures are supposed to have done, but always set so far in the past that none of them can be confirmed. The Elder Ones have drifted out of history and into legend—and are probably better left that way. Only a fool prods a monster with a stick just to see what kind of noise it will make."

"Could they be allies, in our fight against the Big Four aliens?" said Daniel.

"If they are what they're supposed to be, and if you can persuade them to do what you want, it would be like using a tactical nuke to drive a nail into wood."

"They're that powerful?" said Daniel.

"At least," said Alan. "And if you're not feeling pants-wettingly frightened, I'm not doing my job properly."

"Any idea where we might go, to look for them?" said Tina.

Alan sighed. "I know I'm speaking because I can feel my lips moving, so why aren't they listening? No, Tina. No one in my line of business knows where to look, and no one wants to. Let sleeping gods lie, and all that. But if anyone would know . . . it's William Dee of the Albion Club. His family was supposed to have certain unhealthy connections with the Elder Ones—which only goes to prove that some gods will shag anything. It is possible that Dee might be able to put you in touch with them."

"Why are you so willing to talk to us about this?" said Daniel.

"Because I am absolutely fascinated to see what you will do next," said Alan.

"You want the alien bases destroyed, but your bosses don't want to get involved," said Daniel. "Because they're afraid of alien reprisals if you fail. But you're quite happy to use us, at arm's length, to get it done for you. And of course if anything should go wrong, we make the perfect scapegoats to blame it on."

"Couldn't have put it better myself," said Alan. He nodded to Tina. "When you're finished with the Albion we really must get together for lunch, so you can tell me all about it."

"Have you ever been to the Albion Club?" said Daniel.

Alan stared off into the distance. "They wouldn't let the likes of me cross their threshold, even if I had a search warrant and a battering ram."

"I thought you were a man of power and influence?" said Tina.

"Oh, I am," said Alan. "But the Albion dates back to a time when the spy business was strictly a game for gentlemen. Another reason why they belong in the past. One last piece of advice, my dear Hydes: watch your backs."

"Are you talking about the Elder Ones, or the Albion?" said Daniel.

"Yes," said Alan.

"Before you go," said Daniel. "Who do you work for, exactly?"

"Ah," said Alan. "That would be telling. Almost certainly no one you've ever heard of. They don't exist, I never came here, we never had this conversation. Have a nice day."

He rose to his feet and strode off through the park, not looking back. Daniel kept a careful eye on him until he was sure the man couldn't overhear.

"So that's your little spy friend."

"Not friend," said Tina. "Ally would be closer."

"He reminds me of my police contact," said Daniel. "Happy to feed us crumbs of information, in the hope we'll do their dirty work for them."

"We'll just have to find a way to use them to get what we want," said Tina.

"That *is* the Hyde way," said Daniel.

They rose to their feet as though they'd just had enough of the view, and made their way back through the park. And everyone watched the Hydes do it, without actually looking in their direction for more than a moment.

Daniel parked his car highly illegally, in a part of Pall Mall that liked to keep itself to itself. The whole area was the kind of empty that only happens because someone is enforcing it. Daniel and Tina walked down the street until they found a door that deigned to have a visible number, and then they counted their way along to the place they were looking for: a grim and brooding edifice, with three stories of aging stonework and boarded-over windows. The impressively large door had no number, bell, or knocker, just a very discreet brass plaque saying simply THE ALBION. Carefully positioned to be half hidden in shadows.

"I'm getting a strong feeling of nobody home," said Tina. "Like everyone just ran away and left the place to look after itself. Possibly because it had accumulated dangerous levels of gloom. I'll bet even the gargoyles have moved on to another roof."

"That may be what we're supposed to think," said Daniel, "to discourage visitors. What better cover is there, than looking like somewhere no one would want to go?"

He leaned over a small intercom grille set flush beside the door, and then stopped to clear his throat self-consciously.

"I hate using these things..."

"You get shy at the strangest moments," said Tina. "Be a big brave boy, and I'll let you wear my leather choker later."

Daniel addressed the intercom in his best confident tone.

"There are two Hydes here, who want to talk to someone about the Elder Ones."

He waited, but there was no response. Tina pushed Daniel out of the way, and growled at the intercom.

"Let us in, or I'll kick your damned door right off its hinges!"

There was the sound of heavy locks disengaging, and the door swung slowly back before them. Tina smiled triumphantly at Daniel.

"You just have to know how to talk to these people."

Daniel stepped cautiously into a wide and gloomy corridor. Something about the atmosphere immediately raised all his hackles, as though he'd just walked into a trap that didn't care he knew it was a trap. Tina moved quickly in beside him, glaring around her and daring anything unpleasant to emerge from the shadows. The door shut itself firmly behind them, and the sound of closing locks reverberated loudly on the quiet. Tina didn't even glance back.

"Is that supposed to impress us? We're Hydes!"

Daniel frowned as he took in the wood-paneled walls, thick carpeting with a dull and repetitive pattern, and the almost suffocating air of authority and privilege.

"This is a gentlemen's club, all right."

Tina smiled nastily. "And I can't wait to do something appalling in it."

"Try to wait until after we've got what we came here for," said Daniel.

"Diplomat," said Tina.

It quickly became clear that no one was going to come and meet them, so they set off down the corridor. Daniel's shoulders hunched despite himself, all his instincts shouting at him that he was in enemy territory. He glanced at Tina, but if her instincts were telling her anything she didn't appear to give a damn. Daniel frowned, as he realized how dull and muffled their footsteps sounded, as though something in the club's ambience was suppressing all signs of life.

"There aren't any portraits on the walls," he said, just to be saying something. "None of the usual celebrated past members."

"No paintings at all," said Tina. "Not even the traditional insipid landscapes. Maybe they sold everything off when times got hard. I'm starting to wonder if this place is just an empty shell."

"Then who opened the door for us?" said Daniel.

Tina sniffed. "I hate it when you go all practical."

"Somebody has to," said Daniel.

They kept walking, but the corridor didn't seem to have any end. After a while, Daniel started opening some of the doors they were passing, but all they ever contained were echoing empty spaces, bare floorboards, and featureless walls. Rooms long abandoned, because there was no one left to use them. And when Daniel glanced over his shoulder at the front door, it was so far back it was lost in the gloom. Tina stirred restlessly at his side, eager to press on and find someone she could throw against a wall and question.

"It feels like we've been walking for ages," she said, "and we're not getting anywhere."

"I'm starting to think we should have left a trail of breadcrumbs behind us," said Daniel.

"I'd hate to think what might creep out of the skirting boards to eat them," said Tina.

Daniel shook his head. "You had to go there, didn't you?"

Tina glowered around her. "You know what? I think we could use a little more light in here, don't you? Let's rip some of this nice wood paneling off the wall, pile it up, and make a nice fire."

"Nothing like a good blaze, to cheer a place up," said Daniel.

They were actually reaching out to the nearest wall when they heard quiet shuffling feet from somewhere up ahead. A frail old man in an old-fashioned servant's outfit emerged from the shadows. Bent right over by age and infirmity, his head was so low he had to stare at the carpet rather than at Daniel and Tina. He finally lurched to a halt and forced his head up inch by inch until he could glare at them. His face was heavily lined, and his head retained only a few strands of gray hair, but his sunken eyes were still sharp and fierce. He took his time looking Daniel and Tina over, and when he finally addressed them his voice was cold and harsh, without an inch of give in it.

"Hydes, in the Albion. What has the world come to? Ah well, if you've got this far you'd better come and have a word with His Nibs."

It took him a while to turn around, while his back and joints competed to see which could creak the loudest, and then he set off at a slow, steady pace. His back forced his head down again, but he seemed to know where he was going. Daniel followed after, maintaining a careful distance, shooting the occasional sharp glance at Tina when she seemed to be getting impatient.

Almost immediately, the corridor took a sharp turn to the left, and just like that they were walking along a pleasantly lit passageway. Daniel had to wonder if it would ever have appeared if he and Tina had just kept going on their own. The Albion Club's internal geometry struck him as intrinsically treacherous. Daniel turned his attention back to the stooped old man shuffling determinedly along in front of him, and raised his voice.

"I'm Daniel Hyde, and this is Tina. Who are you?"

The servant let out a brief chuckle, but didn't look back. "I'm Fry, the butler. Head cook and bottle-washer as well, these days. And I have to polish all the brass. I am so fed up with brass you wouldn't believe it. But, since I'm all the staff there is . . ."

"Where is everybody?" Tina said bluntly.

"Dead and gone, mostly," said Fry. "Hell of a thing, when a club outlives its members. And its staff. There used to be so many spies and field agents stopping off here, to consult some old book in the library, or pick up some weapon no one but us remembered. I can still see them, sitting in their wingback chairs with their brandy and cigars, having loud hearty chats about tradecraft and secrets and the ins and outs of killing bad things. We had an army of staff on call in those days, just to keep up with them. Our kitchens were famous, not to mention our cellars. We had wines laid down no one even remembers anymore. People knew how to live, in those days. Just not for long, mostly. Being a secret agent didn't make for old bones, particularly when you were going after the kind of abnormal threats the Albion specialized in . . .

"But; the world changed and we didn't. That was the point of the Albion: to preserve the old knowledge, and the old ways of dealing with things. Because the old ways always work. At some point people will realize that, and remember they need us after all."

"You really believe people will come back?" said Tina.

Fry let loose his nasty cackle again. "You're here, aren't you?"

"Is it just you and Mr. Dee, these days?" said Daniel.

"Pretty much," said Fry. "There are still a few ghosts lurking around. I told His Nibs, I told him: I'm not cleaning up the ectoplasm. Not with my knees. I should have retired long ago, but as long as His Nibs still needs me . . . We go way back, you see. Him and me. Back to when Intelligence was a gentleman's affair."

"You were a gentleman?" said Tina.

Fry shot an unpleasant grin back at her. "Bless you no, miss. I was a gentleman's bit of rough. You might not believe it now, but I was considered uncommon handsome in my younger days. His Nibs took a fancy to me, and me to him, and he got me this job so we could always be close." He sniffed loudly. "Job for life . . ."

"Do you still have much to do?" said Daniel.

"You'd be surprised," Fry said darkly. "And not in a good way. The old place still has its share of secrets. Things that have to be looked after, or locked up—or put down, if they start to get out of hand. And anyway . . . I can't leave as long as His Nibs is still here. He couldn't run the Albion without me, and he knows it."

He stopped abruptly, before a door Daniel would have sworn wasn't there a moment before. Fry knocked loudly, raising the echoes, with a gnarled hand like a block of wood. He opened the door without waiting for an answer, and then stepped aside to announce the visitors.

"Mr. Daniel Hyde, and Miss Valentina Hyde, to see the Master of the Albion!"

Daniel found that interesting, because Fry shouldn't have known Tina's full name. It seemed they were expected. He moved carefully past the bent-over butler and, with Tina all but treading on his heels in her eagerness to hurry him on, entered a warmly lit study. The furniture and fittings were resolutely Victorian—large and bulky and made to last. Dusty portraits of unsmiling faces stared back from the walls, while rows of leather-bound volumes packed the bookshelves from floor to ceiling. The deep carpet was a sharp zigzag pattern of black and red, and soaked up every sound Daniel and Tina made. At the back of the room, behind a sturdy writing desk, sat another hunched figure, dressed to the height of 1920s fashion. The old man nodded familiarly to the servant at the door.

"That will be all, Fry."

The butler sniffed loudly. "You sure you don't want me to hang around? They're ugly brutes, even for Hydes."

"I can manage, thank you, Fry."

"That's what you said back in '53," said the butler, "when we were out in Tibet. But I was the one who had to kick the Abominable fellow in the unmentionables, and then throw you over my shoulder and run down the mountainside."

"That will be all, Fry!"

The butler vanished, snapping out of existence like a blown-out candle flame. Daniel and Tina both jumped a little, despite themselves, and the man behind the desk smiled.

"Yes, he's a ghost. The last loyal servant of the Albion Club, who wouldn't let a little thing like dying get in the way of carrying out his duties. Sorry I had to cut him short, but he'd reminisce all day if you let him. Ghosts live in the past. I am William Dee, current Master of the Albion . . . for my many sins. Please, have a seat."

Daniel arranged himself as comfortably as he could on the stiff-backed visitor's chair, while Tina slumped bonelessly on hers. Daniel took a moment to study William: a scrawny vulture of a man with a bald head, a gaunt face, and piercing eyes. He smiled briefly at Daniel, as though he knew exactly what was going through Daniel's mind.

"I really am William Dee, despite all the rumors. I'm older than I look, which takes some doing, but the club looks after those who serve it. And of course I know who both of you are. Welcome to the Albion, Daniel and Valentina Hyde. Killers of monsters, and of Edward Hyde—and good for you. I was also very happy to hear what you did to the Martians and the Bug-Eyed Monsters. Doesn't matter whether they're monsters or aliens, you have to stamp them out like cockroaches or you'll never get any peace."

"Is *everyone* watching us?" said Tina.

"Pretty much," said William.

"You were expecting us," said Daniel. "Did someone tell you we were on our way?"

"Alan Diment phoned me," said William. "He's a good boy. Knows what matters, and what needs doing to get things done. I used to work in the field with his grandfather, back in the day. Just a slip of a lad, but you wouldn't believe what he could do with a garotte."

Daniel considered Alan's age, did the maths, and wondered whether William was pulling his leg. The man looked seriously old, even ancient, but he would have to be . . . Daniel knew William was waiting for him to ask how old he was, so he didn't. Just smiled easily, and waited for him to continue.

"I won't keep you hanging about," said William. "We're not here for pleasantries. You want to know how to contact the Elder Ones."

"Are they real?" Tina said bluntly.

"Bless you, little Miss Hyde," said William. "They're realer than we are, if the truth be told. The Elder Ones don't just come from some other world, but from outside our entire existence, and it doesn't pay to think too much about where that might be. Some things the human mind just isn't equipped to deal with."

He paused for a moment, gathering his thoughts.

"We call them the Elder Ones, because all the more accurate names are just too disturbing. They arrived on this world in the dark days, before human history had even got started. Of course we worshipped them as gods—what else could we do? But eventually Humanity put its shoulder to the wheel and started things moving, and somewhere along the line the Elder Ones were forced into the background. Whether they fell or were pushed from their high station is open to question. They sleep now, in the hidden places, waiting for their time to come round again. They speak to us in our dreams.

"They've been quiet for a very long time. Powerful beyond anything we can imagine, beyond our ability to comprehend or control. And only a fool would seek to disturb them without the direst need."

He stopped, and smiled his unsettling smile, as though to say *The ball is in your court now. Where do you want to go from here?*

"Would the Elder Ones help us against the remaining aliens?" said Daniel.

"There are records of times when they have helped Humanity against their enemies," said William. "All kinds of powers and dominations have established a presence on the Earth at one time or another, but they are all gone, and the Elder Ones remain."

"Why do all these aliens keep coming here?" said Daniel.

William shrugged. "Who can say? They're aliens, and have ways of their own. Presumably, they're here because they want something."

Daniel remembered the Martian slaughterhouse, and the living machines of the Bug-Eyed Monsters, and nodded slowly.

"Why would the Elder Ones agree to help us against the current aliens?" said Tina.

"It's not wise to question the Elder Ones," said William. "We probably wouldn't like the answers."

"Can they be awoken, after such a long time?" said Daniel.

"Of course," said William. "If you know the right way to go about it." He showed the Hydes his unsettling smile again. "The Albion is the only place left that still preserves all the old rituals."

"And you're willing to help us?" said Tina.

William just nodded. "Don't worry, my dear, I'm not about to present you with a bill, or a demand for favors. The knowledge in the Albion is here to be used, in times of need. And it would feel good, to prove to the world that the Albion still has a part to play in the great game. But really, I want to raise up the Elder Ones just so I can see what they look like."

"How long will it take you, to discover the right rituals?" said Daniel.

For the first time, William didn't meet his gaze.

"I shall have to consult the club library," he said. "Sort out the exact words. It's not something you can afford to get wrong. The Elder Ones can be very hard on those they see as being disrespectful."

Daniel nodded. "Talk to our armorer, Patricia. When you're ready."

"Waking the Elder Ones isn't the problem," said William. "It's getting them to go back to sleep again afterward."

He started to laugh. He was still laughing when Daniel and Tina got up and left the room.

The ghost butler, Fry, was waiting for them in the corridor. He shook his head slowly, as Daniel closed the door on William Dee's laughter.

"He's never been all there, where the Elder Ones are concerned. You'd better go. I know how to calm him down. I keep telling him, it's time he handed the reins on to some younger Dee, let them shoulder the burden, but he won't hear of it. Keeps saying none of them are up to the job, and who's to say His Nibs is wrong . . . ? Come with me. I'll get you out of here. And if you've got any sense, don't come back."

Fry led them through the club to the front door, waited for them to step outside, and sniffed loudly.

"Don't call us, we'll call you."

And then he slammed the door in their faces. Daniel and Tina looked at each other.

"Do you think anything useful will come of this?" said Tina.

Daniel shrugged. "We've done all we can here."

"Where to now?" said Tina. "Back to the Jekyll & Hyde Inc. building?"

"Of course," said Daniel. "If we do have to take on the Reptiloids or the Greys without the help of ancient space gods, I want to be carrying something extremely destructive from the armory."

"Guns!" said Tina. "Really big guns!"

"Well," said Daniel. "That goes without saying."

Chapter Seven
DOWN IN THE TUNNELS WHERE THE REPTILOIDS GO

✣ ✣ ✣

EVERYONE IN THE LOBBY stopped what they were doing and looked round sharply as Daniel and Tina slammed through the doors. They all clearly expected to see them looking like death warmed over again . . . and actually seemed a little disappointed when they found that wasn't the case. Daniel and Tina stood together, backs straight and heads held high, so everyone could get a good look at how magnificent they were. Daniel waited until he was sure the point had been made, and then gave the watching crowd his best hard stare, at which point everyone went back to work.

"I do like to see other people being busy," said Tina.

"Even though the armorer isn't here to crack the whip over them," Daniel observed.

"Where do you suppose she's hiding herself?" said Tina.

"Probably taking her ease in her luxurious office on the top floor," said Daniel. "Planning something else we don't know about, and won't like one bit when we do."

"You know," Tina said wistfully, "I'm almost sure there was a time when we were in charge of Jekyll & Hyde Inc."

And then they broke off, as the armorer's favorite came hurrying through the crowd toward them. Joyce slammed to a halt in front of Daniel and Tina and grinned brightly—the same bright and cheerful presence, bubbling over with enthusiasm as she prepared to be useful.

"Hi! It's me again! The armorer—"

Tina glowered at her fiercely. "Stop that, right now. No woman should ever be that eager to follow orders. Stand up for yourself!"

"Well, yes," said Joyce. "But . . . Patricia is the armorer! And she is just so cool!"

Tina shook her head and turned to Daniel. "You talk to her."

"What can we do for you, Joyce?" Daniel said kindly.

Joyce bounced up and down on her toes, grinning broadly. "You remember me!"

"You made an impression," said Daniel. "Now, what is so important you had to run all the way across the lobby to tell us?"

"Patricia instructed me to wait here for you," said Joyce.

Tina scowled. "How long have you been waiting for us to show up?"

"About ten minutes," said Joyce.

Tina looked to Daniel. "How could the armorer know we were on our way back, never mind so close?"

"She has people," said Daniel. "No doubt they report in. Where is Patricia right now, Joyce?"

"I'm to escort you to the armory," Joyce said importantly. "She's waiting to talk to you."

Daniel frowned. "We have to go back to the old building?"

"Oh no," Joyce said happily. "The entire armory has been moved here, and reestablished on our first floor."

"How is that even possible?" said Daniel. "The old armory took up half of the floor, and was packed full of incredibly dangerous things that really didn't like being interfered with."

Joyce shrugged. "None of us were involved in the move. Patricia just announced it as a done deal. And you really don't ask her questions when she's got that look on her face. Besides, most people would rather rip their own heads off than have anything to do with the armory. We've all heard stories . . ." And then she leaned forward, so she could lower her voice conspiratorially. "The general feeling is Patricia found some kind of teleport system in the armory, and used it to transport the whole thing in one go."

"The old armorer never said anything to us about a teleport system," said Tina.

"To be fair," said Daniel, "we never asked. And given that we've spent most of the night beating up aliens, is a teleport really so unlikely? Especially when you consider some of the stuff we do know about."

"Like what?" Joyce said immediately.

"You don't want to know," said Tina. "You'd have nightmares."

"All right, Joyce," said Daniel. "Take us to Patricia."

"I'll take you to the armory door," said Joyce. "But if it's all the same to you, I think I'll wait outside while you go in."

"And disobey a direct order from Patricia?" said Daniel.

Joyce grinned. "I'm loyal, not stupid."

"Good for you!" said Tina. "You'll have a backbone before you know it."

"Play nicely, Tina," said Daniel.

"I will when everyone else does," said Tina.

They took the elevator up to the first floor. It tried to play an easy listening version of the Rolling Stones' "Let It Bleed" at them, until Daniel punched a hole in the steel wall and ripped out the speakers. The elevator continued its journey in a sulky silence. Joyce looked worshipfully at Daniel, and he just knew Tina would never let him forget that. The elevator delivered them to the first floor as quickly as possible, and the doors sprang open with almost indecent haste. Joyce went charging off down the corridor, while Daniel and Tina ambled along in the rear, refusing to be hurried. Daniel looked thoughtfully around him. The first floor still struck him as disturbingly quiet and empty, compared to the hustle and bustle of the lobby.

Tina frowned, as the same thought occurred to her. She called out to Joyce, and she came speeding back to look at Tina expectantly.

"We know the tailors are here," said Tina. "Why hasn't anyone else moved in?"

"You'll have to ask Patricia about that," said Joyce. "We don't get told much."

"I'm sure the armorer will tell us, if we ask her nicely," said Daniel.

"Patricia knows everything!" Joyce said proudly.

"Let's hope not," said Daniel. "Does the armory take up half of this floor?"

"So people say," said Joyce. "But no one I know has felt like coming up here to check. Was it always that big?"

"The Hyde armory is basically one big warehouse, packed full of strange and unusual weapons and devices," said Tina.

"But the war against the monster Clans is over," Joyce said carefully. "And since you and Daniel are doing such a marvelous job of demolishing the alien bases, why do we need so many weapons?"

"Once it was monsters, now it's aliens," said Daniel. "But even after they're all dead and gone, you can bet something else will come along. Hydes always have enemies."

Halfway along the corridor, they were forced to stop when a reinforced barrier sealed off the rest of the floor. The only way through was a single steel door. Joyce took one glance, and ducked behind Daniel and Tina. The Hydes looked the door over carefully. There were no guards, and no obvious defenses or protections. Just a very familiar warning sign above the door: PLEASE DON'T DROP ANYTHING.

"This looks exactly the way I remember it," said Tina. "Not a single change . . . What is that woman up to?"

"Maybe she's feeling nostalgic," said Daniel.

"I don't have a key for the door," Joyce said tentatively. "Maybe you're supposed to knock?"

"Hydes don't knock," Tina said firmly.

"The old armory door was never locked," said Daniel.

"Really?" said Joyce. "I thought you said it was packed full of really horrible things?"

"You don't have to worry about people getting in there," said Tina. "The armory can look after itself. You'd be better off worrying about all the truly appalling things that want to get out."

"Oh, I worry," said Joyce. "I really do."

Daniel approached the door as though he was perfectly ready to walk right through it, and the door fell back before him. Tina moved quickly forward to join him and they strode through the opening, daring anything to have a go at them. And then they both paused and looked back, when they realized Joyce was still standing outside. She shot them a quick and entirely unconvincing smile.

"You don't need me now. I'm sure you can find Patricia on your own."

"Disobedience and defiance to orders are one thing, not doing something because you're afraid is something else," Tina said sternly. "Get your arse in here, right now."

Joyce got as far as the doorway, and then stopped and peered unhappily at the Hydes.

"It's just that I've heard so many rumors..."

"I'm sure you have," said Daniel. "But now you have two big brave Hydes to watch over you."

"And you do want Patricia to be proud of you, don't you?" said Tina.

That clinched it for Joyce. She raised her chin, squared her narrow shoulders, and scurried through the doorway. And then tried really hard not to jump when the door slammed shut behind her. Daniel stared around at the brightly lit armory, which seemed to stretch away forever. It all looked just as he remembered, right down to the general feeling of unease and an overwhelming sense of danger.

"What are you looking for?" said Joyce, and Daniel gave her points for keeping her voice steady.

"It's always wise to keep a watchful eye out for predators when you enter a jungle," said Tina. "Stand tall, Joyce—there are things here that can sense fear."

"It's not that bad," Daniel said quickly to Joyce. "It's just that there are some items that would benefit from being nailed down and having chains thrown over them. And I still wouldn't trust them."

Tina nodded briefly to Joyce. "Don't let any of this bother you. Hydes need unusual weapons because we have to fight unusual enemies. But there's nothing here that won't do what it's told, if you slap it hard enough."

"Take us to the armorer, Joyce," said Daniel.

"You do know how to find her?" said Tina.

Joyce nodded quickly. "She gave me a map."

The hand-drawn map showed a carefully marked route through the maze of shelves. Joyce traced the way carefully with a rose-pink nail, and then set off with something that might have passed for confidence if you didn't look at it too closely.

They passed open shelving, glass display cases, and the occasional large box with spikes on the inside, featuring everything from steampunk antiques to futuristic shapes that made no sense at all. They all possessed a certain threatening glamor, along with a sense of something dangerous just waiting to be put to use. One of them growled at Daniel when he got too close, only to go very quiet when he growled back. There were never any labels, instructions, or warning signs. Because either you knew what something was, or you had no business messing with it.

Joyce finally brought the Hydes to a small office that Daniel was sure used to belong to the previous armorer, Miss Montague. And there was Patricia, sitting behind an entirely ordinary desk, working her way through a pile of paperwork. There were none of the luxuries and comforts that filled her office on the top floor—this was a place where work got done. Patricia briefly acknowledged Daniel and Tina, and then nodded approvingly to Joyce.

"Well done. Extra brownie points for not letting the place get to you. Now get back down to the lobby, and tell everyone to stop slacking off."

Joyce smiled brilliantly at the unexpected praise, spun on her heel, and darted back through the warehouse, with a look in her eye that suggested really bad consequences for anything that bothered her on the way out.

"Our little girl is all grown up," Daniel said solemnly.

Patricia sat back in her chair and gestured for Daniel and Tina to sit down. They did so, and Patricia looked them over, not even raising an eyebrow as she took in their completely undamaged condition.

"How did you get on with William Dee?"

"Dee is well weird," said Tina. "But he said he could make contact with the Elder Ones, on our behalf. I have yet to be convinced that is a good idea."

"How very wise of you," said Patricia.

Daniel looked expectantly at her, but the armorer had nothing more to say. Daniel decided to change the subject.

"How did you move the armory here?"

Patricia actually smiled, just for a moment. "You'd be amazed at some of the things my predecessors acquired down the years... though perhaps *amazed* isn't quite the right word. *Appalled* is probably better. Aliens have been visiting the Earth throughout human history, and left all kinds of things behind, just waiting to be picked up by someone with an eye to the main chance. All I had to do was search through the inventory, locate a teleport device, and talk to it nicely—and here we are." She looked at the warehouse with all the pride of ownership, and then nodded briefly to the Hydes. "Come with me."

She started to get up, and then stopped as Daniel sat firmly back in his chair, to make it clear he had no intention of going anywhere just because the armorer thought it was a good idea. Tina did the same, only more aggressively.

"You did say you wanted weapons," said Patricia.

"Who are we taking on this time?" said Daniel.

"My people have discovered the current location of the Reptiloid base," said Patricia.

"And it's right here in London, isn't it?" said Daniel.

"Yes," said Patricia. "Islington, to be precise."

Daniel shook his head. "Why am I not surprised?"

"Because you are a deeply cynical person," said Patricia.

"I hate to show my ignorance," said Tina, "but what are Reptiloids, exactly?"

"Big humanoid lizardy things," said Daniel. "Some say they're from outer space, others believe they're descended from ancient Celtic snake gods. Basically scales and teeth, tails and claws. And forked tongues. Think intelligent crocodiles with delusions of grandeur."

Tina smiled. "I can handle crocs. I've still got the boots I made from one of the big bastards we fought in the sewers under the British Museum."

Daniel looked thoughtfully at Patricia. "How did your people find the base?"

"By going to bad places, and listening carefully while bad people talked," said Patricia. "It's amazing what people will admit to, once they've been encouraged with free drinks, or just a sympathetic listening ear."

"They have consciences?" said Daniel.

"They like to boast," said Patricia. "What's the point of knowing important secret things, if you can't use them to impress other people? Apparently the Reptiloids are up to something that needs to be stopped right now, before it gets out of hand. So if you'll just come with me, I'll sort out some suitably unpleasant things to take with you."

Daniel shook his head, and folded his arms across his chest. Tina quickly copied him, to demonstrate unity.

"We want a proper briefing," Daniel said firmly, "on the grounds that going in blind has not worked out too well for us. We are not going anywhere until you give us enough advance information to ensure we don't get the crap kicked out of us this time."

"Right," said Tina. "We want to know everything you know."

"You don't have that much time," said Patricia. "Oh very well, I suppose I can fill you in on the basics."

She took a moment to arrange her thoughts, and then launched into lecture mode.

"The Reptiloids have an extensive base in the sewer systems under Islington."

"Oh hell," Daniel said disgustedly. "Not the sewers again . . ."

Patricia fixed him with a cold stare. "What?"

"He's just having a flashback," said Tina. "Don't mind him. Carry on."

"According to Edward's file," said Patricia, "the Reptiloids first occupied the tunnels back in Victorian times. But before they could get anything started, they were found out and fought by Edward, who saw their presence as a threat to the organization he was building to fight the monster Clans. He went down into the tunnels, and it's a tribute to how much Edward scared the Reptiloids that they ended up barricading themselves in so he couldn't get to them. The Reptiloids put themselves into hibernation, and rather than face the time and expense it would take to dig them out, Edward just left them there.

"But now it seems they're waking up, either because something alerted them to the power vacuum left by the destruction of the monster Clans, or because Edward finally died. Or maybe because all the other alien bases were getting busy. Either way, Reptiloids are roaming the sewers again, and putting new plans in motion."

"What kind of plans?" said Tina.

"We don't know," said Patricia. "Their human agents are too scared to talk, because the Reptiloids eat people who disappoint them. But something is definitely in the offing, and the general feeling is that when we find out what it is, we're really not going to like it. So it's vital you get into the Reptiloid base and destroy it, while they're still getting started."

"Do you have an address?" said Daniel. "Islington covers a pretty large area."

"I have a map of the sewer system," said Patricia, "but that's all. Some of my people went down into the tunnels to take a look, and none of them came back. You'll just have to go down there and follow your nose."

"Since you know so much," said Daniel, "why are all the alien bases situated in London?"

"Because that's where the monster Clans were," said Patricia. "The aliens wanted to keep an eye on their enemies, so they could take over from them when the opportunity finally presented itself. Aliens take the long view."

She produced her map and laid it out on the desk. Daniel and Tina leaned forward, to get a better view. The map was very detailed, but there was nothing to suggest which tunnels were controlled by the Reptiloids. Daniel gave Patricia his best hard stare.

"If we're going down into the sewers again, I want hazmat suits."

"I have something better in mind," said Patricia. "For now, concentrate on the map. You'll have to work your way through the system, tunnel by tunnel, until you encounter the Reptiloids."

"The longer we stay down there, the greater the chance we'll be discovered," said Daniel. "Don't you have anything on your shelves that could help us locate the aliens?"

"Reptiloids are cold-blooded," said Patricia. "Which means the usual heat-seeking devices won't work."

"Give me a minute," said Tina. She got out her phone.

"Who are you calling?" said Daniel.

"I'll give you three guesses and the first two don't count," said Tina. "Now hush . . . Ah! Alan, it's me!"

Daniel pushed his head in beside hers so he could listen in, just in time to hear Alan Diment's resigned sigh.

"I haven't even got back to bed yet," he said. "All these years without so much as a Christmas card, and now you won't leave me alone. What do you want, Tina?"

"It's about the Reptiloids," said Tina. "Apparently they're up to something."

"We know," Alan said immediately.

"Why didn't you tell me that before?" said Tina.

"You didn't ask," Alan said reasonably.

"Well, we're asking now," Daniel said loudly.

"Hello, Daniel!" said Alan. "Honestly, how do you put up with her?"

"Being a Hyde helps," said Daniel. "Listen, while we're here, do you know where the Reptiloids come from?"

"Some of the older reports pointed to Venus," said Alan. "Though given what we know now of that world's appalling surface conditions, that now seems unlikely. Other reports claim the Reptiloids were cloned shock troops, genetically engineered by one of the other alien races, until they broke free and went their own way. There are also stories about Celtic snake deities, which only goes to prove some people will believe anything."

"Do you know what the Reptiloids are up to?" said Daniel.

"All we can be sure of that they're planning an attack," Alan said carefully. "I have planned a response, and placed the details before my superiors, but I'm still waiting for authorization. Of course, if you were to go down there and start some trouble . . ."

"I'm amazed you survived this long without Hydes to lean on," said Tina. "Do you know where we should look for the Reptiloid base?"

"We've got a pretty good idea," said Alan. "I'll send you a map."

There was a brief pause, and then Alan's map appeared on Tina's phone. It looked much the same as Patricia's, with one section of tunnels helpfully highlighted. Along with useful entrance points from the streets above.

"Some of those manhole covers haven't been opened in ages," said Alan. "Workmen are supposed to go down into the sewers at regular intervals to check out conditions, but it would seem money has been going into the right pockets to make sure that didn't happen. The Reptiloids have a lot of human agents protecting them."

"More bloody Renfields," Tina growled.

"Why haven't you done something about these people?" said Daniel.

"We know about the ones we know about," Alan said carefully. "But we also know there are more that we don't know about. If we wipe out the agents in our files, the others would just disappear and we might never find them. The only thing we can be sure of, is that more and more Reptiloids are emerging from hibernation—and they won't stay down in the sewers for long."

"How do you know that?" said Daniel.

"I have people inside their people," said Alan.

"Of course you do," said Tina. "Thanks for the information, Alan." She put her phone away and smiled happily at Patricia. "You're not the only one who knows things."

"I didn't know you knew Alan Diment," said Patricia.

"We didn't know you knew him," said Daniel.

"I know what I need to know," said Patricia.

"Have you found out yet who sent that fleet of assault helicopters to destroy our old building?" said Tina.

Patricia shook her head. "Lots of people are claiming responsibility, just for the bragging rights, but it's hard to discern who was actually behind the attack. There's no shortage of credible suspects, because so many people have good reason to hate Hydes. It would have helped if you could have hung on to a few soldiers for questioning."

"We were fighting for our lives!" said Daniel. And then he stopped, and looked at her thoughtfully. "What are the chances of another aerial attack, on this building? You've gone out of your way to make sure everyone knows Jekyll & Hyde Inc. is alive and well and back in business."

"I have people watching the skies," said Patricia, "and weapons systems in place on the roof. If any helicopters show up here, they're in for a really unpleasant surprise."

"Hold it," said Tina. "Why weren't there any defenses on the old roof?"

"There were," said Patricia. "Unfortunately, you'd driven away the people who should have been manning them. Don't worry, I brought them all back, and supplemented them with my own people."

"It sounds like you have your own private army," said Daniel.

"I didn't waste my time after I left Edward," said Patricia. "I kept busy."

"Doing what?" said Daniel.

"Ah," said Patricia. "That would be telling."

"Why haven't we heard of you before this?" Tina said bluntly.

Patricia showed the Hydes her brief cold smile again. "Because I am a professional."

"And that's how you know Alan Diment," said Daniel.

"Concentrate on the Reptiloid base," said Patricia. "Whatever they're up to, we need to slam the door in their face. Show me Alan's map again."

Tina got her phone out.

"The highlighted tunnels still cover quite a large area," said Patricia. "There's no telling where the center of operations might be."

"And Alan didn't even offer a guess as to how many Reptiloids have emerged from hibernation," said Daniel. "We could end up facing a whole army of the things."

"Which means we're going to need weapons," said Tina. "Really nasty and unpleasant weapons."

"What she said," said Daniel. "Only with even more bullets."

"I think I can help you with that," said Patricia. "If you'd care to follow me . . ."

By the time she was up on her feet, Daniel and Tina were already standing waiting for her. Patricia sighed quietly, and then led the way out of her office and into the maze of passageways.

"Guns!" Tina said loudly to Patricia's back. "We want guns!"

"No, you don't," said Patricia, not even glancing back over her shoulder. "Firing guns in such a confined space could cause all kinds of problems—everything from ricochets to giving away your position to the Reptiloids. And anyway, I thought you were all about the joys of hand-to-hand combat?"

"There were times in the other bases when we could have used some long-distance weapons," said Daniel.

"To thin the herd down to more manageable numbers," said Tina.

"Good to hear you thinking tactically, for a change," said Patricia. "But standard weapons won't help you in the sewers."

Tina sniffed sulkily. "Want a gun."

"Well, you can't have one," said Patricia. "But dry your eyes and blow your noses, my children, for I have toys and party favors to bestow that will put a smile on your faces and a bounce in your step, because I am a Hyde armorer."

She stopped before one particular shelf, opened an unlabeled box, and showed Tina the contents.

"Atomic knuckle-dusters," Patricia said proudly.

Tina grinned broadly. "Really?"

"Well, no, not precisely," said Patricia. "But they are the next best thing. These brass knuckles have been charged with serious explosive energies, so when you hit somebody you can be sure they'll stay hit."

"Cool!" said Tina. She thrust her hand into the box and brought out the knuckle-dusters.

"Don't try them on here!" Patricia said immediately, and frowned at Tina until she slipped the brass knuckles into her pockets. "If you can't play responsibly with your toys, you won't be allowed to have them."

"Try and get them back," said Tina.

"What do I get?" said Daniel. "Nuclear nunchucks?"

"Sorry," said Patricia. "Someone else is using those."

She set off through the maze again, leaving Daniel and Tina to hurry after her. The armorer finally stopped before another shelf, tapped on the side of an aquarium until the contents stopped fighting, and then reached into the murky waters and brought out three yellowed finger bones, wired together.

"You've heard of killing bones?" Patricia said to Daniel. "Point one at somebody, and they drop down dead? Here we have three such bones connected by silver wire personally blessed by a defrocked pope. Just point these bones, concentrate on the killing word I will murmur into your ear in just a moment, and your enemies will explode—suddenly and violently and very messily. All the destructive power and range of a gun, without any of the associated drawbacks, like recoil, ricochet, and something else beginning with *R* that I can't be bothered to think of at the moment."

"Very nice," said Daniel, making no move to accept the bones. "What's the catch?"

"What makes you think there's a catch?" said Patricia.

"Experience," said Daniel.

"You are, of course, entirely correct," said Patricia. "You can only use the bones a limited number of times before you use up all the stored energies . . . and we have no record of how many times they've been used in the past."

"I'll take them anyway," said Daniel.

"Thought you would," said Patricia. She dropped them into his hand, and then leaned forward to murmur the activating word. Daniel blushed, just a little. Tina looked at him curiously, but he shook his head firmly.

"And that is all the weapons I am going to give you," said Patricia.

"What?" said Tina, ominously.

"Hold it right there, Armorer," said Daniel. "You don't get to make decisions like that. We will decide what we need to carry out a mission successfully."

"What he said," said Tina. "Only with even more authority."

"As armorer, I am in the best position to decide what you need," said Patricia. "If you have a problem with that, get yourself another armorer. If you can find anyone prepared to even enter this place without filling their underwear."

"Won't the Reptiloids have weapons?" said Daniel.

"Quite possibly," said Patricia. "What do you want me to do—go down into the sewers with you and hold your hands?"

"Oh, would you?" said Tina. "That would make us feel so much better."

Patricia gave her a hard look. "They probably won't use weapons for the same reason you can't: because too many things could go wrong. Think positive."

Daniel scowled. "What about the hazmat suits? Those sewers are full of filth and disease. The microbes are so big they lurk around in side tunnels, waiting to jump out and mug you. I am not going down into the sewers again without proper protection, and industrial-strength nose plugs to keep out the smell."

Tina nodded. "I remember smells so bad they could turn your nose inside out."

Patricia shook her head. "Hazmat suits are so last decade. I think we can do better than that."

She set off again, darting this way and that without hesitating, and finally stopped before a taller than usual set of shelves. She went up on her toes to reach for something right at the back, which immediately shifted away out of reach. Patricia glared at it.

"Don't make me have to come up there."

There was a pause as something thought about that, and then a grubby cardboard box launched itself off the shelf and into the armorer's hands. She took out two silver circlets, and tossed the box over her shoulder.

"Fasten these torcs about your throats, and not only will they protect you from the general appalling conditions, they will also conceal you from your enemies... as long as you're not standing right in front of them. Don't say I never do anything for you."

Daniel and Tina stuffed the torcs in their pockets.

"What about flashlights?" said Daniel. "It's going to be very dark in the tunnels."

"We need to see what we're fighting," said Tina.

"Flashlights would only warn the Reptiloids where you are," said Patricia. "The torcs will allow you to see clearly no matter how dark it gets."

Daniel looked thoughtfully at the armorer. "You've been giving this mission a lot of thought."

"That's my job," said Patricia.

"But no more weapons?" said Tina.

Patricia sighed. "You don't need any more. Daniel will give the Reptiloids the explodo, and you can beat up any still left standing."

"It's not enough just to take down the Reptiloids," said Daniel. "We have to destroy the whole base, to send a proper message. And after having to improvise an explosion in the Martian and Bug-Eyed Monster bases, I think we need to take something bomby with us this time. The previous armorer was very good when it came to bombs."

"I can do that," said Patricia. "In fact, I have just the thing in mind. Follow me, and don't stray from the path. There are wolves in the wood."

"Bring them on," said Daniel.

"Yeah," said Tina. "We're feeling peckish."

Patricia gave them a look that said she was going to rise above that, and set off through the passageways again. Daniel and Tina trudged along behind her. Tina moved in close so she could murmur in Daniel's ear.

"We shouldn't have had to ask for a bomb."

"A bomb should come as standard, for a Hyde armorer," said Daniel.

"No whispering in class!" Patricia said loudly. "Or you can all stay behind in detention."

She stopped abruptly before a glass display case, lifted the lid, and brought out a single particularly unimpressive item.

"That is a brick," said Tina.

"No, it isn't," said Patricia.

"With a big red button on it," said Daniel.

"If that's a bomb, it's a really good disguise," said Tina.

"You don't want a bomb," said Patricia. "Anything powerful enough to blow up that many sewer tunnels would collapse the whole area. However, think of the old story about placing a frog in a bowl of water. If the water is too hot, the frog just jumps out, but if you put it in cool water and then heat it gradually, the frog won't notice. He'll just keep paddling away and boil to death. And that's what we're going to do. Reptiloids are cold-blooded, and only function properly in warm temperatures."

"So we lower the temperature gradually," said Daniel, "and the aliens will go back to sleep."

Tina scowled. "But what am I supposed to do with a brick? Throw it at a Reptiloid?"

"The device is currently configured to look like a brick," Patricia said patiently, "so you can just leave it lying around and no one will notice. Be grateful. Considering where you're going, I could have made it look like something much worse. All you have to do is set this as near the center of the base as possible, and then hit the button to activate it. The device will immediately start lowering the temperature. Its field should be powerful enough to cover the entire sewer system."

"Should?" said Daniel.

Patricia shrugged. "It's an imperfect world."

She handed the brick to Daniel, and then handed Tina what appeared to be a remote control with a big red button on it.

"Why does everything have to have a big red button?" said Daniel.

"So you won't get confused," said Patricia. "Once you've set the brick in place and activated it, get the hell out of the sewers. Try not to get seen doing that. We don't want the Reptiloids to work out what's happening, and leave the tunnels before you hit the button on the remote and set off the brick's secondary function, sending a wave of intense heat racing through the tunnels."

"Why did the Reptiloids set their base in the sewers in the first place?" said Tina.

"Maybe it reminds them of home," said Patricia.

"Good answer," said Daniel.

"I thought so," said Patricia.

Tina glowered at Daniel. "Suddenly you're on her side?"

"Only when she's right," said Daniel.

"Good answer," said Tina.

"Don't touch the remote until you're safely back on the surface," said Patricia. "Once you hit that button, the flames will incinerate every living thing in the sewers. And be sure to stand well away from the manhole opening."

"Won't the intense heat damage the sewer systems?" said Daniel.

Tina shook her head. "Always the Boy Scout."

"Somebody has to be," said Daniel.

"The brick is not a bomb," said Patricia, holding onto her patience with both hands. "It's an incendiary. The flames will just remove all the accumulated crap. Victorians built their sewers to last. Always assuming the device does what it's supposed to."

Tina shot the armorer a hard look. "Run that last part by me again."

"No one has checked this particular item out in ages," said Patricia. "And it's not like we can test it. With devices like this, a certain amount of unpredictability comes with the territory."

"I can live with that," said Tina.

"As long as we keep a safe distance," said Daniel.

"Precisely," said Patricia. "Now off you go, my children. Hop like bunnies, have fun, and this time try not to come back looking like you've been fed headfirst into a giant Cuisinart. My supplies of pick-me-up are limited."

"We are not going anywhere," Daniel said firmly, "until we have got on the outside of a really big meal and some serious drinks. There's nothing like trashing alien bases to work up a real appetite."

"What he said, only with even more stomach noises," said Tina. "Have you set up a canteen yet?"

"Oh please," said Patricia. "We have a staff restaurant, with our very own chef."

"At some point," said Daniel, "there needs to be a very serious discussion about your operating budget."

"Of course," said Patricia. "How are you with spreadsheets?"

"Food!" Tina said loudly. "Right now, if not sooner!"

Patricia shook her head. "Go back to the armory door. You'll find Joyce waiting for you. She can take you to where you need to be."

"How do you get her to jump at your every instruction?" said Daniel.

"She thinks I'm cute," said Patricia.

"There's no accounting for taste," said Tina.

One meal of many courses and repeated desserts, washed down with the finest wines and brandies in creation later, Daniel and Tina set out across London in their stolen police car. It was getting close to midday, and the streets were packed with the usual bad-tempered traffic, but there's nothing like a police car driven with speed and enthusiasm to convince everyone else to get out of the way. When they finally got to Islington, Tina connected Alan Diment's map to the car's satnav, and a posh female voice guided them to an especially ugly back alley. Daniel and Tina got out of the car and took a good look around them, but there didn't seen to be anyone else about.

It was all stained and crumbling brick walls, with not even a single window overlooking the alley. Filth and garbage had piled up against the walls, as though carried there by some unseen tide. Tina turned up her nose.

"Who lives in a place like this?"

"This isn't the kind of place where anyone lives," said Daniel. "It's just somewhere people pass through. Probably to do something illegal, immoral, and entirely unwise."

"My kind of place," said Tina, and they shared a smile.

It didn't take them long to locate the manhole in the middle of the alley. Daniel bent over the grime-encrusted steel cover, and it stared back at him like a diseased eye, daring him to do his worst. He struggled to get a good grip, and then hurt his back trying and failing to shift the damned thing. He straightened up, and massaged his lower back muscles with both hands.

"We should have brought crowbars," he said stiffly. "And possibly a stick or two of dynamite."

"Just Hyde up and move the bloody thing," said Tina.

Daniel punched the steel cover so hard it bent in the middle, and the edges rose into the air with unpleasant sucking sounds. Daniel ripped the cover free, and threw it away so hard it hit the wall and dug in. He leaned over the dark opening, took a quick sniff, and then retreated quickly, shaking his head hard to try and drive out the horrible smell that had got in. He quickly took out his silver torc, and snapped it into place around his throat. He didn't feel any different, but when he moved cautiously back to sniff at the opening again he couldn't smell a thing. Tina moved in beside him, her torc already in place, and they stared down into the darkness that filled the opening.

"After you," Tina said brightly.

"Oh no," said Daniel. "Ladies first."

"I'm no lady," said Tina. "I'm a Hyde. Now get your arse down there."

Daniel descended a ladder of iron hoops hammered into the brick wall. They all gave disturbingly under his weight, and he was careful not to test their strength for too long. He jumped the last few feet, and then stepped quickly out of the way as Tina came hurrying down after him. Daniel pulled a face as he looked at the water filling the bottom of the curved tunnel. It was dark and scummy, and had things floating in it that made him wish he wasn't ankle deep in the stuff. Tina dropped down beside him, looked at what she was standing in, and then glared at Daniel as though it was all his fault.

The brick tunnel had curved walls, floor, and ceiling, and was only just big enough to hold the two Hydes. Daniel felt as though he'd entered a subterranean artery, or some other less pleasant part of the body. The brickwork was cracked and pitted, and stained so badly in places it looked almost diseased. Thick mats of blue and purple moss clumped here and there on the walls.

Tina grinned. "They say if you smoke that stuff, it can give you serious insights into the mysteries of the universe."

"Are these the same people who told you drilling a hole between your eyes would make you smarter?" said Daniel.

"I'd still like to try that some time," said Tina.

"I think not drilling a hole in your head is a pretty good sign that you're already intelligent enough," said Daniel.

"Hold everything," said Tina. "There's no light down here, but I can see perfectly clearly."

Daniel looked up and down the tunnel. There were no working lights, just the shaft of daylight dropping down through the opening, but Daniel could still make out every detail in the tunnel.

"It's the torcs," he said.

"These things really are amazing," said Tina. "You could burgle anywhere with these. No way I'm giving them back when this is over."

"Let's go look for some Reptiloids," said Daniel.

He set off along the tunnel, and Tina trudged along beside him, muttering under her breath. A rat the size of a cat swam past them, pursued by something larger that Daniel didn't recognize. After a while the tunnel branched off in several different directions. Daniel peered into one arched opening after another, but they all looked the same.

"The Reptiloids are supposed to be all over this section," Tina said quietly. "So why haven't we bumped into any yet?"

"Maybe they're hiding from us," said Daniel.

"That would be the sensible option," said Tina.

And then both their heads snapped round as they heard something moving in one of the side tunnels, splashing through the waters and not giving a damn if anyone heard them. Tina grinned at Daniel.

"What say we go check out the suspicious noises?"

"We are supposed to be in sneak mode," said Daniel.

"Aren't you curious to see what a Reptiloid looks like?" said Tina.

"You just want to hit something," said Daniel.

"And you don't?"

"Okay," said Daniel. "You knock it down, and I'll trample it."

"Good plan," said Tina.

They set off down the side tunnel, but only managed a few yards before they had to duck back around a corner to avoid being spotted by an approaching crowd of Reptiloids. Daniel and Tina found an indented archway and pressed their backs flat against the moss-covered brickwork. And then they both stood very still as the aliens passed by, so close Daniel could have reached out and tapped one on the shoulder. But the Reptiloids didn't even glance at the Hydes, because the aliens didn't have torcs that let them see clearly in the dark.

The Reptiloids were roughly human in shape, but so tall they had to bend right over to avoid banging their heads on the ceiling. Broad-shouldered and barrel-chested, with long tapering waists, the arms were so long their hands hung down to their knees. The curved fingers ended in vicious claws that looked designed for tearing and gutting. The Reptiloids had scaled hides, mostly gray but with raised patches of red and purple, and their faces thrust forward in long muzzles packed full of teeth. The eyes were a dull red, glowing like the last coals in a guttering fire, full of ancient inhuman knowledge.

They turned the corner into another tunnel, and Daniel slowly relaxed. The Reptiloids were the first aliens that looked like they could go one-on-one with a Hyde. Daniel took out his killing bones and looked to Tina, who held up her brass-knuckled fists.

"You were born to wear those," said Daniel.

Tina beamed at him. "You say the sweetest things."

"But let's not rush to start anything," said Daniel. "We're here to plant the brick."

"Don't I get to hit anything?"

"Let's let the incendiary do the heavy lifting."

Tina sniffed. "Well, you're no fun."

They moved on, darting from one tunnel to another whenever they heard something approaching, and trusting to the shadows to keep them hidden. Reptiloids came and went on unknown missions, occasionally pausing to communicate in short bursts of hissing, like angry steam whistles. Daniel kept pressing forward, trying to reach the center tunnels highlighted on Alan Diment's map, but every way he tried was blocked with Reptiloids. Tina leaned in close to murmur in his ear.

"I think this is as far as we're going to get. This might not be the center of the base, but it's so densely populated we must be close. Let's just drop the brick and get the hell out of here. The longer we spend in these tunnels, the more likely we are to be spotted."

Daniel looked at her. "I said that, back in the armory."

"I know," said Tina. "I was listening."

"Let's try just a little farther," said Daniel. "A lot of Reptiloids have been heading down this particular tunnel, and I'd like to know why."

Tina shrugged. "I never was any good at being the voice of reason."

A few sharp turns later they entered a single huge chamber, where long ranks of hibernating Reptiloids stood stiffly together, wrapped in thick gray shrouds. Silent and still, they had been set shoulder to shoulder, leaning back against the brick walls. Daniel moved slowly forward, his killing bones at the ready, while Tina kept an eye on the way they'd come. Daniel pushed his face right into a sleeping Reptiloid's, but there was no reaction. He tested the gray shroud, pulling gently at it with his fingertips. It felt like greasy cobwebs. The Reptiloid stirred, and Daniel froze where he was. The alien stopped moving, and Daniel carefully pulled his hand back.

He moved on into the chamber, and Tina hurried after him, determined not to be left out of anything. And right at the back they discovered a great pile of human bodies, looking as though they'd just been dumped there. At first Daniel thought they were dead, but when he moved in closer he could see they were breathing shallowly. He shook a few shoulders, but none of them responded.

"Are they hibernating, like the Reptiloids?" said Tina.

"There's no shroud around any of them," said Daniel.

He took a firm hold on one man and hauled him out of the pile. He turned the unresponsive figure over onto his back . . . and that was when he saw the alien egg. Dark, scaly, the size of a man's fist, it protruded from the man's bare belly, with thick purple veins disappearing into the pale flesh as though pumping some alien poison. Patches of crocodile scales showed clearly on the man's skin, and there was something wrong in the length of his arms and legs. Claws were forming on the fingertips.

"What the hell is this?" said Tina. "Some kind of hybrid?"

"Worse than that," said Daniel. "The Reptiloids are implanting their eggs in living human hosts, and the eggs are transforming these people into Reptiloids. The aliens are creating their own invasion army . . . out of us."

"They couldn't have just gone up onto the streets and abducted people," said Tina. "Someone would have noticed."

"I've been wondering why we haven't bumped into any of the aliens' human agents," said Daniel. "And now I think I know why. The Reptiloids must have decided they didn't need their agents anymore, except as hosts for their eggs."

"Bastards . . ." said Tina.

"It doesn't matter whether it's Martians, Bug-Eyed Monsters, or Reptiloids," said Daniel. "To aliens, humans are just something to be used."

"What are we going to do about this?" said Tina, gesturing at the pile of unmoving bodies.

"As long as these people are here, we can't use the incendiary," said Daniel. "The flames would kill them."

"But how many people might die if we don't shut down this base?" said Tina. "Alan seemed pretty sure the Reptiloids were on the brink of starting something awful."

"I couldn't save anyone in the Bug-Eyed Monsters base!" said Daniel. "I have to help someone here!"

Tina met his gaze steadily. "Do you know any way to reverse their condition?"

"If we can get them back to the armory, Patricia might be able to do something."

"We can't carry this many people back through the tunnels."

"I won't give up on them! I have to try!"

"Of course you do," said Tina.

Daniel raised the man before him into a sitting position, and slapped his face hard. The eyes snapped open, and they were red and alien. They locked onto Daniel, and the expression on the man's face had nothing human in it. He opened his mouth to scream a warning. Daniel grabbed the man's head with both hands and broke his neck, and then lowered the body to the floor as gently as he could. Tina put a comforting hand on Daniel's shoulder.

"Sometimes you have to concentrate on the people you can save. Let's just plant the brick and go. I've had enough of this place."

Daniel removed the brick from the container he'd improvised inside his jacket. He pressed the big red button to activate it, and then tucked the brick out of sight under the pile of bodies. He looked at them for a long moment, trying to find the right words, but there didn't seem to be any. So he just turned his back on the hibernation chamber and moved off into the sewers, with Tina sticking as close to him as she could.

"Do you know where you're going?" she said, after a while.

"I memorized the route as we came in," said Daniel.

"Of course you did," said Tina.

And then they rounded a corner and found a whole group of Reptiloids blocking the tunnel. The aliens didn't hesitate, just launched themselves at the humans with clawed hands and snapping teeth. Daniel pointed his killing bones, concentrated on the activating word, and then raked the bones back and forth. The nearest Reptiloids exploded, one after another. Heads were blown off, bellies burst apart, and purple blood splashed across the tunnel walls.

The surviving aliens pressed forward, vaulting over their own dead to get to the intruders. Tina went to meet them, lashing out with her knuckle-dusters, smashing Reptiloid skulls and staving in their chests. She laughed out loud as she danced among the aliens, striking them down and trampling their writhing bodies underfoot. Daniel couldn't use his killing bones with her in the way, so he tucked them away, and went to kill as many Reptiloids as he could with his bare hands.

Alien after alien crashed into the filthy tunnel waters, and did not rise again. Because nothing could stand against Hydes in their hate. Daniel and Tina killed them all, and when they finally stopped and looked around at the piled-up Reptiloid bodies, it didn't seem too many. Daniel looked back down the tunnel.

"I can hear more of them coming."

"Where from?" said Tina.

"Everywhere."

"Time we were leaving," said Tina. "It's never a good idea to outstay your welcome."

They hurried on through the sewer tunnels, splashing through the deepening waters. The sound of pursuit grew louder. Daniel threaded his way through the maze of tunnels without pausing, but when the Hydes finally returned to their entrance point, they found the way blocked by more waiting Reptiloids. Daniel and Tina showed the aliens their teeth, in fierce happy grins. The Reptiloids raised their muzzles and hissed like insane steam whistles. Daniel raked his killing bones back and forth and Reptiloid after Reptiloid exploded in bloody messes, decorating the tunnel walls with blood and gore and splintered bone.

More of the aliens surged forward, and a flailing claw slapped the killing bones out of Daniel's hand. They dropped into the filthy waters and disappeared from sight, and the Reptiloids fell on the Hydes with cold remorseless fury. Tina moved to the front, because she still had the charged knuckle-dusters. Daniel turned and set his back against hers, so he could face more aliens as they came charging down the tunnel to join the fight. The Hydes lashed out with all their strength and all their rage, and there wasn't a Reptiloid who could stand against them—but there were always more to take the place of those who fell.

Tina forced her way forward, foot by foot, heading for the ladder on the wall, laughing joyously as she slaughtered everything before her. Daniel moved back with her, step by step, but the numbers crowding in on him were so overwhelming all he could do was strike out at the alien faces before him, and put himself between Tina and the endless lashing claws that cut into him again and again. His blood dripped into the murky waters, mixing with that of the aliens. He never made a sound, because he didn't want Tina to know what his defense of her was costing him. He lowered his head and hunched his shoulders, and killed every alien he could, ignoring the snapping teeth and claws that gouged his flesh.

He was a Hyde; he could take it. So Tina wouldn't have to.

And then he realized that the Reptiloids were slowing down. He was dodging and ducking more of their blows, and the ones that landed seemed to have less strength behind them. His breath steamed on the air before him, and Daniel smiled suddenly. The brick was lowering the temperature in the tunnels.

Tina cried out triumphantly as the last of her Reptiloids fell back into the murky waters with its head smashed in. Daniel yelled for her to get to the ladder, and heard Tina grunt with effort as she pulled herself up the iron rungs. He lashed out with his broken bloody hands, clearing some space, and then he turned and went up the rungs after her. He was right behind Tina when a clawed hand closed around his ankle and hauled him off the ladder.

He crashed back into the filthy waters, and grappled with the Reptiloid as they rolled back and forth, tearing at each other like maddened animals. Daniel swung the alien over onto its back, straddled the struggling thing, and thrust its head underwater. It took its time dying, and when Daniel finally let go of it and forced himself onto his feet, a crowd of Reptiloids were staring at him with unblinking bloodred eyes. He smiled at them, and the Reptiloids stayed where they were, frozen in place by Hyde hate and the lowering temperature.

"Daniel!" Tina yelled down through the sewer opening. "Get your arse up here!"

"Hit the button on the remote!" Daniel yelled back.

"Not till you're out!"

Daniel started up the ladder, hauling himself up one rung at a time. His muscles ached, his back was screaming at him, and blood dripped steadily from his wounds, but he had enough strength to keep going. *I am getting really tired of having the crap beaten out of me,* he thought, *but I saved Tina.* He looked up as she called his name. Tina was leaning right down through the opening, one arm stretched out to him. Daniel reached up and grabbed her hand, and she hauled him up and out into the alleyway. Tina made a shocked sound as she took in Daniel's wounds, but he just gestured at the remote control in her hand.

"Hit it."

Tina pressed the big red button, and a fountain of flame burst up out of the sewer opening, seething and roaring as it climbed high into the sky. The heat was so extreme it drove Daniel and Tina all the way back to the end of the alley. Eventually the fiery column collapsed back into the sewers, and soon only a few wisps of smoke emerged from the opening. Daniel would have liked to hear some screams, but he supposed you couldn't have everything. He turned to Tina and raised a hand, and the Hydes solemnly high-fived each other.

"One more base down," said Tina. And then she stopped, and looked closely at Daniel. "Your wounds are closing. And your bruises are disappearing even as I look at them."

"I feel great," said Daniel. "And I don't think it's anything to do with Patricia's little pick-me-up still being in my system. It's just my body remembering it's a Hyde, and learning how to cope with all the mess we've been going through."

"So we don't need to rely on Patricia anymore," said Tina.

"I don't think we ever did," said Daniel. He stretched luxuriously. "No one left but the Greys now. Maybe we won't need the help of the Elder Ones after all."

Tina shook her head sadly. "You had to say that . . ."

Chapter Eight
ENEMIES AND ALLIES

✣ ✣ ✣

DANIEL PUT AN ARM across Tina's shoulders, and they leaned companionably against each other. It had been a long hard night and day, full of blood and suffering and the slaughter of aliens, but both Hydes were content with the feeling of a job well done. And that was when Daniel's phone rang. He took it out and glared at it for a long moment, before answering.

"What?" he said loudly.

"You need to get back here right now," said Patricia. "We have visitors."

The phone went dead before Daniel could say anything. He put it away and sighed deeply. The moment had lost it savor.

"It could be the mercenaries," said Tina. "Back for another go at us."

"In broad daylight?" said Daniel.

"We have been very successful," said Tina.

"I knew we shouldn't have put our name on the front door," said Daniel.

"Do you think it's the mercenaries again?" said Tina.

"I think Patricia would have mentioned them, if that was the case," said Daniel. "And I'm pretty sure we would have heard the explosions in the background."

"But we are going?" said Tina.

"Where else were we going to go?" said Daniel.

"Can I drive this time?" said Tina.

Daniel smiled. "Try and keep most of the wheels on the ground, most of the time."

"No promises," said Tina.

✣ ✣ ✣

Tina powered her way through the midday traffic with such style and enthusiasm that even hardened London bus drivers hurried to get out of her way. Tina whooped and hollered as she pressed the accelerator to the floor, and worked dark miracles with sudden gear changes. Daniel was almost sure he saw traffic lights turn to green the moment they saw Tina approaching, rather than risk upsetting her. One bike messenger stubbornly refused to get out of her way, and Tina hit him from behind so hard that he and his bike ended up on the top of a taxicab. Many people applauded.

The police car finally screeched to a halt outside Jekyll & Hyde Inc., and parked itself half on and half off the sidewalk. Daniel and Tina bailed out of the car, and looked quickly around for anything that needed coping with. But there was no obvious damage, no fires or broken windows, and even though Daniel craned his head right back he couldn't see any attack helicopters buzzing around the roof. He relaxed a little, and turned to Tina.

"If the building isn't under attack, why call us back so urgently?"

"Maybe Patricia felt lonely," said Tina.

"'Visitors' covers a lot of ground..." said Daniel. "Who else knows we're here?"

Tina shrugged. "It had better be someone I want to talk to, or there's going to be trouble."

"Well," said Daniel. "That goes without saying."

He strode into the lobby, with Tina only a step behind. It was still full of Patricia's minions, rushing back and forth as they put the finishing touches to Jekyll & Hyde Inc.'s new public face. And then they all stopped, and broke into loud applause. Every single one of them was grinning broadly, and pounding their hands together in what appeared to be genuine enthusiasm. Daniel and Tina stopped where they were, and moved a little closer together.

"Are we in the right building?" said Daniel.

"We must be," said Tina. "Here comes Patricia's little favorite."

"Doesn't she have anything else to do, except hang around and wait for us to show up?" said Daniel.

"That is an important job," said Tina.

Joyce came hurrying forward to join them. She wasn't applauding the Hydes, but looked as though she wanted to. She slammed to a halt before Daniel and Tina and bounced up and down with excitement, her eyes shining.

"Word of your success is all over the building!" she said happily, raising her voice to be make herself heard over the applause. "No one can believe you took out three alien bases so quickly, and walked away!"

Daniel nodded to the grinning crowd, and raised his voice. "Thank you very much, all of you; now knock it off! Too much and it sounds like sarcasm."

The clapping died away, amid general laughter.

"And get back to work," growled Tina. "Before Patricia notices you're slacking."

Everyone smiled and nodded and went back to being busy. Daniel looked at Joyce.

"Why the sudden change in attitude?"

"Because you earned it!" said Joyce.

"I'm not used to being popular," said Tina.

"Don't worry," said Daniel. "It won't last." He fixed Joyce with a steady stare. "What is so important that we had to be summoned back in such a hurry?"

"Beats the hell out of me," Joyce said cheerfully. "Patricia just told me to escort you up to her office on the top floor. We have to go there right now! It must be something big, because that whole floor is Patricia's special territory. Well, that and the armory, obviously."

"You're babbling, Joyce," Daniel said kindly. "Take a deep breath, turn around twice and spit, and give us your best guess as to what's going on."

Joyce leaned in close, and lowered her voice. "No one gets invited to the top floor unless it's really important. But Patricia insisted I should be the one to take you up there! I think she's taking a special interest in me."

"Go for it, girl," said Tina.

Daniel wasn't sure that Patricia taking an interest in anyone was necessarily a good thing, but kept that to himself.

"Is anyone already up there with Patricia?" he said.

Joyce nodded quickly. "Some very important people are talking with Patricia in her office. She let them go up on their own!"

Tina frowned. "Without an escort?"

"I know!" said Joyce. "Lots of us were ready to volunteer, but Patricia sent word no one was to bother these people, so we didn't."

"Any idea who they are?" said Daniel.

"I only saw them from a distance," said Joyce.

Which would have been a perfectly good answer, if Joyce hadn't suddenly found it difficult to meet the Hydes' gaze. Which suggested that she did know, but had been told to say she didn't. Daniel wasn't a fan of surprises where the armorer was concerned, but couldn't find it in him to pressure Joyce. He was still in a good mood from knowing he wasn't going to have to fight off another army of mercenaries, and besides, it would have felt like bullying a puppy. He gestured to Joyce to lead the way to the elevators, and she shot off as though someone had just fired a starting pistol. Daniel and Tina followed after her in their own good time, and everyone else fell back respectfully. A few looked like they wanted to clap Daniel or Tina on the shoulder as they passed, but wisely thought better of it.

All the way up to the top floor, the elevator refrained from playing any music, and Daniel refrained from doing any more damage. Someone had cleaned up the mess he'd made the last time, but he could still see dents in the metalwork. The elevator chimed politely as it delivered them to the top floor, and then hurried off to be somewhere less worrying.

Joyce led Daniel and Tina down the corridor to Patricia's office, knocked politely, and then pushed the door open. She stepped back, and gestured grandly for them to enter.

"Hold it," said Daniel. "Aren't you coming in with us?"

"I wasn't invited," said Joyce. "This meeting is for movers and shakers only."

"I am not leaving you hanging around out here," said Daniel. "You come in with us, Joyce."

"Right," said Tina. "We'll just tell Patricia you're our minder, and we'd be lost without you."

"Oh no," Joyce said quickly. "I really couldn't. Given who's already gone in there, you're going to be discussing seriously hush-hush things that I'm pretty sure I don't want to know about." She smiled suddenly. "Patricia will invite me in, when she wants to see me."

"Young love," said Tina. "You'd think there'd be a cure by now. Don't worry, Joyce, I'll put in a good word on your behalf."

"Please don't," said Joyce.

Daniel entered Patricia's office with Tina glaring at his side, and Joyce closed the door firmly behind them. And then Daniel stopped dead in his tracks as he saw Patricia talking quite casually with Alan Diment and Commissioner Jonathan Hart. Daniel looked to Tina.

"Small world, isn't it?"

"Apparently," said Tina. "So these are the visitors Patricia wanted us to know about . . ."

"I should have guessed," said Daniel. He waited a moment for the others to acknowledge him, and then kicked a potted plant so hard it flew across the office and exploded against the far wall. Patricia and her guests stopped talking to look at him.

"I liked that plant," said Patricia.

"You can probably put it back together again, if you try really hard," said Tina.

Daniel looked steadily at Alan. "I didn't know you people knew each other."

"Oh, we're all good chums," said Alan. "We go way back."

"We've worked with Patricia before," said Johnny. "On certain off-the-books operations."

Tina fixed the armorer with a cold stare. "And you never thought to mention this before?"

"You never asked," said Patricia.

Daniel took a moment to note that Alan and Johnny had both made an effort to dress up for the occasion. Alan was wearing a smart city suit, complete with old-school tie, while Johnny had put on his dress uniform, complete with gold piping. Patricia was still wearing her signature outfit of black over black, including the black leather gloves she never took off—either because she was making a statement, or because she didn't have any other outfits.

A quick glance around confirmed there weren't any more visitors' chairs, so Daniel and Tina stood together and struck their most impressive pose. The one that strongly suggested they were ready to punch anyone through a wall who didn't show them the proper respect. If Patricia and her visitors were impressed, they did a good job of hiding it. Tina smiled sweetly at Alan.

"What brings you here, Mister Very Secret Agent?"

"I have been sent by my superiors to offer you the department's official congratulations," Alan said easily.

Tina shook her head. "Your department never offers anything that doesn't come with a price tag."

"How very hurtful," said Alan.

"I notice you're not denying it," said Daniel. He turned to Commissioner Hart. "What are you doing here, Johnny?"

"Give me a minute, Danny boy, and I'll show you."

Johnny talked quietly into his phone. He'd only just put it away when there was an official-sounding knock at the door. The new arrival didn't wait for Patricia to invite them in, just slammed the door open and marched into the office. Tall and saturnine, they wore a uniform that Daniel recognized immediately. He'd seen it often enough before, as a great many people wearing it had been doing their level best to shoot him full of holes. The mercenary crashed to a parade rest in the middle of the room. Tina made a low growling sound, her hands closed into fists.

"This is Major Boughton," Johnny said loudly. "He's with me."

Daniel shook his head. "You always did have a weakness for bad company."

"It got me where I am today," said Johnny. "Major Boughton is in charge of the company of soldiers who were hired to attack your old building."

"How does a Commissioner of Police know a major of mercenaries?" said Tina.

"We've had occasion to work together," Johnny said carefully. "To deal with certain well-connected terrorists or criminals I wasn't allowed to touch—officially. Edward brought us together, in the beginning."

Daniel stared at him. "You worked for Edward Hyde? You were one of his creatures?"

Johnny stirred uncomfortably on his chair. "I wouldn't put it that way."

"I would," said Daniel. "No wonder you never supported me, when I was raving about being attacked by monsters. You couldn't afford to attract attention to your own extracurricular activities."

"Precisely," said Johnny. "No hard feelings, I trust?"

Daniel looked at him. "What do you think?"

Johnny turned away, rather than face what he saw in Daniel's eyes. He nodded quickly to Major Boughton, who took a step forward to draw everyone's attention back to him.

"My company was hired by human agents in the employ of aliens. We did not know who was behind the contract when we agreed to it, and now the truth has been revealed we no longer feel bound by its conditions. We will not work for enemies of Humanity. I am here to offer our services to Jekyll & Hyde Inc., in your fight against the Greys."

"You blew up our building and shot the shit out of us!" Tina said loudly.

The major met her blazing gaze with unblinking calm. "You killed a great many of my people. Good soldiers, who were only following their orders. But professionals don't let their emotions get in the way of getting the job done. You shouldn't take these things personally, young lady."

Tina tensed dangerously.

"I was the one who informed the major who he was really working for," Johnny said quickly.

"How did you find that out?" said Daniel.

"While I was busy digging up information on your behalf," said Johnny.

"My people may be killers for hire, and we may have done questionable things," said the major, "but there is a line in the sand we will not cross. We stand ready to join your war against the aliens."

"Fine," said Tina. "We can always use a few good men. But first . . ."

She surged forward, grabbed a handful of the major's jacket, and lifted him off his feet. She marched him across the room, slammed him against the wall, and thrust her face in close to his.

"But don't think for one moment that all is forgotten and forgiven, Major."

She dropped him back on his feet, and went over to stand with Daniel. The major took a moment to regain his balance and dignity, and tug his uniform back into place.

"And don't call me *young lady*!" Tina said loudly.

"You'd make an excellent soldier of fortune," said the Major.

"I am ready to be your intermediary," Johnny said quickly, "between Major Boughton and Jekyll & Hyde Inc. And I have to say, Danny boy, going by what people have been telling me about the Greys, you're going to need an army of professional killers to back you on this one."

"The commissioner is entirely correct," said Patricia. "My people are telling me that the Greys pose more of a threat than the Martians, Bug-Eyed Monsters, and Reptiloids put together. That's why I called you back here to meet these gentlemen."

Daniel smiled coldly at Johnny. "I should have known you'd find a way to weasel in, and grab some glory for yourself."

"You know I hate to be left out of things," said Johnny. "Especially when there's power and privilege to be had."

He rose to his feet and nodded to the major, and they left the office together, closing the door quietly behind them.

"I thought they'd never go," said Alan.

Daniel glared at Patricia. "You really think it's a good idea to let people like that roam the building unaccompanied?"

"The commissioner is *your* contact," said Patricia. "And your friend."

"I still wouldn't trust him further than I could throw a wet camel," said Daniel. "Johnny is a political animal, always looking for a chance to grab the next gold ring. But really, I was talking about the major."

"Damn right," said Tina. "His people have already had one good stab at putting Jekyll & Hyde Inc. out of business. And you let him wander around our new building, so he can see all our defenses and protections?"

"The major has been shadowed by my people all the time he's been here," said Patricia. "Making sure he doesn't get to see anything we don't want him to see—but very politely, because we're going to need his soldiers. The Greys present a bigger threat than anything you've encountered so far."

"Do you believe in the major and his convenient conscience?" said Tina.

"Not necessarily," said Patricia. "We'll keep a close eye on him, and the commissioner. And the best way to do that is to keep them close."

Tina scowled at Alan. "You know everything. What kind of a man is the major?"

"He has a reputation for being a first-class soldier," Alan said carefully. "In mercenary terms, that means you can trust him to do what he's been paid to do, or die trying. And I can tell you for a fact that he has turned down contracts that would have brought him into conflict with this country's best interests. Despite everything, Boughton remains a patriot. Which of course makes him that much easier to manipulate."

Daniel looked thoughtfully at Alan. "We know why Johnny was here, but what about you? Do you have new information for us?"

"In a way," said Alan. He paused for a moment, choosing his words carefully. "I have been keeping my superiors informed about your triumphs over the aliens. Constant surveillance is the price you pay, for including me in your little war. But now, I have to tell you my superiors have decided that you have become just a little too successful. They see Jekyll & Hyde Incorporated as a threat—not only to the department, but to the entire status quo."

He paused to see how Daniel and Tina were taking this, and then continued.

"There must always be checks and balances. No group can be allowed to become too independent. It has therefore been decided, at the very highest levels, that I should present you with the following ultimatum: Either Jekyll & Hyde Incorporated agrees to place itself under my department's control, or steps will be taken to shut you down. Permanently."

Daniel and Tina looked at each other, and then at Patricia. She stared calmly back, making it clear the response was up to them. Daniel looked at Alan long enough for him to stir uncomfortably on his chair.

"You expect us to take orders from you?" Daniel said finally.

"That is the price of your being allowed to do business," said Alan.

"And you really think you can shut us down?" said Tina.

Alan smiled. "My department doesn't deal in open attacks, like the major and his soldiers. And we have access to weapons and devices Major Broughton can only dream of."

Daniel turned to Tina. "You know him better than me. Is he bluffing?"

Tina's face was full of a terrible cold anger. "Probably not."

"Please understand," Alan said smoothly, "that destroying Jekyll & Hyde Incorporated is not our preferred outcome. My superiors see a bright future with you and your people tucked safely under the department's wing."

"You want us to be your attack dogs," said Tina.

"I'm so glad we understand each other," said Alan.

Tina took a step toward him, and everybody tensed. "I thought we were friends, Alan."

"We are, my dear," Alan said earnestly. "That's why I volunteered to come here, and break the news to you personally."

"You want to muzzle us," said Tina. "Put us on a leash, and make sure we only go after the people you don't like. If you really were my friend, you would have protected me from this."

Alan sighed. "It's one thing to act out like a wild child when you're young and carefree, but now it's time for you to grow up and accept that there's a bigger picture. You must learn to do as you're told."

"Never," said Tina.

She surged forward, lifted Alan out of his chair with one hand, and strode over to the nearest window. She drew back a fist to smash the glass, but the window obligingly opened itself for her.

"Tina, please think this through!" said Alan. "You don't want to do this!"

"Oh, I really think I do," said Tina.

She threw him out the window, and turned her back on his rapidly fading scream. The window closed itself behind her.

"I thought you liked him," said Daniel.

"I did," said Tina. "But no one betrays me and gets away with it." She looked coldly at Patricia. "Send some of your people to clean the mess off the sidewalk."

"Of course," said Patricia.

She got on her phone and murmured quiet instructions. Daniel moved in close beside Tina, but didn't try to touch her. She was so tense she looked as though she might break.

"Should we be concerned about retaliation from his superiors?" he said carefully.

"He's not that important," said Tina. "They'll understand this is just a message not to mess with us. And besides, we have an army of mercenary soldiers to back us up now."

"I'll have a quiet word with Johnny," said Daniel. "He can use his position as commissioner to run interference. Good thing I didn't throw *him* out the window, like I wanted to."

"I've always admired your restraint," said Tina. She gave him a look that said she was about to change the subject. "At least now we know who was behind the attack on our old building."

"But why did the Greys decide to launch a preemptive strike?" said Daniel.

"The Greys are more entrenched in our society than the other aliens," said Patricia. "They've learned to think like us. Including *Get your retaliation in first*."

"Who knew we'd have so much in common?" said Tina.

Patricia's phone rang. She listened, murmured a few words, and put it down again.

"It seems we have another visitor on the way up."

Tina smiled at Daniel. "You can defenestrate this one."

"You're so good to me," said Daniel.

Tina's smile widened. "I am!"

"While we're waiting," said Patricia, "you can give me your report on what happened at the Reptiloid base."

"They're dead," said Daniel.

"Very dead," said Tina. "And good riddance."

"I'll expect a written report on all your actions at some point," said Patricia.

Daniel looked at her. "Hydes don't do reports."

"I'm afraid I must insist," said Patricia.

Tina smiled easily at her. "Do you want to lose another desk?"

Perhaps fortunately, the door swung open at that point, and William Dee entered the office as though he was on a state visit. He lurched across the room, leaning heavily on a wooden stick with a silver wolfshead handle. He was wearing a smart and surprisingly fashionable suit, though he was so thin he looked like he'd rattle around inside it if he coughed. He headed for the nearest chair and sank down on it with a sigh of relief, before nodding familiarly to Patricia.

"Hello, Pat. Been a while."

"Hello, William," said Patricia.

Daniel stared at the armorer. "Do you know everybody?"

"Pretty much," said Patricia. She looked thoughtfully at William. "I didn't think you ever left the Albion, these days. That you needed its protections, to keep you safe from all the enemies you've made."

"That's what I want them to think," said William. "But there are some seriously old tunnels under the Albion, just waiting to connect me with all kinds of useful places across London."

"Why are you here?" said Daniel.

William turned stiffly on his chair, and fixed Daniel with a cold, implacable gaze.

"This is my world, and I will do whatever it takes to protect it—including hauling my ancient bones all the way across the city to talk to you in person. The Greys are more powerful than you know. More powerful than anyone knows. You don't have a hope in hell of defeating them without the support of the Elder Ones."

"We've done all right so far," said Tina.

"Brute strength and stubbornness can only carry you so far," said William. "The Greys aren't like the other aliens."

"Do you know where their base is?" said Daniel.

"The Greys don't have a base," said William. "They live among us, because they can fool us into seeing them as humans."

"Okay . . ." said Tina. "Major game-changer."

Daniel frowned. "Are we talking about actual shape-changing, or some kind of illusion?"

"More like a telepathic instruction," said William, "to make us see what they want us to see."

"So anyone we meet could be a Grey?" said Tina.

"Of course," said William. "They're everywhere."

Daniel thought about that. If anyone could be a disguised Grey, that would have to include a certain armorer who just turned up out of nowhere, and seemed determined to take control of Jekyll & Hyde Inc.

Tina gave William a hard look. "How can we be sure you're not a Grey, come to feed us misleading information? How can we be sure of anything you're telling us?"

"You can't," said William, flashing her his unpleasant smile. "Welcome to my world."

"Is this why you choose to live alone?" said Daniel.

"No," said William. "I just don't like people much."

"Then why are you so keen to save them?" said Tina.

"When everything else has been taken away from you, because you've lived too long," said William, "you still have your duty. A cold comfort, but better than none."

Daniel looked at Patricia. "Is there anything in the armory that would let us see a Grey as it really is?"

"Let me check some of the darker corners," said the armorer.

And if you can't find anything, or say you can't, thought Daniel, *does that tell me something?*

"Greys have infiltrated all the corridors of power," said William, "quietly steering important people to make the decisions they want."

"What do the Greys want?" Daniel said bluntly.

"Our world," said William. "But why risk destroying it by fighting a war, when they can persuade us to just hand it over?"

Daniel turned to Tina. "Could this be behind Alan Diment's ultimatum? Might one of his superiors be a Grey, trying to take us off the table before we can do anything?"

"Could be," said Tina. "And maybe that is what's behind Commissioner Hart's sudden decision to deal himself in."

"No," said Daniel. "He's just a creep."

"He's your friend," said Tina.

Daniel shook his head. "It's like we can't trust anyone."

Tina snorted. "Like we ever did."

"The Greys are our secret masters," said William, rapping his stick loudly on the floor to get their attention, "and you have removed all the other alien races who might have got in their way. You have to stop the Greys *now*, before they can take advantage of the situation you created."

"No good deed goes unpunished," said Daniel. "Do the Greys at least have a center of operations?"

"No," said William. "They use us to get their work done. You can't attack them without destroying our own infrastructure."

"Then how are we supposed to stop them?" said Daniel.

"By gathering all the Greys together in one place," said William. "And then we wipe the bastards out."

Daniel looked at Patricia. "Do we have a bomb that big?"

"I'll check the inventory," said Patricia.

"Aren't there any nice aliens?" said Tina, just a bit plaintively.

"If there are, they don't come here," said William.

"How do we get all the Greys in one place?" said Daniel. "Bait a trap with some alien cheese?"

"By presenting them with a threat so dangerous, they'll have to turn out in force to stop it," said William. "I will allow word to get out that I plan to summon the Elder Ones back to this world. The Greys will know it'll take everything they've got to stop that."

Daniel frowned. "Do the Greys have anything powerful enough to stop the Elder Ones?"

"The Elder Ones could be vulnerable when they first appear in our world," William said carefully. "They have to download themselves from their higher dimension in order to take on a physical form, and, just possibly, the Greys could interfere with that process."

Daniel met William's gaze steadily. "The Elder Ones could be a worse threat to us than the Greys. We can fight aliens, but alien gods?"

"And how can we be sure you're not persuading us to do what the Greys really want?" said Tina.

William dropped Daniel a roguish wink. "I like her. She's crafty." He showed Tina his unpleasant smile again. "You don't have any choice. The Elder Ones are the only weapon you can use against the Greys."

"But what are we supposed to do, after the Elder Ones have dealt with the Greys?" said Daniel.

"Make a deal with them," said William. "They're not interested in running this world. They just don't want anyone else to have it."

"I thought the Elder Ones used to have dominion over the Earth?" said Tina. "And that ever since we booted them out, they've been trying to get back in so they can reign again?"

"That's human thinking," said William. "They're so much bigger than that."

Daniel wasn't sure he believed that, but said nothing.

"What location did you have in mind, William?" said Patricia.

But before he could say anything the door swung open, and

Alan Diment strolled in. He stopped and smiled easily about him, so they could all see how completely unharmed he was. Daniel and Tina moved to stand closer together. Patricia let one hand slip under her desk, as though reaching for a concealed weapon. William swiveled round in his chair, and fixed Alan with a cold, calculating stare. Alan looked from face to face, and his smile never wavered once.

"Hello, everyone. Did you miss me?"

"Next time, I'll throw you from somewhere higher," said Tina.

"Wouldn't do you any good," said Alan. "Some time ago, my superiors decided I was too valuable to be allowed to die while they still had need of me. So they had me remade and refashioned. I was not consulted. I agreed to a lifetime of service, not a life sentence. But in the end, I knew where my duty lay."

"You're immortal?" said Daniel.

"Ask me in a thousand years," said Alan. "The good news is, I don't take outbursts of temper personally. I'm still ready to work with Jekyll & Hyde Incorporated to bring down the Greys . . . once you've agreed to operate under my department's authority. There's nothing like a mutual enemy to bring all sides together. Isn't that right, William? I overheard your plan, by the way, while I was waiting outside for just the right moment to make my entrance."

"We won't work for you," said Patricia. "But . . . what if we were to offer you something your superiors would want even more than that?"

Alan raised a polite eyebrow. "What did you have in mind?"

"A bottle of the Hyde Elixir," said Patricia. "For your scientists to study."

Alan nodded slowly. "Yes . . . that might just do it. But I would have to take the bottle with me, right now."

Patricia's hand came up from under the desk, holding one of the bottles Edward had left in the armory. Patricia set it carefully on her desk, and Alan moved quickly forward to snatch it up before she could change her mind.

"A fine vintage, I'm sure."

"Hold it," said Daniel. "If you were waiting outside in the corridor, why didn't Joyce warn us?"

"I'm afraid she's not around anymore," said Alan.

Something in his voice put a chill in Daniel's heart. He hurried over to the door, and looked out into the corridor. There was no sign of Joyce anywhere. He turned and glared at Alan.

"Where is she? What have you done with her?"

"Coming back from the dead always leaves me feeling very hungry," said Alan. "I'm afraid I just gobbled her up, shoes and all."

Daniel's face went very cold. He started forward, and Tina grabbed him quickly by the arm.

"Not now, Daniel. Not while we still need him."

Daniel looked at her, and then nodded tightly. "We won't always need him."

"No," said Tina. "We won't."

Daniel turned back to Alan. "You must have passed lots of people on your way up here. Why choose Joyce?"

"Because he knew her death would hurt you most," said Tina. "Isn't that right, Alan?"

"You know me so well, my dear," said Alan.

"But I was the one who tried to kill you," said Tina. "Why not hurt me?"

"Haven't I?" said Alan. "By hurting him?"

"Does Joyce's death mean we're even?" said Patricia.

"Oh, of course," said Alan. He hefted the bottle of Elixir. "This pays for all. For the time being."

Daniel glared at Patricia. "Joyce liked you! She really liked you!"

"I know," said Patricia. "But she's gone, and I have to deal with what's in front of me."

Daniel turned his glare on Alan. "I *will* find a way to kill you."

"Good luck," said Alan. "I couldn't, and I tried really hard. Now, I really must be going."

"I never knew you at all, did I?" said Tina.

Alan looked at her steadily. "You never knew *all* of me. Because I only showed you what I wanted you to see."

"I'll walk with you, Alan," said William, levering himself out of his chair with the aid of his stick. "It would appear we have much to discuss."

"Of course, William," said Alan.

They left the room together. Daniel turned on Patricia.

"I can't believe you just gave him the Elixir!"

"His scientists can examine it all they want," said Patricia. "They won't get anywhere."

"I want a bottle of the Elixir," said Daniel. "Right now."

Patricia looked at him thoughtfully, and then produced a second bottle from her desk. She held it out, and Daniel took it.

"How did you know I had another bottle?" said Patricia.

"Because I know how you think," said Daniel.

"I rather doubt that," said Patricia.

"Why do you want the Elixir, Daniel?" said Tina.

"So that if Diment drinks it, to make himself a Hyde, I can force a second dose down his throat and turn him back," said Daniel.

"Good thinking," said Tina.

Chapter Nine

WHAT YOU DO, WHEN HARD CHOICES ARE THE ONLY CHOICES YOU HAVE

✣ ✣ ✣

"WE CAN'T DO ANYTHING until William Dee puts his plan together," said Patricia, "so why don't you take some time out, and try to relax? Some of the offices on this floor are very comfortable. There are couches to doze on, televisions to watch, and minibars you can empty."

Tina looked at Daniel. "It does sound tempting. Particularly the minibars."

"I'm not staying where Joyce was murdered," said Daniel.

Tina put a hand on his arm. "That wasn't your fault."

"I should have protected her," said Daniel.

"There was nothing you could have done," Tina said steadily. "If anyone's at fault, it's me. I trusted Alan."

Daniel put his hand on top of hers. "You thought he was your friend."

"I really did," said Tina. "But I should have known better, because I always knew what he really was."

Daniel let his breath out slowly. "He didn't even leave us a body to bury. I will make him pay for that, once this mess is over. And then I think I'll pay his superiors a visit, for inflicting something like him on the world."

"Not until we don't need him anymore," Patricia said firmly. "If you don't want to stay here, where do you want to go?"

"Back to the original Jekyll & Hyde Inc. building," said Daniel. "I think I could rest there."

Tina shrugged. "At least we can be sure no one will bother us in that death trap."

Daniel started toward the door, and then paused to glance back at Patricia.

"Phone us the moment you hear from Dee. When it's time for us to do something."

"That building really isn't safe," said Patricia.

"Where is?" said Daniel.

The two Hydes walked back down the corridor, both of them lost in their own thoughts. They remained silent in the elevator—Daniel because he had nothing to say, and Tina because she couldn't think of anything to say that would help him. In the lobby, everyone stopped what they were doing and watched silently as the Hydes walked through. There was no applause, and no admiring glances. They'd heard about Joyce's death. Tina shot an angry glance at Daniel.

"How can they treat us like this, after everything we've done?"

"They're mourning," said Daniel.

"We can't protect everyone," said Tina.

"Then what use are we?" said Daniel.

They walked down the street, staring straight ahead, angry about different things. There was no one else around, even though it was well into the afternoon.

"Where is everybody?" Tina said finally.

"Probably keeping their heads down, and watching out for more helicopter attacks," said Daniel.

"Maybe we should send a mass-mailing to our neighbors," said Tina. "Tell them there's nothing to worry about anymore, because the mercenaries are on our side now."

Daniel looked at her. "Are they?"

"The major did seem quite upset over how he'd been treated," said Tina.

"I'm not sure mercenaries do upset," said Daniel.

"You don't trust anyone, do you?" Tina said admiringly.

They came to a halt outside the old building, and looked it over. The fires had finally gone out, and smoke had stopped rising from the ruined roof. Most of the glass in the front of the building was cracked or shattered or had fallen out, but someone had cleared all the broken fragments and fallen debris off the sidewalk. The lobby door still hung loosely, half blown off its hinges.

"Something else we couldn't protect," said Daniel.

Tina gave him a look. "Daniel, either you snap out of this, or I will slap the self-pity right out of you. We are still the cutting edge of Jekyll & Hyde Inc.! We are the ones who get things done!"

"But we're not in charge," said Daniel.

"Do you want to be?" said Tina. "No, stop a moment and think about it. We never were very good at making decisions, and running things. We've always been more hands-on when it comes to solving problems. The way things are now we get to do the things that matter, while Patricia does all the hard work. Let her be in charge, if that's what she wants. We have more important things to do." She slipped her arm through his. "Do you really want to hang out in this dump?"

"Yes," said Daniel. "I really do."

"Then let's find somewhere we can put our feet up in as much comfort as possible, until Patricia sounds the call to action. And then you can take your mood out on the Greys."

"Sounds good to me," said Daniel. "Have you still got your atomic knuckle-dusters?"

"Of course," said Tina. "You know I never give up anything fun."

Daniel tried the front door, and it came away in his hands. He dropped it on the pavement, and led the way into the lobby. He had to stop for a moment, to take in the extent of the damage. The walls were stitched together with cracks, the floor was half hidden under fallen debris, and the ceiling had slumped dangerously low in places, looking as though the whole thing might collapse at any sudden sound. Daniel gave it a warning look.

"Don't even think about it. I am really not in the mood."

He moved slowly across the lobby, stepping carefully over bits and pieces of his past. He remembered when he first came to Jekyll & Hyde Inc., a disgraced and broken ex-cop who'd thought his life was over. Until Edward Hyde gave him the Elixir, and changed his life forever. He remembered how impressed he'd been by the great open space, with its style and luxury and gleaming parquet floor. Now he walked through the ruins of the way things used to be, and the bright light shining through the cracked upper windows only made the scene seem more desolate. Sudden echoes rose up, and he looked round to see Tina moodily kicking at the rubble. She caught his eye, and shrugged quickly.

"We can't stay here, Daniel. There isn't even anywhere to sit down."

"I thought we might go up on the roof," said Daniel.

Tina stared at him. "Why would we want to go there?"

"Because that's where all of this started," said Daniel. "When we looked out over London and thought we could have it all, just because we were Hydes."

"The roof is where it all started to go wrong," said Tina. "One moment we were lords of everything we beheld, and the next the night sky was full of attack helicopters."

Daniel smiled at her. "We needed a wake-up call."

Tina sighed. "How would we even get to the roof? I doubt the elevators are working, and I wouldn't trust them if they were."

"We'll walk," said Daniel.

Tina stared at him, and Daniel laughed.

"Come on, I'll race you to the top."

The climb was so long and hard it put even two Hydes out of breath, though they did their best to conceal it from each other. They were finally brought to a halt a few floors short of the roof, when the stairs became completely blocked by debris and wreckage, and both of them were glad for an excuse to pause and get their second wind. Daniel took his time evaluating the situation, and then started smashing slabs of stone and plaster with his fists, and throwing everything he could lift back down the stairs. He was making good progress until he was suddenly forced to stop and step back, as sparking electrical cables dropped out of a gap in the wall, writhing around the stairwell like spitting snakes. Tina stepped quickly past Daniel, took a firm hold on the cables, and yanked them out of the wall. They drooped lifelessly in her hands, and she shook them a few times to make sure they'd run out of sparks, before tossing them carelessly over the handrail.

Daniel cleared his throat carefully. "That could have gone horribly wrong."

"But it didn't," said Tina.

Daniel smiled briefly. "Shocking behavior, Tina."

"Fun time!" Tina said happily.

Step by step and stair by stair, the Hydes fought their way up the last few floors, moving or hitting anything that got in their way, and climbing over any obstacles that looked too big to break apart. Tina let Daniel take the lead. She could see he'd decided that nothing was going to stop him getting to the roof.

Eventually they reached what was left of Edward's office. The furniture and fittings had been crushed into firewood by fallen debris. Great holes in the ceiling and walls let in the sunlight, while gusting breezes prowled around the room. The door to the stairway leading up to the roof was riddled with bullet holes. Daniel tried to open it, but the door was wedged solidly in place. He hit it once, and the heavy wood split from top to bottom. He ripped the broken door out of its frame and threw it to one side, and then started up the stairs. The door at the top was in even worse condition, with so many bullet holes the light streamed through like miniature spotlights. Daniel looked back at Tina.

"Moths," he said solemnly.

Tina nodded. "I think they've been getting at the Elixir."

Daniel made his way carefully up the blood-spattered stairs, and gave the door a good shove. It toppled backward onto the roof, and Daniel walked out into the open air. There didn't seem to be much left of the roof itself, just craters, fire damage, and the kind of general destruction usually only associated with war zones. But surprisingly, what remained was firm enough under his feet. He gestured for Tina to come out and join him, and she emerged cautiously into the bright sunlight, glaring around her.

"I suppose there could be a more desolate spot on the Moon somewhere, but I wouldn't put money on it."

"Edward meant his building to survive, no matter what was thrown at it," said Daniel.

Tina sniffed loudly. "I'm still not seeing anywhere we could sit down."

"I thought we might admire the view," said Daniel.

He set off across the shattered roof, stepping carefully around the gaps and crevices. Some of the craters were so deep rain had pooled in them, and there were crevices wide enough he could look down into Edward's office. Most of the roof's boundaries were simply gone, blasted into jagged chunks of concrete and steel, and the massive air-conditioning unit had been blasted into pieces. He kept pressing forward, heading for the one intact edge. He finally chose a reasonably intact section, stamped on it a few times, and then and sat down, letting his legs dangle carelessly over the drop. Tina took her time joining him, but finally settled down at his side. They leaned companionably together, and looked out over London. Endless rows of glass frontages stretched away before them, shining in the sunlight like so many vertical jewels. The wind blew briskly about them, as though on its way to somewhere more civilized.

"I like looking at the buildings," said Daniel. "Thinking about all the people who work in them—wondering who they are, and what they're doing."

"Probably plotting how best to kill us," Tina said darkly. "Sometimes I think the whole world has a grudge against us."

"They're just jealous, because they're not Hydes," said Daniel.

The sunlight was warm and soothing, and the clear air was refreshing after the dust-choked stairwells. It all seemed very peaceful.

"What are we doing here?" said Tina.

"Thinking," said Daniel. "Once we've killed all the aliens . . . what do we do then?"

Tina shrugged. "You said it yourself: Hydes have a lot of enemies. There'll never be any shortage of people to fight."

"But will they be someone worth fighting?" said Daniel.

"Picky picky," said Tina. "The fight is what matters."

"I'm not so sure of that anymore," said Daniel. "What's the point of fighting a war you know will never end?"

Tina looked down at the long drop, and kicked her legs idly. "What else is there?"

"We could walk away from Jekyll & Hyde Inc.," said Daniel. "Turn our backs on the past, and make new lives for ourselves."

"Doing what?" said Tina.

"That's the problem, isn't it?" said Daniel. "It would have to be something worth doing."

"Why can't you be content with what you are?" said Tina. "What's wrong with just being a Hyde, and being with me?"

"Because when we relax and take our eye off the ball," said Daniel, "that's when this building happens. That's when Joyce happens."

Tina rested her head on his shoulder. "You always want to take the weight of the world on your back. Let it go, Daniel. Nothing that happened to Joyce was down to you. Same with this building. I say keep it simple. What is it you really want?"

"I want to kill all the Greys," said Daniel. "And then, I want to kill Alan Diment. And his superiors."

"And then?" said Tina.

"That's what I'm asking you," said Daniel.

"We'll think of something," said Tina. She sat up straight again and looked out over London. "I don't believe in too much planning. Just let the world come to you, and take what you want from it. We're Hydes, which means all of this is just here for us to have fun with."

"That's how Joyce used to think," said Daniel. "But the world proved her wrong."

"If Joyce was here," said Tina, "she would slap you a good one, just for considering giving up."

Daniel smiled briefly. "Well, she'd think about it."

His phone rang, and for once he was quick to answer it.

"You need to go back to the Albion Club," said Patricia. "William Dee says he has something to show you."

"Does he have a plan?" said Daniel.

"Apparently," said Patricia. "Now go. Time is running out."

"Isn't it always?" said Daniel, but the armorer was already gone. He rose to his feet and took one last look out over London, while Tina stood up and brushed the dust from her clothes.

"Why doesn't Patricia ever phone me?" she said. "I have a phone."

"Patricia thinks I'm easier to intimidate," said Daniel.

"Ah," said Tina. "I knew there had to be a good reason."

They took their time driving across London, for which the midafternoon traffic was suitably grateful. Daniel let Tina drive again, because he was still thinking.

"You know," Tina said finally, "you could brood for the Olympics, and pick up a bronze in glum. I thought you couldn't wait to get stuck into the Greys?"

"We're missing something," said Daniel. "We've been so busy

running back and forth, slapping down the aliens that we haven't had time to think about the big picture."

"We're Hydes," said Tina, expertly manuevering the car through a brief opening in the traffic and ignoring the outburst of protesting horns. "We don't do subtle. We just hit things until they break."

"That might not be enough this time," said Daniel.

"Are you still worrying about the Elder Ones?" said Tina.

"The ancient alien space gods?" said Daniel. "What could possibly go wrong with summoning something like that into our world?"

"We'll just have to make sure they're pointed in the right direction," said Tina.

She parked outside the Albion Club, happily blocking the sidewalk. As they approached the club's front door, it swung briskly open before them. Daniel stopped, and looked at it suspiciously. Tina stirred impatiently beside him.

"What's wrong now?"

"I'm not used to being made welcome," said Daniel.

"It just shows we're expected," said Tina.

Beyond the door, there was nothing but darkness. Daniel eyed it distrustfully.

"That wasn't there the last time."

"William has probably arranged something special for us," said Tina.

"You say that like it's a good thing."

"Am I going to have to pick you up and throw you through the doorway?" said Tina.

"The only reason to be that dark is to hide something that someone else doesn't want us to see," said Daniel.

Tina paused. "You think it might be a trap? That there might be something in there waiting for us? Good. I am really in the mood to hit something."

"Never knew you when you weren't," said Daniel.

They walked through the doorway, and just like that they were somewhere else.

When the darkness fell away from their eyes, they were standing on a stone ledge looking out over a massive underground cavern.

Tina grabbed Daniel's arm, and they both took a careful step back from the edge.

"A dimensional gate," said Daniel. "A shortcut between two places, via underspace."

"You have no more idea how that works than I do," said Tina.

"This is true." Daniel looked out over the huge cavern. "Good thing we were just on a high rooftop, or this drop would be seriously freaking me out."

"Maybe we could get the tailors to whip up some of those gliding parachute outfits," said Tina. "You know, the ones with bat wings."

"Indoor bat-suit gliding," said Daniel. "I like it."

The rough stone floor was a long way down, the ceiling went up even farther, and the cavern stretched off into the distance for a lot farther than Daniel felt comfortable with. Glowing rocks shone fiercely from the cavern walls, bright enough to illuminate the whole interior. Daniel couldn't tell whether they'd been set in place, or if it was some natural phenomenon, but he knew which way he'd bet.

"What's going on down there?" said Tina.

She pointed, and Daniel concentrated on the cavern floor. Somewhere at the back stood a ring of standing stones, like Stonehenge, but more primitive. Just rough stones, dragged into position. In the middle was a single flat slab, like a sacrificial altar. Two men were standing over it, discussing something with great enthusiasm. One of them was William Dee.

Daniel looked at the sacrificial slab and thought, *Just what is that man's plan, exactly?*

"Looks like William thinks he's found the perfect spot for his summoning," said Tina. "But why choose such a large cavern?"

"Because he believes it'll take that much space to accommodate the Elder Ones when they appear," said Daniel.

Tina took in the amount of space between floor and ceiling.

"Well," she said, "that's not in the least intimidating. Is it too late to go back to Patricia, and ask her to find us a spiritual bazooka?"

"You really want to risk annoying the big spooky space gods?" said Daniel.

Tina nodded reluctantly, and gestured at the cavern. "Where do you suppose we are?"

"Underground," said Daniel. "Apart from that, your guess is as good as mine. The dimensional door could have dropped us off anywhere."

The same thought struck them at the same moment, and they both looked quickly behind them to make sure their exit was still there. The glowing outlines of a door hung on the air, like a child's drawing superimposed on reality. Daniel turned his attention back to the cavern, and gestured at the stone walls.

"I can see cave mouths, tunnel openings, and what look like ancient galleries carved out of the stone. Not necessarily by anything human. I can also see a great many people occupying those places."

"What kind of people?" said Tina, narrowing her eyes.

"Since they're all wearing very familiar uniforms, it would appear the major and his soldiers got here before us," said Daniel. "They all appear to be heavily armed, and I'm also seeing really big gun emplacements, which suggests they're getting ready to ambush the Greys when they arrive." And then he stopped, and looked down the stone steps connecting the cavern floor to the ledge. "Someone is heading our way."

A single figure made its way up the steps, and Daniel and Tina relaxed a little as they recognized Major Boughton. They could have gone down the steps to meet him, but Daniel felt it important they make it clear who answered to whom. Otherwise the major might try giving them orders. He finally came to a halt before them, out of breath from the long climb but trying not to show it. He had a gun holstered on each hip, and two bandoliers of bullets crisscrossing his chest. He nodded brusquely to the Hydes.

"Mr. Dee is too busy to brief you, so he asked me to bring you up to speed. Because of course I don't have enough duties and responsibilities."

"Get on with it," said Tina.

"My people have established themselves in the best positions," said the major. "We have uninterrupted lines of fire, and a truly impressive amount of firepower."

"What's the plan?" said Daniel.

"Wait for the Greys to show up, wait a little longer to make sure they're all here, and then open up on them with everything we've got."

"So we're not needed?" said Tina, just a bit dangerously.

"These are Greys we're talking about," said the major. "Who knows what tricks they might pull? You're the backup, in case we're not enough."

Tina nodded. "How long before the Greys arrive?"

"Mr. Dee will begin the summoning any time now," said the Major. "Apparently the Greys will immediately detect this, and come in force."

Daniel gestured at the circle of standing stones. "Who is that down there with his back to us, talking with William?"

The major frowned. "You can see them? From here?"

"Hyde eyes," said Tina. "Beats the hell out of binoculars."

"That is Mr. Diment," said the Major. "He is very interested in everything to do with the summoning."

"What about Johnny Hart?" said Daniel. "When can we expect him to grace us with his presence?"

"The commissioner sent a message, saying that while he supports our endeavor he will not be joining us in person." The major kept his voice perfectly level. "He assured me he is very busy making sure no one notices what's going on here."

Tina scowled. "Why is he so ready to miss out on all the action?"

"Because he's not stupid," said the major. "We're going to be facing an unknown number of Greys, with unknown weapons. Add to that the arrival of the Elder Ones, and simple logic suggests not all of us are going to make it out of this alive."

Tina fixed Boughton with a thoughtful look. "If you think the odds suck that badly, why are you and your people here?"

"Because it's our duty," said the major. "We still remember the soldiers we used to be."

"Why did you become a mercenary?" said Daniel.

The major smiled briefly. "For the money, of course."

"Of course," said Daniel.

Boughton looked steadily at Daniel and Tina. "Mr. Dee wished me to explain why so few people ever try to summon the Elder Ones—apart from the obvious danger to our world. It seems the price of summoning is the death of the summoner. Only the willing sacrifice of the summoner's life can lower the barriers between our reality and theirs."

"Why would William agree to that?" said Tina.

"Because he's lived too long, and he knows it," said the major.

"What do you think the Elder Ones are?" said Daniel. "Aliens, space gods, or monsters from the great beyond?"

"That is way beyond my pay grade," said the major. "Hopefully we'll kill all the Greys before the summoning is completed, and then we'll never need to know. Now, I have to make the rounds of my people and shout at them in an encouraging way. Because we only have one chance to get this right."

"Hold it," said Daniel. "What are *we* supposed to do?"

"Hold your ground, and guard the dimensional door behind you," said the Major. "Once the Greys arrive Mr. Dee will close their door, so yours will be the only way out."

Tina scowled. "I wanted to punch out some Greys."

"Once the slaughter begins, I think you can expect a great many highly motivated aliens coming up these stairs," said the major.

"Good," said Daniel.

The major nodded briefly. "In my job, it's often not clear who the good and bad guys are. It helps to be sure, for once."

He set off back down the steps. Daniel looked after him, wondering if there was something else he should say, and then his attention was caught by a sudden blaze of light on the far side of the cavern.

"The Greys!" he shouted. "They're here!"

A horde of leaping, scuttling things burst through a massive circle of dazzlingly bright light: tall spindly figures with skin the color of flesh that had been dead a long time. Their arms and legs had too many joints, their heads were too big, and their eyes were just patches of darkness. The Greys swarmed through their dimensional gate in wave after wave, and sudden beams of light leapt out from within the horde, illuminating the caves and galleries where the major's people were waiting. The mercenaries were so badly dazzled they didn't get off a single shot before ravening energy beams shot out from the Grey horde, and blew great holes in the cavern walls. Caves and galleries exploded, sending bodies and body parts flying through the air. The energy beams struck again and again, slamming home with merciless precision.

It was all over very quickly. Daniel never did see what happened to Major Boughton. The Greys kept firing until they were sure there was nothing left to fire at, and then the energy beams snapped off. Fires blazed out of caves and galleries all over the cavern walls. The Grey horde swept forward across the cavern floor and overran the circle of standing stones. Tina grabbed Daniel's arm.

"How could the Greys know where to aim their guns?"

"Someone told them," said Daniel. "They came through that dimensional gate already knowing exactly where their ambushers were. Someone here has betrayed us."

He looked down at the standing stones. William Dee's summoning never even got started. Two Greys were holding him firmly, with a long-fingered hand clapped over his mouth. William wasn't even trying to fight them. He locked shocked, and lost.

"How do we stop this?" said Tina.

"We can't," said Daniel. "Even if we could get down there without being picked off by the energy beams, there's just too many of them."

"Then what are we going to do?" She was gripping his arm painfully hard now.

"We get the hell out of here," Daniel said steadily. "We go back through the dimensional gate, and guard it from the other side. We call Patricia, and have her empty out the armory, arm all of Jekyll & Hyde Inc.'s people, and bring them to us. And we bring them back here, and lead them against the Greys. Because this is the only chance we have."

"I'm afraid you're not going anywhere," said a familiar voice behind them.

Daniel and Tina spun round. Standing between them and the dimensional gate was Alan Diment. Except there was something wrong, something off, about the way he stood and the way he looked at them. As though he couldn't bother to pretend anymore.

"Greys can look like anyone," said the man who wasn't Alan Diment. "I looked like this so I could move among you and learn your plans. I talked with William Dee and the major, and they told me everything I needed to know." He showed them a brief and entirely inhuman smile. "I can't believe you swallowed that story about me being immortal. I just used Grey technology to break my fall."

"Then why did you kill Joyce?" said Daniel.

"Because she was there," said the Grey Diment. "Because I wanted to keep you off-balance. Does it matter?"

"You can't always have been Alan," said Tina. "I would have known."

"Would you?" said the Grey Diment. "We're very good at showing people what we want them to see." He gestured at the Greys on the cavern floor. "Your war is over. You never stood a chance. And now the summoning has been stopped, all that's left is you."

"You can't replace us," said Tina. "We're not just people."

"Our scientists are already busy unlocking the secrets of your Elixir," said the Grey Diment. "Soon we'll have a legion of Grey Hydes, and then we won't need to work from the shadows anymore. We'll just take what we want. You helped make that possible, by destroying all the aliens who might have been our competitors. I should say thank you, for all your help . . . but I don't think I will."

A strangely shaped gun appeared in his hand, and he fired a beam of shimmering energy at Tina. She let out the quietest of sighs, and collapsed bonelessly to the ground. Daniel started forward, only to stop abruptly as the Grey Diment turned the gun on him.

"She's not dead, only sleeping. But when she wakes she'll be lying on the sacrificial slab in the circle of stones. This is why I wanted you here. This is why our weapons didn't target you, even though we knew where you were. William's death would have opened a door to allow the Elder Ones into our reality—but the death of a Hyde will seal that way forever.

"Stay here, Daniel. I want you to watch, as the death of your beloved ensures our triumph. And don't think you can come down and sneak among us, to rescue Tina. We have scanners in place that can detect a Hyde's presence."

"Why not just kill me now?" said Daniel.

"Because this is more fun," said the Grey Diment. "I like to think of you watching, trying to come up with some last-minute plan to save the day, and finally despairing when you realize there's nothing you can do. Sometimes I wonder if we've spent too long living among you people, but discovering a sense of humor has been absolutely delightful.

"Of course, you don't have to stay here. You could go back through the dimensional door, and run to Jekyll & Hyde Inc. for help. But if you do, you give up all chance of saving Tina. So I think you'll stay to the very last moment, hoping you'll think of something . . . only to see all hope die as we kill the woman you love.

"You can leave, then. We'll come and get you, when we have enough Grey Hydes to tear down Jekyll & Hyde Inc. Well, I've enjoyed our little chat, but I have so much to do. Goodbye, Daniel. Enjoy the show."

Diment disappeared, replaced by a Grey alien. It picked Tina up, threw her effortlessly over its bony shoulder, and then moved carefully around Daniel, covering him all the time with its gun. And then it loped off down the steps to the cavern floor, leaving Daniel standing alone.

He'd never felt so helpless in his life. All his Hyde strength and speed were worthless. If he tried to go after the Grey it would hear him and stun him like it did Tina, and by the time he woke up it would be too late to save her. He had to be smarter than that.

He couldn't go down to the cavern floor, because the Greys had something that would warn them of his presence. The only way to get down there . . . was to not be a Hyde. He reached inside his jacket and brought out the bottle of Elixir he'd brought with him. He unscrewed the cap and raised the bottle to his lips, and then hesitated. The Elixir wouldn't just turn him back into a man, it would make him the weak and broken thing the monsters had made him. But there was no other way. Tina needed him. Everyone needed him.

And he had to do something.

He smiled suddenly, as he realized that everything he'd been through so far, with the Martians and the Bug-Eyed Monsters and the Reptiloids, had all been leading up to this. Fighting and suffering and pushing himself far beyond his old limits so he'd be strong enough to do this. And despite himself, despite everything, he laughed quietly.

He had to be Daniel Carter, to save the day.

He swallowed a good dose of the thick, oily liquid and his flesh seemed to melt, surging this way and that over his rapidly shrinking frame. He cried out in pain and horror as his body turned in upon itself, giving up the glory of being a Hyde for something much smaller. He dropped to his knees, shaking and shuddering. He finally was a man again. A poor, broken, crippled thing, again. Pain raged through him, shaking him like a dog shakes a rat—all the forgotten hurts of old injuries, and shattered bones that never properly healed.

The monsters had broken him with malice aforethought because they were Frankensteins, and understood all the torments that flesh is heir to. He collapsed onto his side and curled into a ball, breathing harshly as he forced the pain back through an effort of will. He couldn't have done that for himself—but he could do it for Tina.

After a while, the pain subsided to a more manageable level, and his breathing steadied. He pulled his knees in under him, and forced himself back onto his feet. He stood swaying, beads of sweat breaking out all over his face. His hands were trembling, and his leg muscles twitched and shuddered just from the strain of holding him up. He wondered what he looked like, and turned to study his reflection in the mirror on the wall.

Tall and painfully thin, a scarecrow of man looked back at him, withered away by constant pain and a lack of anything like health. His once handsome face was all bone and shadow, and his eyes were those of a dead man walking. His clothes hung loosely about him, meant for a much bigger frame. His back was crooked, his limbs were twisted, and he looked like one good breath of wind would blow him away. A man who had been hurt by professionals, who wanted to make sure he stayed hurt.

"Well," said his reflection. "You look like something that was dug up and then hit over the head with the shovel. Not exactly the man who's going to save the day."

"Help me," said Daniel.

"Why should I?" said his reflection.

"Because you're the part of me that always tells me the truth," said Daniel, "whether I want to hear it or not. How do I do this? How can I save Tina?"

"Forget being a Hyde," said his reflection. "Forget fighting and winning. Slow and sneaky does it. Stick to the shadows, take your chances when you find them, and remember: it's all about getting close enough to make a difference."

Daniel's reflection winked at him and then disappeared, taking the mirror with him.

Daniel considered the stone steps falling away before him. It was so long since he'd been this small broken thing that he'd forgotten how bad it was. Or perhaps he just hadn't wanted to remember. He wanted to lie down and sleep, and never have to wake up again to this terrible life, but he didn't have that luxury. Not while he was all there was to save Tina. He thought of how angry she would be, at having to be saved again, and that was enough to put a smile on his lips. He gathered what strength he had, and started down the steps.

Ready or not, here I come.

He winced at every impact of his feet on the unyielding stone, every step driving a spike of pain up his legs. Each movement was agony, and he had to struggle to keep himself moving. He couldn't let himself think of how far he had to go, or how long it would take. He just lurched from one step to the next, like a scarecrow with broken legs.

He paused before a cave mouth that had been occupied by the major's troops. All that remained were scattered bits and pieces, and a stench of burned meat. He grieved silently for fighting men whose names would never be known, and moved on. For a while, it seemed unseen presences walked with him, giving him what comfort and support they could. The ghosts of the fallen.

The steps seemed to go on forever.

When he finally reached the cavern floor, there were Greys everywhere. He stayed in the shadows, not moving. None of the aliens or their unknown machines reacted to his presence, because he wasn't a Hyde. He was Daniel Carter, who still remembered a few useful things from his police training. He waited till a Grey came within reach, and then punched it viciously on the back of the neck. He felt as much as heard bones break, and the Grey collapsed. He dragged the body back into the shadows, and a quick search produced a gun similar to the one the Grey Diment had used on Tina. It felt good in his hand.

He looked out over the packed cavern floor. He couldn't hope to sneak through that many Greys without being noticed; so he'd have to go round. He dropped to his hands and knees and crawled slowly along the cavern wall, always careful to stay in the shadows. The long journey hurt him more than descending the stone steps, and he had to grit his teeth to keep from crying out. Drops of sweat fell from his face to the floor. His bare hands tore and bled on the rough stone. Daniel didn't need to look back to know he was leaving a trail of blood behind him.

He was tired, so horribly tired, but he used the pain to keep himself awake. He made himself concentrate on getting just a few feet farther, and a few feet more, because that meant he was getting closer to Tina. Finally, Daniel forced his aching head up, and saw the standing stones right ahead of him. Grey aliens danced and leapt around the circle of stones, in strange ungainly celebration. Dancing, to celebrate their long-awaited triumph. Daniel smiled slowly, at the thought of taking that away from them. Of making them pay for all the awful things they'd done, and the worse thing they'd made him do to himself.

Tina was lying on her back on the sacrificial stone. Her eyes were closed, but she was twitching and groaning as though some instinct was trying to force her awake. Daniel allowed himself a slow sigh of relief. He'd got there in time. He turned his head painfully slowly to see William Dee was standing beside the slab, two Greys holding him up as much as holding him in place. Shock and failure had dug deeper lines in his face, and left his eyes wide and vague.

On the opposite side of the slab stood another Grey. Daniel was sure he recognized something of Alan Diment in the way it held itself. Daniel stayed on his hands and knees, keeping very still, well back in the shadows. Daniel Carter had brought him this far; now he needed Daniel Hyde.

He eased a trembling hand inside his jacket, and carefully brought out his bottle of Elixir. There was still a fair bit left, and Daniel almost wept at the thought of losing his pain and being strong again. But even as Daniel Hyde, he knew he couldn't fight off this many Greys to rescue Tina. He wouldn't get half a dozen steps before one of them would shoot him down. He needed a plan, a strategy . . . but he had nothing.

And that was when a harsh familiar voice called him by name. Daniel's head came up, and standing right in front of him was Fry, ghost butler of the Albion Club. An old man in an old-fashioned servant's outfit, bent over by age and infirmity, or at least the memories of them. His deep-sunk eyes were sharp and fierce, and when he spoke his voice was cold and certain, without an inch of give in it.

"Well, stab me, look what the cat dragged in. You looked rough enough when you were a Hyde. I knew when I let you into the Albion it would only lead to trouble. Now here we are in the arsehole of the world, with His Nibs needing me to bail him out again."

Daniel gestured to Fry to keep his voice down, but the ghost just kept talking.

"They can't see or hear me. Only you. Unless I let them." He smiled a terrible smile. "In a moment I will take my aspect upon me, and let them see what death is like as it goes walking through the world. And while they have no eyes for anything but me, you go Hyde again, wake up your girlfriend, and hold the Greys off while I join with William to complete the summoning. The Elder Ones will put the fear of God into these Grey bastards. Just the thought of them manifesting is enough to scare the crap out of me, and I'm dead. Come on, boy! Drink your magic potion; there's work to be done."

Daniel knocked back the Elixir, and then grinned like a wolf as flesh raged back and forth over his thickening bones. He surged to his feet, huge and powerful and every inch a Hyde: a predator in a world of prey. He nodded to Fry, who nodded easily back, and then strode out past the standing stones to show the Greys his true nature. Suddenly, his presence beat on the world like the tolling of some cold iron bell. Far more than a ghost, he brought death itself into the world, and everything that came after, and shoved it in the Greys' faces. The aliens let out an awful sound and fell back in disarray, unable to cope with something so outside their experience.

Daniel burst into the circle of stones, his stolen gun held out before him. He shot the two Greys holding William Dee before they could react to his presence, and they crashed to the ground. William stared at his rescuer with wide shocked eyes.

"Finish the summoning!" Daniel yelled.

But William just stood there, struggling to pull his scattered wits together. Daniel grabbed him by the shoulders and turned him around, so he could see Fry manifesting to the Greys, and William's mouth snapped shut as new purpose filled his eyes.

"I can do this!" he said. "Just buy me a little more time. If I can only find the strength . . ."

The ghost Fry turned his back on the trembling Greys, and walked back to stand before William.

"I'll be your strength, my love. One last time."

He walked inside William, and disappeared. William stood up

straight, and launched into the ritual. His voice sounded out strong and fierce as he spoke the ancient words, and a great desolate cry went up from the surrounding Greys.

Daniel sat Tina up on the sacrificial slab, and put his face right next to hers.

"Tina, it's me."

Her eyes snapped open, and she smiled at him. "Took you long enough."

"You would not believe what I had to go through to get here," said Daniel.

"I'll pin a medal on you later." She jumped down off the slab. "Let's go kick some Grey arse."

The Grey that had been Alan Diment was already moving forward, no longer held at bay by the ghost Fry's presence. It aimed its gun at Daniel and fired, but he ducked under the shimmering energy beam and launched himself at the Grey. He could have used his own gun, but that wouldn't have been enough. He needed to make this personal. He got in close before the Grey could fire again, and punched his fist right through the alien's chest and out its back. Black blood spouted. The alien stood very still. Daniel jerked his fist out and the Grey collapsed, as though that had been all that was holding it up. Daniel looked down at it, and kicked it in the face.

"For you, Joyce."

He grabbed up the gun the Grey had dropped and tossed it to Tina. She snatched it out of midair, and as Daniel went to join her she produced something else from an inner pocket. Daniel recognized it immediately as the device she'd taken from Patricia in the armory.

"I don't think this is a weapon," said Tina. "Given that it has a big red button on it, I'm guessing it's a bomb."

"Hit the button," said Daniel. "And then throw it as far as you can. And let's hope it's got a decent time delay."

Tina laughed, hit the button, and threw the thing out over the Greys' heads. They looked up to follow its trajectory, and when it exploded its light filled the whole cavern. A great blast of force tore hundreds of aliens apart, and the following shock wave sent hundreds more crashing to the ground. Daniel and Tina had tucked themselves away behind separate standing stones, but were still hard pressed to keep their footing.

When they emerged, the possessed William was coming to the end of the summoning. The surviving Greys pressed forward from all sides. Daniel and Tina opened fire with their stolen guns, dropping alien after alien, but the guns soon ran out of whatever powered them, and the Hydes threw them away. Tina put on her knuckle-dusters, and winked at Daniel. And then they went forward to meet the Grey horde.

There were only so many ways the aliens could enter the circle, and Daniel and Tina guarded them all. She struck down every Grey that came before her, crushing skulls and smashing in chests, while Daniel tore off long gray arms and used them to smash in Grey heads. The numbers seemed endless, but Daniel didn't give a damn. He was a Hyde, doing what he was born to do, and glorying in it.

And then William Dee shouted the last word of the summoning, and everything changed.

The Elder Ones arrived.

The Greys stopped where they were, every head raised to stare in horror at what hovered above them. The Elder Ones filled the whole top half of the cavern, vast and powerful, their great wings beating on the air. Impossibly beautiful, they shone like the sun, their faces full of a terrible understanding, and a cold implacable justice.

Oh my God, thought Daniel. *They're angels. The Elder Ones are angels.*

The Greys cowered and fell back, like wayward children whose parents had unexpectedly returned. Daniel made himself stare at the Elder Ones, despite the blinding light they radiated. He had paid for this moment in blood and suffering. The Elder Ones looked on the Greys, and every single one of them disappeared. Not a trace remained of the living or the dead, in all the great cavern. And then a great voice sounded in Daniel's head.

We have sent them back to their own world. Along with a warning, to stay away from Earth—or else. We only have so much mercy in us. We will also pass this message on to any other aliens who have taken an undue interest in the Earth.

And then the Elder Ones were gone, and the world seemed that much smaller.

Daniel looked at Tina, and she nodded to show she'd heard them too. Daniel turned to William, but he was lying dead on the stone floor. The summoning had taken its price. But just for a moment Daniel thought he saw two handsome young men dressed to the height of 1920s fashion, walking out of the stones hand in hand. Daniel turned back to Tina.

"It's over. Let's get out of here."

They headed back to the stone steps, and the dimensional door, leaning heavily on each other.

"I knew you'd come and save me," said Tina.

"And you're not mad at me?" said Daniel.

"Well," said Tina, "don't make a habit of it."

They walked companionably together.

"What are we going to tell Patricia?" said Tina.

"Beats me," said Daniel. "She's never going to believe this one."

"Hell," said Tina, "I was here, and *I* don't believe it."

Chapter Ten
DIDN'T SEE THAT COMING

✣ ✣ ✣

IT WAS A PLEASANT afternoon, as Daniel and Tina drove back across London. Bright sunshine, obnoxious traffic—just another day in the big city. Daniel was driving, because he was just in the mood to make someone feel nervous. Tina stared silently through the windscreen, and Daniel just knew she wasn't seeing London.

"So," she said finally. "Angels . . ."

"Well, sort of," said Daniel. "I'm pretty sure the Elder Ones only allowed us to see as much of them as our minds could cope with."

"Even so," said Tina. "*Angels . . .*"

Daniel shrugged. "We've seen stranger things."

"This is true." Tina shot him a sideways look. "Do you think the alien threat is over now?"

"There's no one else left to hit," said Daniel.

Tina nodded. "Good answer."

Daniel brought the car to a halt outside Jekyll & Hyde Inc., and left it parked somewhat on the pavement and somewhat on the road, confident the car could look after itself. Tina kicked thoughtfully at one of the tires.

"Are we keeping this car?"

"I don't see why not," said Daniel. "There's nothing like driving around London in a stolen police car to give you that real outlaw feeling. I'll have a word with Johnny, and he'll do what's necessary to keep the flies off."

Tina sniffed loudly. "He owes us big time, for not showing his face when it mattered."

Daniel was suddenly distracted by all the people walking up and down the street. They nodded politely to him and Tina as they passed, but ignored the police car—because one of the first rules in any business area is that everyone minds their own business.

"Maybe things are finally getting back to normal," said Tina.

"I'm not so sure . . ." said Daniel.

He indicated to Tina to look farther down the street. Where the old Jekyll & Hyde Inc. building used to be there was now nothing but empty space. A great gap between two buildings, like a pulled tooth. Nothing to show the old building had ever been there.

"I guess someone decided it was surplus to requirements," said Tina.

"And I think we can guess who," said Daniel. "I'll miss the old place."

Tina looked at him. "Really?"

"I had some good times there," said Daniel.

"Ah yes," said Tina. "Killing Edward. That was a good day."

Daniel shook his head. "You get sentimental about the strangest things."

He led the way into the lobby of the new building, and then stopped dead to look around him. It was completely empty, spotlessly clean, exactly the way it used to look when Daniel first saw it. Right down to the long list of fake company names scrolling proudly down the wood-paneled wall, with JEKYLL & HYDE INC. right at the top in dignified gold leaf.

"About time you got back here," said Patricia.

Daniel looked round sharply. The armorer was standing right before him and Tina, even though he was sure she hadn't been in the lobby when they entered. It occurred to him that she looked exactly the same as she always did, every time he saw her. Not just the same outfit, but the same look and the same effect, as though she was concentrating on presenting one particular image so he wouldn't see something else. The word *Grey* crossed Daniel's thoughts, and not in a good way.

"Well done, both of you," said Patricia. "The Greys are gone, the alien bases have been very thoroughly trashed, and thanks to you every alien species with an unhealthy interest in the Earth has just received a warning they'll never forget, courtesy of the Elder Ones."

"Did you know they were angels?" Tina said bluntly.

Patricia raised an eyebrow. "I suppose that's one way of looking at them."

"Are you responsible for the disappearance of the old building?" said Daniel.

"Who else do you know who could get the job done that quickly?" said Patricia.

"But how did you . . . ?" said Tina.

"It wasn't as if you needed the old place anymore," said Patricia. "This building is an exact duplicate of the original, down to the very last detail."

"Yes . . ." said Daniel. "I've been meaning to ask you about that. Why remake the old place so completely?"

"Because I'm not creative," said Patricia, "just extraordinarily efficient. And now, I really must be going."

"What?" said Tina. "Why?"

"I've achieved everything I was sent here to do," said Patricia. "You must have realized by now that I was never your old armorer. I just took on the role because it made it easier for you to accept me."

"Why are you here?" said Daniel.

"Because you needed me," said Patricia. "You were about to walk away, but only you could deal with the threat of so many aliens getting ready to make their move. I was sent here to give you the boot in the arse you needed, to get you involved."

"Who sent you?" said Tina.

"Pray you never find out," said Patricia. "Now, I really must be off. I've been called back to over the hills and far away. I present to you a fully restored Jekyll & Hyde Inc. What you do with the organization is entirely up to you. I also leave you a new executive officer, to help you run things."

She gestured at the far end of the lobby, and there was Joyce—alive and well and waving cheerfully. Daniel grinned broadly at her and waved in return, and Joyce raced across the lobby and threw herself into Daniel's arms. He hugged her tightly, an old pain slowly easing in his chest. He was almost afraid to let go of Joyce even for a moment, in case he lost her again. And then Tina moved in and hugged them both, to make sure that could never happen. After a while, they all let go of each other, and smiled. Daniel turned back to Patricia.

"How...?"

She smiled, briefly. "I told you: I restore things to how they used to be."

"I always knew you had something special in mind for me," said Joyce. "Do you have to go?"

"My time here is up," said Patricia. "I'm needed somewhere else now."

"Who are you, really?" said Tina.

"Not all aliens are monsters," said Patricia.

She turned into a pillar of blazing light, which quickly faded away and was gone.

"Okay..." said Daniel. "I can honestly say I did not see that coming."

"It's been that sort of a day," said Tina. "So, what are we going to do with Jekyll & Hyde Inc.?"

"Oh," said Daniel, "I'm sure we'll think of something."

He grinned at Tina, and then at Joyce, who was already bouncing up and down on her toes in her eagerness to get to work for them.